The Brazilian Husband

REBECCA POWELL

COPYRIGHT

All characters and events in this publication, other than those clearly in the public domain, are fictitious and any resemblance to real persons, living or dead, is purely coincidental.

Copyright © 2016 Rebecca Powell

All rights reserved. No part of this publication may be reproduced, stored in a retrieval system, or transmitted, in any form or by any means, without the prior permission in writing of the author.

Cover design by Paper and Sage at
www.paperandsage.com

ISBN-13: 978-1533372055
ISBN-10: 1533372055

First edition.

For Rosemary and Lyn Powell, my Mum and Dad,
with love and thanks.

I will never forget the day my daughter first called me Mummy, but I will always regret not being there the night she was born.

PROLOGUE

Recife, July 1978

He didn't hear her calling until the glass rolled out of his hand and shattered on the stone floor, jerking him awake; even then he mistook her voice for bats feeding in the trees outside his window. He slowly prised his head from the desk, scratching at his unfamiliar stubble, and reached for the near-empty bottle of cachaça. He stayed there a moment, listening to the insects in the yard and the click-clack of the ailing fan above him, wondering if he had imagined her voice, but then she cried out again, and this time there was no mistaking it.

She was calling his wife's name.

Fumbling to his feet he rubbed the back of his neck and flapped loose his white shirt, which had stuck to his skin in the heavy heat. Still dazed, he stumbled out of the office and along the hallway, where he slid back the bolt on the front door.

He thought whoever it was had gone but then he heard the panting. A figure lay crumpled at the foot of the steps: a child, shivering even in the heat of the night, her feet bare, her forehead buried in the tattered door mat, struggling to catch her breath. He staggered down and scooped her up as she screamed again, clutching her swollen belly. She swore at him and asked for his wife. He said nothing but carried her back through the courtyard to the kitchen where he hoped there would still be water.

"Quero minha avó," she kept saying, "I want my Nan."

He didn't know her Nan, but he knew her. Even with her split lip and the raw gash across her cheek there was no mistaking her.

Once in the kitchen he lay the girl down gently on the floor and gave her a stick of corn to bite on, pushing her feet back during her contractions, just as the midwife had shown him hours earlier. The shock of her had shaken him awake but the alcohol still left him confused and the tessellated patterns on the floor tiles made his head spin.

The baby slid like a skinned mango into his cupped hands. It didn't cry and his heart tightened. He opened its mouth, ignoring the girl's insults in his intense concentration. The whole world had been reduced to saving this little life. He dug his index finger into the tiny mouth and a thick black mass came out like pondweed. He patted its back and rubbed its twig-like arms, whispering,

"Live."

And it must have heard him, as it sputtered to life, kicking its legs into his chest.

Wrapping the baby in a tea towel he cut the cord with the cook's bread knife. The girl lay on the cold, hard floor, blood trickling like veins between the tiles, her hands still clutching the table leg. His hands shaking, he held the baby out to her.

"It's a girl," he said.

"Take it away," she hissed.

He stood in the humming light of the kitchen, the broken window hanging open on the thick night, and heard the first drops of long awaited rain start their tentative dance on the dry ground. He breathed in the smell of wet earth and the decaying fruit of the cashew trees as he cradled her in his arms, this new little life already sucking at his knuckle, and lost in his own pain, and in the hopeless perfection of the child he had somehow delivered, his tears finally came.

Her life was in his hands now, he thought.

It would be many years before he came to realise that it was his life that was being held in hers.

CHAPTER ONE

London, March 1994

When we got married, even I only gave us a year. I'd been giving us a year for the past fifteen years.

That summer was our anniversary and I was planning a surprise for Edson – not that we ever celebrated anniversaries - we weren't that kind of a couple – and in any case, there hadn't been much cause to celebrate over the last few years. We'd covered it all: for better and for worse, in sickness and in health, but that evening, despite it all, despite all those nights alone with a bottle of gin, and those often equally lonely nights together with our backlog of baggage, I was determined we were going to celebrate.

It was dark before it should've been, the cold London night devouring the last crumbs of the miserable end-of-winter day. My feet were throbbing after a double shift on the jewellery counter. As my new trainee Denise locked up the display cabinets, I slipped out of my blistering heels and stretched my toes, imagining sinking them into the soft, warm sand of a Brazilian beach, thousands of miles away from this crummy job;

this crummy weather. That was going to be our celebration – my anniversary present to Edson; my apology for the past and a promise for the future.

It had taken me the best part of two years to save up for the trip – squirrelling away the pennies and the pounds, steadily, stealthily, secretly building up enough to take us all away - and at lunch time I'd finally done it; I'd walked in to the travel agents across the road and booked our first ever two-week holiday as a family: me, Edson and Rosa. I couldn't help but grin as I imagined the look on their faces when I showed them the tickets later that night.

A voice interrupted my daydreaming.

It was Mike, our manager. He'd flung open the double doors and was striding over to the counter.

"Which of you lot was the last one in the stock room?"

The rest of the staff hurried towards us.

"Anyone want to own up?"

No-one made eye contact with anyone else, and for a moment it looked like no-one would admit to anything, but then beside me I saw Denise slowly start to raise her hand. Denise was twenty-one and a single mother of two boys. She was bordering on incompetent but I liked her refusal to let lack of skill or experience curb her enthusiasm. She was like a little clockwork mouse; wind her up and off she went, smiling, helpful, eager, as long as I pointed her in the right direction.

"Would any of you go out and leave your house without locking the front door?" Mike asked, "Well? Would you?"

I felt everyone hold their collective breath, waiting to see what he'd do. The week before he'd fired Suzanne from lingerie because she'd knocked over a display and torn an expensive dress. I glanced at Denise. She was biting her lower lip and staring at the floor, her hand hovering by her hip. Her mum, who'd promised to look after the boys whilst she was at work, had flown off to Ibiza with a man she'd just met and Denise was having to fork out for childcare. I didn't know what she'd do if she lost her job - she'd only been there two months; she was still on probation. I, on the other hand, had been there two years and had a perfect record. I couldn't let him fire her over something so inconsequential. Besides, I was still buzzing from the high of finally booking our holiday.

I reached out and gently lowered her hand.

"Sorry, Mike," I said, "that was my fault."

"It doesn't take a genius to lock a door." He was looking at Denise.

"Like I said, it was my fault and I'm really sorry."

"And you're absolutely sure you want to take responsibility for this?" he asked.

I had been, until he'd said that. Nevertheless, I nodded. The most I'd get would be a wrap on the knuckles. I'd had worse. It'd be worth it if it meant Denise got to keep her job.

"Well, because the door of the stock room was left open, some idiot has made off with half our stock – including the watches."

I looked up, horrified.

Shit.

Mike glanced at the others and then back at me, flicking his finger towards the door, "Collect your things and leave," he said, then looked around, addressing everyone, his voice a warning, "Zero tolerance, you all know that. One strike and you're out. I don't care who you are."

"But," I started, only he was already heading back out the door to the stairs. I looked at Denise, who was staring at me with tears in her eyes. I turned and ran after him.

"Come on, Mike," I called up over the banister, taking the stairs two at a time to catch up with him, "you're not serious, right?"

He stopped and watched me as I stumbled up the last few steps towards him, still barefoot, pink-faced and puffing.

"It wasn't your mistake to own up to," he said. He didn't sound angry, he sounded disappointed.

"Then don't fire me."

"I have to."

"Why?"

"Because you lied."

I looked at him, mouth open as if to speak, but nothing came out. I couldn't stop shaking my head.

"You lied to me, Jude, in front of all those people. What was I meant to do?"

"Come on Mike, you know I really need this job."

"That's not what it sounded like to me. Sounded like you wanted to play the Good Samaritan. Sounded like you were doing what you always do - flying to the rescue of yet another lost cause."

"Mike," I called after him but didn't move. I knew this was about more than the stockroom.

I hadn't known he was married when it started, or else it wouldn't have started at all. I already knew it was beneath me, sleeping with the boss, but I couldn't help it. He'd made me feel like I still had something; could still feel something - until that afternoon, when I'd found out he was married and naively asked him when he was planning on leaving his wife.

"I'm not leaving my wife," he'd laughed, "no more than you're ever going to leave your pathetic excuse for a husband."

As he'd said it, I knew it was true. I wasn't going to leave Edson, but I realised that I'd simply wanted him to want me to.

"You don't understand," I'd said, but then stopped. He was married. It no longer mattered what the truth was about Edson and me; about our arrangement. I'd been an idiot and it was over. And Mike had clearly welcomed this excuse to clear up his mess and get rid of me.

He paused as he reached the top of the stairs and looked back, "It's been fun though, right? No hard feelings."

I watched as his office door clicked shut behind him.

I knew Edson would have been expecting me home hours ago, but not trusting myself to hold it together in the tomb-like tunnels of the underground, I'd sought refuge huddled against the window at the back of the night bus, staring at the pale reflection of my face as life hurried past outside.

"No need to come in again," Mike's personal

assistant had told me, slipping on her jacket and reaching for her handbag to let me know we were finished. "I'll forward you the necessary paperwork." She'd looked down her nose at me with what was either pity or disdain, I couldn't decide. She was half my age, newly engaged and one of those people who still believed that there were no problems, only solutions. She hadn't a clue.

I leant my forehead on the cool glass and felt my heart sink. I'd messed up everything. I'd been planning this evening for so long; the evening where I'd tell Ed about our holiday to Brazil; where I'd listen as he told me again of the beautiful house on the beach where he grew up; of his surgeon dad and his politician mother; of his beautiful sisters and his successful friends. I'd wanted to wait until I was sure we could afford it; a surprise; the best present I could ever give him; the one thing he longed for more than anything in the world – to go home. I'd even taken up Portuguese classes again, like he always wanted me to. Only now I'd gone and ruined everything.

A group of young girls giggled in the seats in front of me. I shut my eyes and listened. How had I got there? Crumpled on the late bus, alone, thirty-eight years old and out of a job – again. My life was being sucked away from under me and what was I doing about it? Just ignoring it, letting myself fade away, like that was normal, like this was all my life was ever meant to be. I knew Edson would be disappointed if he knew about Mike. He'd always been my biggest fan, the person who believed in me, even when I stopped believing in myself. He'd say 'what were you thinking?'; he'd say I deserved better. That was easy to say though, wasn't it? Doesn't everyone think they deserve better? As if the world owed any of us anything. But where would we be if we all got what we deserved?

I pushed open our peeling blue front door and felt the stale warmth of home hit my face. I slipped off my shoes and felt the worn carpet, rough under my feet. Adding my hat and coat to the pile of paraphernalia already hanging over the banister, I made my way as quietly as I could past the living room door and into the kitchen. A holdall seeping dirty washing told me that Rosa was home from whichever friend's house she'd been staying at these last few days. She'd been staying over more and more of late and when I asked where she was, she'd avoid the question and just say that Dad had said it was okay.

"Jude? That you?" Edson's voice came from the front room, his Brazilian accent still thick even after fifteen years in London.

He'd always be waiting for me to come home after a day on his own. I'd change his catheter and we'd laugh together as I told him about some daft thing someone had done at work, or the palaver I'd had with a particularly obstreperous customer. At least, that's how it usually went, except when he was deep into one of his depressions. After almost fifteen years, he was still my best friend in the world and I loved him with every part of me. I knew he couldn't control his depression, the doctors had told us it was to be expected, and I tried not to blame him. It came in cycles and we dealt with it the best we could, but those last few weeks he'd been worse than I'd ever seen him; monosyllabic at most. I hadn't managed to get even the hint of a smile out of him. I knew it had something to do with the call from his ex-lover, but he refused to discuss it. Instead, we'd discuss what he wanted for dinner; he'd want something I didn't have and then he'd try to goad me into an argument about it. I'd make his bed, tidy away his left-over lunch and pretend I hadn't heard, telling myself that it would all be forgotten once I told him about the holiday I was planning.

Only now there wasn't going to be a holiday. I'd blown it. I was going to have to go and persuade the travel agent to give me a refund. We'd need the money to see us through the next few months, whilst I looked for another job.

"Just a minute," I forced a breeziness into my voice as I reached in to the cupboard for the bottle of gin, only to remember I'd drunk the last of it the night before. I stood staring at the empty shelf. How could I tell him I'd lost my job? How were we going to manage without my wages? I couldn't lay that worry on him, not when he was like he was. I'd promised him a long time ago that I'd take care of everything and I wasn't about to let him down.

"Jude!" He was getting impatient. Dinner would have to wait.

I kicked the bag of clothes toward the washing machine and gathered the dirty mugs, glasses and plates from the worktop just as Rosa decided to turn up the stereo in her bedroom and the ceiling started to vibrate.

"Hey!" I shouted up, noting the growing watermark emanating from under the bathroom. One more thing to add to my interminable to-do list. When there was no response, I shouted again. And again.

I stormed to the bottom of the stairs and called up.

"Rosa!" Shouting made my head hurt.

No reply.

"Rosa!" I yelled, my frustration mounting, my anger at Mike and at myself for being such an idiot making it far worse than it should've been.

"What?" came the reply.

"Turn that music down!"

"What?"

Just then Edson called again, "Jude!"

"In a minute, Ed," I snapped. At times like that I resented his dependence on me. I craved freedom. I wanted to be elsewhere, anywhere, for just one night: one night when I had no one to look after. I suppose that had been the allure of my sad affair with Mike.

The music clicked off. I lifted my head to shout up again but was caught off guard by Rosa's face appearing over the banister. At fifteen she was so tall, so awkward with her still undecided beauty.

"Alright Mum?"

"Where have you been?"

"At Sal's."

"I thought you were at Jenny's."

"Same difference," shrugged Rosa, slouching down the stairs and rummaging under my things to find her bag.

"And who do you think is going to do all

that washing in the kitchen?"

"Don't start, Mum."

"Why, where are you going?"

"Out."

"Who with?"

"Darren."

"I thought you were with Kenny."

"I just said don't start, Mum."

"I'm not starting. I liked Kenny, that's all."

"Kenny's a shit."

"There's no need to..."

"What?"

"Well, I just hope you're being careful."

"Careful?"

"You know what I mean."

"God, Mum, shut up, I'm not a kid."

"You're still only fifteen. And I don't want you regretting anything, that's all."

"Hello, this is the twentieth century."

"That doesn't mean you can go around being a..."

"A what, Mum?"

"Never mind."

"No, go on, say it."

"I said forget it."

"You think I'm a slapper, that's it, isn't it?"

"Watch your tongue." I knew I sounded like my own mother and cringed. When had I let myself become such a nagging middle-aged cliché?

"Oh my God, that's what you think I am, isn't it?"

"Of course it isn't." Who was I trying to kid? I wasn't talking about Rosa. At least Rosa was having fun.

"Better than being a frigid old cow," Rosa

shouted.

I slapped her hard across the face. I didn't mean to, it just happened. We froze; both of us knowing a line had been crossed, unsure where to go from there.

Just then Ed called me again, this time more urgently.

"Jude!"

I stormed in to the living room, shaking and angry with myself.

"What?" I snapped, then fell silent as I saw him, lying between the television and his wheelchair, the remote control on the floor next to an open bottle of tablets.

"Rosa!" I screamed into the hallway.

The front door slammed shut.

CHAPTER TWO

Over the Atlantic Ocean, July 1994

My eyes stung from the intensity of the tiny screen in the otherwise darkened cabin. I took off my headphones and rubbed the back of my neck. Beside me, eyes glazed, immersed in a story of beautiful people in 'High Octane Entertainment' sat Rosa, her body turned pointedly away from me, the guide book I'd given her on her lap.

We'd left Heathrow over ten hours ago, Rosa as tight-lipped and sullen-faced as she had been for the past three months, headphones permanently plugged in, eyes always elsewhere.

"Don't see what difference it'll make," she'd said, when I'd tried to explain why I had to keep this promise to her father, "It's not like he's going to know."

It had crept up on me, gradually stifling me: the silence of the house without Edson. The rooms echoed with his absence. The activity of the days that followed his death had buoyed me along in an artificial cocoon of funeral arrangements and paperwork. But once the anchor of activity had been wrenched from beneath me; the funeral dealt with; the last guest gone; the healthcare equipment returned, the life had simply fallen out of me. I was all alone, jobless and husband-less, breathing in the emptiness of a house that no longer needed me. And I missed him. For so long I'd been cursing the constant care he needed from me, that, for all my complaining, it had never dawned on me how much I needed him.

The flight attendant came past to collect the trays of food. I handed over my untouched tray. I'd lost track of which meal it was supposed to represent, stuck as we were in the limbo of long haul. As I was closing up my table, the man from the window seat next to me, who'd clambered over us both in the middle of the meal, reappeared from behind the flight attendant. I'd had a polite conversation with him as we'd left Heathrow, the way people feel obliged to do when thrust together with strangers on a journey. He was a journalist travelling to Brazil to cover the country during the World Cup, only he'd been delayed, I couldn't remember why.

"Didn't I read that the World Cup was in America this year?" I'd asked.

"Oh yes, it is, but Brazil is tipped to win it again, so I've been sent to cover the reaction when they do."

"You mean 'if'," I'd corrected him.

"No, no, I mean 'when', trust me," he'd said knowingly, handing me his card, as if offering me his credentials for such a remark. He had been so very excited about the football and bubbling over with the names of all the important people he knew from previous trips. I'd hardly said a word, smiling politely, but had nevertheless sighed with relief when he'd pulled on his eye mask and tugged his complimentary blanket from its thin plastic film.

Now, ten hours later, he looked positively frazzled, smiling apologetically as he shuffled past Rosa's already bent legs. He attempted to make it over me in one giant step but caught his foot on the strap of my bag, which I'd neglected to push under the seat in front of me, and finished the movement with a thud as he fell hip-first into his seat, leaving one extremely long leg hovering inches from my face. Seemingly unembarrassed, he calmly manoeuvred it back in to his seat and refastened his safety belt. He was a little younger than me, I guessed, or maybe it was just the natural ease with which he moved, in contrast to the awkward ache of my own exhausted body, which gave that illusion. I wondered how he could bear to be so cramped for so many hours with legs that long.

"Sorry about that," he said and I realised he'd caught me staring.

I smiled, embarrassed.

"See you in the sunshine," he grinned, shuffling down in his seat and closing his eyes, pulling his blanket back up to his chin like a little boy on school camp.

Watching him, so peaceful, so at ease with himself, made me feel suddenly, terribly alone. Since Edson's death, since he'd gone and left me like that, I'd been drifting through the days, lost, without a clue how to navigate my way back to who I'd been without him. The one thing that had kept me going, that had given me a morsel of hope to cling to, was this trip with Rosa. But sitting there on the plane, the weight of solitude bore down on me so strongly that I had to fight an overwhelming urge to snuggle up to this bear-like man, nuzzle into his shoulder and be wrapped up beside him in his blanket, where I could close my eyes, feel his warmth and let everything else melt away.

Instead I bent down and gathered together the things that had slipped from my handbag when my clumsy neighbour had caught his foot on it. Mostly it was Edson's papers. He hadn't brought many things with him when he'd left Brazil. He'd left in a hurry, although he'd never told me why. I'd found the few papers he did have stuffed in an old ice-cream container under his bed: among them a faded photograph of his parents; a couple of dog-eared postcards of São Paulo, addressed to Edson R. da Silva, and his passport of course, together with that of his ex-wife, Flavia. I looked at each of them in turn before putting them back in the bag, lingering over my favourite: a photo of Edson as a young man, grinning proudly in front of a long, low building, one arm slung around a man's shoulders, the other around the waist of a heavily pregnant woman. I flipped it over. Scrawled on the back were the words 'Ricardo e Flavia, Braços Abertos, julho 1978.'

I shut my eyes and tried to visualise Edson as a young man again, playing football, laughing.

He'd been 25 when we'd met, although he'd always seemed so much younger, with his boundless energy and unrelenting optimism. I'd just about hit rock bottom at the time. I remember it clearly - my head wedged behind the men's toilet at the restaurant where I was working, cleaning up after a visit from Frank, a barely-tolerated regular, who, at ninety years-old, and with hands that trembled like a tramway, refused point blank to sit down and 'pee like a girl'. I was coughing, having had a cold for weeks - putting the heating on in my flat had been a luxury I just couldn't afford at the time - and had accidently inhaled the stench of Frank. I retched, only instead of throwing up, I burst into tears.

When I eventually emerged from the cubicle, I stared at my face in the mirror; the vacant eyes, the grown-out perm with dark roots. This was not how I'd imagined my life at the age of 23.

A voice behind me made me jump.

"Girl, you gotta listen to Miss Franklin and go get yourself some of that there R.E.S.P.E.C.T." It was Dan, fellow waiter and long-time confidant. I liked Dan. Dan liked Aretha Franklin and hated my boyfriend, Steve.

Steve had charmed me, like he charmed everyone. He had the gift of the gab, but not much else, it turned out. He liked to tell people he was an 'entrepreneur', although as far as I could see, this pretty much translated as 'fencing things off the back of a lorry'. He never made any money, or at least, none that I ever saw. Of course, at first, I thought he was the epitomy of cool, all very edgy and anti-establishment. He was gorgeous and witty and I couldn't believe he'd chosen to be with me.

"Hey sweet cheeks, lend us a fiver," he'd say when I got in from work. I told myself I was helping him fulfil his potential, but who was I trying to kid? I'd fallen for a fake. He'd started spending his days sprawled on the sofa, smoking pot, hands down his pants, watching Cheggars

Plays Pop, and telling me not to worry as Thatcher was going to sort the country out.

I told Dan all this in the toilet at the restaurant.

"You have *got* to get yourself outta there, girl."

Dan was from Stepney, but I was pretty sure he thought he was from New York. That's when he offered me his spare room and revealed his big idea for dragging me out of debt and back to life: Edson.

"This is Edson," Dan pulled me by the hand through the crowd at the bar until I found myself face to face with my husband-to-be.

"Judith!" he cried, as if we were old friends reunited, instead of the complete strangers we actually were. He kissed me on both cheeks and handed me a bottle of beer.

"So, how long have you been in London?" I asked, struggling to unwind my scarf and pull off my gloves in the tight space afforded us, all the time looking around, as if the whole bar could tell why I was there.

"About nine months."

Even in these three words, Edson's accent was as thick and as warm as my grandmother's eiderdown.

"Your English is really good." I smiled to hide my nerves.

"Oh, you know..." he grinned. The truth was, his English was atrocious, but he hid it well.

"I love your hair," he swiftly deflected conversation away from himself.

I touched my snow-dampened hair,

embarrassed. It needed a wash. I'd come straight from the restaurant and it smelt of boiled broccoli and the onions that André the Chef had burnt, while busy flirting with the new waitress – the younger, blonder girl, newly arrived from somewhere near Russia. I'd caught them together and in my attempt at making a dramatic exit, I'd managed to knock over a bottle of red wine. And so now, despite the muggy heat of the bar, I insisted on keeping my coat buttoned up to hide the enormous stain on my previously white shirt.

André the Chef had been my on/off boyfriend before Steve – the latest in a long line of let-downs. My mother had made it clear from a very young age that my sister had the brains, me, the looks. I'd mistaken sexual attention for emotional connection so many times that I'd learnt to trust neither and yet repeatedly fell into the same trap. I'd been on the rebound, of course, and André had been no different to the rest of the men in my life. And yet still, with each one, I always thought I could make everything all right if I just loved them enough. But they always left me, and more often than not, left me in debt, just like Steve had. So when Dan suggested I meet his gay Brazilian friend, I thought 'Why not?' A contract. Cash. No scroungers, and most importantly, no heartache. All I had to do was fill out a few forms, and I wouldn't have to see the guy ever again. I'd be free of debt; free of Steve. I could finally get on with my life.

And so there was Edson, who quite obviously didn't need saving, eyes wild with the possibilities of youth and his new life in London.

"What do you do?" I asked.

"You know," he said, smiling at me, "what I do, it's no me, so I'm no answer this question."

I looked around for Dan, but he'd found himself a tall blond-haired man who looked as if he'd just come back from skiing.

"Okay, so who are you?" I ventured.

"Oh, my Judith, I am like a little mouse in a fish bowl."

He'd obviously been at the bar a while, I thought.

"You know, many moons since I run from cat, big cat," he gestured with his hands to show how big the imaginary cat was, "and then I meet fish and the fish say 'yes, little mouse, we understand you frightened, why you don't come live with us?' And so I jump in bowl and then, oh yes, it's wonderful, cat cannot find me, but oh no! What's this? I cannot breathe under the water, and I cannot swim, and help I'm... how do you say?" he mimed drowning.

"Drowning?" I offered, already lost.

"Yes, drow-ne-ning!" he stumbled over the unfamiliar word, "and the fish say, 'but we have beautiful castle here in our fish bowl', and the fish, they don't understand why I don't want living in their castle. Oh, these fish," he sighed, world-weary, "they understand nothing of the little mouse."

He took a swig of his beer and studied me.

"Are you a fish who understands, Judith?"

"Well," I said, unsure who exactly I was meant to be in his bizarre scenario, "I think I'm probably a mouse who's learnt to swim."

There was a silence as we both drained our drinks, then Edson banged his bottle down decisively.

"So, what you say a summer wedding little mouse?"

He didn't mention Rosa at that point, but it wouldn't have mattered. I knew on leaving the pub and heading towards the bus stop that I would take this grinning, imp of a man for better or for worse.

I'd felt so radical marrying Edson. The money had certainly come in very handy – the money supplied by his still-in-the-closet stockbroker boyfriend Gavin – although I would've married Edson for nothing. He'd waltzed into my life and transported me to another world. How I'd longed to go back to Brazil with him, to meet his family and discover the mystery, the passion, the exoticness of his beloved country. Right now though, Brazil was the last place I wanted to be heading. I wished the pilot would find a reason to turn the plane around and take me back to the familiarity of the house in Wembley. I felt so completely out of my depth. What had I been thinking?

A hand on my arm made me jump. It was the man in the window seat. He rubbed his fingers through his dishevelled hair as he handed me a folded piece of newspaper.

"I think this must have fallen out of your bag," he said, sleepily.

"Thank you," I said, taking the piece of paper, and found myself wondering if he'd ever been married, and if so, at what point in the marriage his wife had cottoned on to the fact that she would always take second place to twenty-two men and a ball.

The pilot announced our descent into Recife, the regional capital of the Northeast. We would soon be in Brazil; it would soon be time to take Edson's ashes home to his family. And then, maybe, we could start to rebuild our life together, mother and daughter. I looked over at Rosa, her strong jaw; her dark eyes; the thick, stubborn curl of her deep brown hair; her slender 15-year old body folded easily in the too-tiny seat. Already frayed beyond recognition, our relationship was being held together by this trip and the memory of Edson. Rosa had announced at the departure gate, in a deliberately poised manner, that on our return she would be moving in with Darren: Darren, who she'd known all of three months.

I unfolded the page the journalist had handed me. It had been torn from the newspaper I'd found on the living room floor when I'd got home from the hospital three months ago. On it, scrawled in biro, the words which had brought me here: Edson's final request, and a request I was determined to honour. I smoothed the page and heard his voice as I read the words:

'Take me home.'

CHAPTER THREE

Recife

We emerged from the air-conditioned artifice of the aeroplane in to a burning wall of heat. It felt like someone had thrown a steaming-hot towel over my face and thrust me in an oven. I could feel the sweat instantly oozing out of me. I stupidly hadn't thought to pack my sunglasses in my hand luggage before I'd left the overcast evening in London, and found myself squinting as I made my way unsteadily down the metal staircase, my legs apparently having forgotten how to walk during our twelve hours of cramped sitting. As I stepped on to the melting tarmac, I was still having trouble steadying my breathing. It was like there wasn't enough air – and it smelled different to anywhere I'd ever been – a mixture of the sea, of the earth after rain, and of my grandad's greenhouse on a hot summer evening in July.

It was a relief to step back in to the fresh, air-conditioned comfort of the arrivals hall, where the familiarity of the blue displays and lumbering luggage belts helped ease my growing panic at the world that awaited me beyond customs.

We stood side-by-side, mother and daughter, each a world away from the other. Rosa stood as if leaning against an invisible Mercedes, the picture of cool, as if she arrived in the northeast of Brazil every day. I hunched next to her, marvelling at my daughter's unconscious ability to make me seem so small.

One by one the passengers faded away, merging into the hubbub of the airport. Rosa shifted her weight from one foot to the other, her eyes on her fingernails, whilst I scanned and rescanned the carousel for our suitcases.

"You keep an eye out here," I said, "I'm going to check the other carousels. You never know, they might've got mixed up somewhere along the line."

My optimism soon dwindled however, as I watched a ragged pink pushchair rattle around the adjacent carousel, until the monitor above it eventually flickered off. Admitting defeat I turned to head back and smacked straight into a heavy canvas bag being hauled over its owner's shoulder. It caught me square on the chin and I yelped.

"I'm so sorry," a voice said.

I looked up. It was the bright-eyed journalist. He instantly dropped the bag and took my chin in his hands. His thumb brushed over my skin with such familiarity that for the briefest of moments I found myself wondering if we actually knew each other.

"Did I hurt you?"

I pulled away, embarrassed at not doing so sooner.

"I'm fine, really, it's nothing. My fault entirely, serves me right for not looking where I was going." I could feel my cheeks starting to burn.

The journalist picked up his bag.

"I thought I'd gone and broken your chin. That'd be a great way to spend your holiday, wouldn't it? Holed up in hospital."

"It's fine, really."

"Promise not to sue?" he grinned.

"Promise." I smiled and held out my hand, immediately regretting the ridiculously formal gesture, but knowing it would look far worse if I were to withdraw it now.

He shook my hand.

"Tom."

"I know, you gave me your card. I'm Judith, Judith Summers - Jude."

"Pleased to meet you Ms Summers - Jude."

The journalist, Tom, hauled his bag on to his shoulder once more, nodded a goodbye and strode towards customs. I touched my fingers to my chin and watched him go, a part of me wishing I could run away with him on whatever adventure he was about to embark.

Back at our carousel Rosa still had no suitcases either. Next to her, a middle-aged man, whose hair still bore the impression of the headrest of his seat, looked with the same dwindling hope at the empty carousel. A lone suitcase drifted through the rubber strips and, as he hobbled forward to claim his belongings, my eyes finally dropped. I tried to think of a suitably upbeat way of telling Rosa that all her clothes, make-up and new bikini had apparently disappeared somewhere between Heathrow and Recife, along with, rather more worryingly, the metal urn containing her father's ashes.

CHAPTER FOUR

Rosa

What the guidebook says:

- Brazil is the fifth largest country in the world.
- Literacy in Brazil is just 86% (over 280,000 adults unable to read or write).
- Up to eight million children are estimated to be living on the streets in Brazil.
- Brazil has the world's largest population of crack-users.

And it is to this corner of 'paradise' that my mother, in the infinite wisdom of someone desperate to make amends, has dragged me; 4,600 miles across the Atlantic ocean (according to the guide book Mum has made me read) in search of what? Forgiveness? Redemption? 'Closure'? (as the over-analysed neurotics on American sit-coms would say). Whatever it is she thinks she's proving by coming over here, I just wish she'd found a way of doing it without involving me.

"If you don't want to do it for me," she said before we left, "then do it for Dad." She knew I couldn't argue with that. It's her win-all, fail-safe argument: 'Do it for Dad.' She says she was planning for us all to go together, but she left it too late to tell Dad. "It's the thought that counts though," she said.

"No Mum, it's the stuff you actually do that counts. Maybe you should've thought of that earlier."

She looked completely crushed when I said that, and I felt pretty bad. She was just trying to make things better. She's had a lot to deal with these last few months, and I know I haven't been much help, but then it hasn't exactly been a joyride for me either.

She said, "You could use the trip for your GCSE geography project; take photos, make notes, do some research." She even gave me this travel guide with all these facts about Brazilian history, geography, culture and stuff. I'm only reading it because it gives me an excuse not to talk to her. Dad's only been gone a couple of months and she's already having a go at me about my GCSEs, like I give a shit about any of that now. Why does she always have to look on the bright side? It drives me crazy. There is no bright side. Dad's dead. Going half way around the world isn't going to bring him back.

I told Mum, as soon as we get back, I'm dropping out of school and moving in with Darren. I know she thinks I'm too young and that I don't know what I'm doing, and I know that Dad really wanted me to get a good education, but honestly, what's the point? We all die. Everything else is just killing time.

Darren's got a bedsit on the Kilburn High Road and says he can get me a job in the furniture shop where he works. I know it's not the Ritz or anything, and I haven't actually told him 'yes' yet, but I can't say I'm not tempted. I don't want to take any exams. I'm lucky because school work has always come easy to me; it's fitting in that's always been the problem. I hang out with Sal and the others because it's better than being alone, but I've always felt I was different; apart, somehow. But then isn't that how teenagers are supposed to feel? The teachers say I could get in to a good university and that I should definitely stay on and do A-levels, and to be honest, that *had* kind of been the plan, until now. But what happened to Dad, well, that puts it all in to perspecctive, doesn't it? I mean, he was from a good family, had the perfect childhood, had everything a boy could ever want. And now he's dead. I know it's not as simple as that, but I just don't see the need to prove myself to anyone by taking a bunch of pointless exams. Anyway, maybe a fresh start will stop me being so angry all the time and give me space to figure out what it is that I want to do with my short, pointless little life.

I never used to be like this, and I really don't mean to be. I wake up and I think, today I'm going to talk to Mum, we'll have a laugh and it'll be like how it used to be between the two of us, but then I look at her and its like she's become this solid brick wall of numbness, like she's forgotten how to feel. It's like she just doesn't get it. At all. She asks if I've done my homework and it's such a pointless, banal question, which clearly has nothing to do with how either of us are feeling or what we're going through, that I get angry straight away. It's like she can see I'm covered in petrol but has gone ahead and lit a match and flicked it at me anyway. And I know I shouldn't be angry at her, but I don't know who else to be angry at. At school I've started bunking off and going up behind the gym for a smoke. Sometimes Darren comes and meets me there, but mostly I'm on my own. Darren doesn't get it either. He hates his dad. He buggered off when he was little, but not too little to have seen what he did to his mum. So a dead dad for Darren, well, that's a cause for celebration.

My dad had his demons, I know that. He never talked about them, but we talked about loads of other stuff. Mostly he talked about Brazil; about when he was a boy; about wanting to take me there. I used to get so bored listening to the same stories over and over; stories that had nothing to do with me. I'd just zone out and pretend I was listening, only now that I'm actually on my way there, to Brazil, I feel such a total shit for doing that. It doesn't feel right to be going there without him, like I'm betraying him somehow. I want to ask him so many things about his life there, about what he was like as a boy, what his friends were like, where he lived, what he did in his spare time, who he loved. If he'd just come back, just for a day, I'd do anything, give up smoking, stay on at school, anything he wanted, just to have him back, just to hear him laugh at my stupid jokes, let him stroke the back of my hand as he talked about the past, tears in his eyes, like he did that last day, only this time I'd stay and listen; this time I wouldn't walk out the door.

CHAPTER FIVE

Recife

The badly air-conditioned bus wove its way through the late evening labyrinth of office blocks and shop fronts. Staring out into the foreign night, I listened to the unfamiliar rhythms of the other passengers' voices. After nearly fifteen years with Edson my Portuguese wasn't bad, but it was still strange to actually be in a country where everyone spoke it.

Back at the airport the customs official had started to get exasperated with my pale attempts to describe the contents of our bags, with the obvious omission of the urn secreted among the beach towels and underwear.

"I suggest you get yourselves a hotel and wait for your bags," he'd finally said.

I hadn't entirely understood what the problem with our bags was, other than it involved a place called Salvador and an aeroplane.

"How long?" I'd managed, unable to get rid of the image of Edson's ashes exploding out of my suitcase in some airport a thousand miles away.

"A day or two, maybe more, depends."

I wasn't sure what it depended on but the man was already ushering us out of the door and I hadn't known what else to say.

"You've got the hotel details I gave you though, right?" I'd asked Rosa, already knowing what she was about to say.

"They were in the suitcase."

As the bus headed into the city, rocking over one of the old bridges criss-crossing the river, I was reminded of Edson proudly claiming that his city was the 'Venice of Brazil'. I couldn't see any gondolas, but there was no denying the beauty of the city lights dancing on the water below.

We drove on past a hotchpotch of office blocks, shop-fronts and shabby-chic colonial corner houses. In the pools of light from the streetlamps I snatched disconnected details: a white church at the top of a cobbled street; grill-fronted shops shut for the night or for good; bicycle tyres and hungry dogs; bare feet, high heels and cigarettes. My back ached and my neck was stiff from the flight. I let my forehead rest on the glass and watched it mist up with my breath.

As the reality of Brazil seeped through the dust-smeared windows I thought of Rosa's real mother, Flavia.

Edson had told me she'd died in childbirth and his refusal to discuss her any further had initially fuelled my jealousy. If he'd once been in love with a woman, then why not with me? I'd learnt to live with it however, and soon we'd found a way of becoming a family, of sorts, and I'd come to think of Rosa as my own. And she was now, officially. After he'd come out of hospital we'd hired a lawyer to make sure of it. The curiosity had never left me though, and part of me wanted to tell Rosa the truth about her mother, if for nothing else, to have someone with whom to share the borrowed memory. I knew I should have told her long ago, but I'd never gotten around to it and in any case, Edson had made me promise not to. There was a time, when we were really close, when I could've probably told her, but it was too late now; the lie had gone on too long.

Peeling ourselves off the plastic seats, it was with a mixture of relief and trepidation that we stepped off the bus into the city. Even at this late hour the pavements were littered with newspaper kiosks and tired-eyed street vendors, the roads still crawling with bicycles and buses. The air smelled of rotting vegetables from the half-cleared market stalls; of petrol fumes mixed with drains and the scent of the sun on a thousand bodies. I put my hand on Rosa's shoulders but she shrugged it off. How I longed for a cool shower and a soft bed.

As we crossed over to the line of waiting taxis, I tried to look relaxed and confident, although I was acutely aware that I stuck out like a pig at a prom. When the first taxi driver refused point blank to take us where we wanted to go, we obediently moved along to the next taxi, bewildered, and showed the driver the piece of paper, on which the girl at the tourist information desk had scrawled the name of a cheap hotel. He waved it away.

"What's he saying?" I turned to Rosa, knowing my daughter's understanding of Portuguese was far better than my own, even if she refused to speak it.

"He says you must be out of your mind and

we should turn 'round and go back to wherever it is we came from," Rosa said.

"And those were his exact words?"

"What do you think?"

"Rosa, I appreciate you want to go home, but I could really use your help here, you know."

Rosa shrugged. I really didn't have the energy for her attitude this evening. Apart from anything else, I needed a drink.

"It's not like any of this is my fault," I said, "I didn't just wake up one morning and say to myself 'hey, you know what? I think I'll drag my daughter over to the other side of the world and completely ruin her summer. I'm doing this for Dad."

"Bollocks you are."

The driver was shouting at us to make way for his other customers and pointing up the street.

"Come on," I said, trying to sound more decisive than I felt. Rosa rolled her eyes and shoved her hands back into her pockets but followed me nonetheless.

As we made our way in the direction indicated by the taxi driver, my bravado about making my way in to the interior of Brazil to find Edson's mother shrank away. All I could hear was the voice of my own mother asking what on earth I was thinking, taking my child to a place like Brazil.

I soon realised why the taxi drivers had dismissed my request for a lift so readily. The hotel was hardly two minutes away. After winding through a series of narrow side-streets, between graffitied walls, neon shop signs and once-ornate buildings now left in ruins, we finally turned a corner and found ourselves in a wide, bustling boulevard. Through the traffic and trees I could make out the lights of a little square, towards the back of which I saw the front door of our modest hotel, nestled neatly between two much grander buildings.

Stepping into the foyer, my relief at finding shelter was short-lived, however. The term 'hotel' was quite obviously employed to describe anywhere with a roof and a front desk, although even that was an exaggeration as the roof above the reception desk had partially collapsed and there were no signs of repair work. Neither did there appear to be anyone around.

"Don't just stand there," I said to Rosa, who was still on the doorstep.

"There's no way I'm staying in this dump," Rosa said, folding her arms and looking back out at the square.

I was on the verge of agreeing with her when a smoky-eyed young man emerged from behind the reception desk and flashed her a grin.

"Bem-vindo," he said, striding past me to take Rosa's bag. I watched as my daughter unfurled before my eyes, happily letting herself be led into the hotel under the spell of this smooth young man and his 'welcome'.

He took us to a room on the ground floor: a cramped concrete box, the walls the fading blue of lapis lazuli, paint peeling off like sunburnt skin. He lingered in the doorway, watching Rosa as she flopped on to the double bed.

"You girls on your own then?"

I took the key from his hand and shut the door with a brusque "Boa noite – good night".

"It's not all that bad," I said to Rosa, who was rubbing her bruised elbows and scowling at the barely-disguised block of concrete, which served as a bed.

"I think he liked you," I added, thinking this might elicit a smile.

"So?"

"So, I'm just saying."

"Saying what exactly?"

"Well, you're a beautiful girl."

"And?"

"Look, we're not at home anymore, that's all."

"Your point being?"

"Just be careful who you flutter your eyelashes at here, okay?"

"Get a life, Mum."

How did everything I say manage to end up so twisted?

Rosa pulled a pillow over her head. Arguing had become our default setting and I didn't know how to change it. It had been the same with me and my mum. I'd thought that that would've made it easier, but it didn't. If anything it made it worse. I could see exactly what was happening but couldn't make her understand. I'd left home at sixteen, so I knew how she felt, but I didn't want Rosa making the same mistakes I had.

Through the small metal grill, which stood in for a window, came the drunken banter of a group of men on the balcony upstairs. Unfamiliar music spilled out of the cafés in the square, a hoard of hidden wildlife singing in a cacophony of accompaniment, celebrating the relative cool of the night: relative. I wondered if Edson had still been able to conjure up the sound of the night in this city as he lay in our converted living room in Wembly, or if it had been permanently blotted out by the rattling of the trains to Watford Junction.

Feeling like a boiled sweet on a beach I peeled off my long-sleeved top and heavy trousers and stepped behind the thin half-wall which partitioned off the shower and toilet. As hot as I was, the water from the greening copper pipe jutting out of the wall was still numbingly cold against my skin. It was just one more addition to the fast-growing list of reasons why I should never have left London. I could still hear my mother's words.

"I don't know what you're trying to prove, Jude, but you won't find the answer by running off to the other side of the bloody world."

As I hopped, shivering, in and out of the jet of freezing water, eye to eye with a staring gecko, I knew my mother was right. I didn't know what I was trying to prove or what it was that I was hoping to find, but I knew there was only one man who could help me figure it out.

First thing in the morning I would start my search for Ricardo.

BRAÇOS ABERTOS STREET PROJECT #14

Tapescript 1

Date: 17th August 1977
Name: Luciana
Age: 11 years

Flavia: You can sit here on the wall next to me if you like.
Luciana: It's okay. I'm fine over here.
Flavia: Why are you holding your arm like that?
Luciana: Jaru didn't come home again last night so Grandad hit me instead.
Flavia: Jaru's your brother, right?
Luciana: Yeah.
Flavia: Where's he now?
Luciana: Dunno. No one's seen him all night, but he'll be somewhere down here at the beach.
Flavia: What do your grandparents say when you come home alone, without your brother?
Luciana: So, last night Grandad says 'go and do something useful like your brother.' And I say 'What's so useful about not even coming home?' And Grandad takes a swipe at me and falls off his stool and the other men laugh and Grandad shouts at me but

	I've already run into the house, I'm not stupid.
Flavia:	Does your grandad have a job?
Luciana:	No, and he can't get one, on account of his legs and the fact that he hasn't got any because of that machine that crushed them in the factory, so me and Jaru, we've always had to work.
Flavia:	Doing what?
Luciana:	I started by selling ice-pops. We used to freeze them in Dona Lucia's fridge-freezer. She's the only one in the street who's got a fridge-freezer and she lets us use it, which is really good of her, as I know people who have fridges in other streets and apparently they don't let anyone use them. They're all mean about it, like it makes them better than everyone else, just because they've got a fridge.
Flavia:	Why ice-pops?
Luciana:	Because that's what people wanted and because I didn't know how to do anything else. But like Jaru says, "No one knows how to do things until they do them." I didn't know how to sell ice-pops, until one day I started selling them, and then I knew.
Flavia:	How old were you then?

Luciana: Dunno. Little.

Flavia: Did you sell them on your own?

Luciana: Nan used to come with us to the beach with her box of pastries, but then one time she tripped and fell and a man had to help her up and everything. Then, that night I heard her arguing with Grandad about money and about Mum and how she never sends us any anymore, and the next morning she gave me her box of pastries and her hands were shaking. She said we'd have to manage without her. I asked her what about the ice-pops and she said it's finished with the ice-pops, that's for kids. Her hands shake all the time now.

Flavia: And your brother? Does he help you?

Luciana: You're kidding, right? Jaru says he can look after himself, but I don't know. Valkiria told me that Valdimar, the boy from the house by the bus stop, went missing last month and they never found him. If I say stuff like that to Jaru he just laughs and says he's going to marry a rich girl from Boa Viagem and live with her family and never have to work. He probably will too.

Flavia: What do you mean?

The Brazilian Husband

Luciana: Jaru always gets what he wants. Once he needed money to pay off a hotel porter and he got 100 cruzeiros from Neginho to take his dog away and kill it because it barked too much and bit his hand when he hit it. He took it to the highway and threw it in front of a lorry. He laughed when he told me that, like he was telling a joke. It was only a puppy. I still think about that puppy, but mostly I think about the way Jaru's eyes shone when he laughed.

Flavia: Does your brother often sleep on the street?

Luciana: Sometimes. Hey, you got any food?

Flavia: I told you; we'll get something after, okay?

Luciana: Yeah, okay. I'm just worried, you know, 'cos Neginho said there was a squad out again last night. Jaru got caught by them once before and came back looking worse than that time he fell under a bus. He drank a lot of cachaça and when he came to bed he told me they'd kept him in a cell with another boy and beaten him and made him do things to the other boy. He didn't say what. Then I woke up in the night because I needed the toilet and I heard him crying in the hammock above me, like a little kid. I didn't dare move or he'd know I'd heard him, so I lay as still as I could and Nan beat me in the morning when she saw my wet mattress.

Flavia: Do your grandparents beat you a lot?

Luciana: [pause] Can we get some food now?

CHAPTER SIX

Recife

As every morning, I awoke with the feeling that there was something I'd forgotten to do; something terribly important, only I couldn't remember what. When the confusion finally abated, the nausea set in, as my memory seeped back through the heavy morning fug: Edson was dead. Gradually I became aware of the sounds of the city filtering in through the metal grill. The sun was already high and the heat almost unbearable. I heard a man's voice and my heart skipped a beat as I imagined for a second it was Edson, come to join us. This was his home, after all; these were his people; this was the place he had so wanted to take us. It seemed I'd finally made it to paradise, but it didn't feel the way I'd thought it would.

Drenched in sweat from a fitful night I showered and dressed before shaking Rosa gently by the shoulder.

"Come on love, let's go and explore," I whispered, steeling myself for what I knew Rosa's reaction would be. She pulled the thin sheet back over her shoulders and grunted.

"Come on love, we can sleep later. I want to see if I can find this Ricardo before lunch."

Rosa drew her legs up to her chest and didn't turn towards me.

"I'm not going anywhere," she mumbled, "I've only just shut my eyes."

"That's just the jet-lag. Come on, get up."

"I need sleep," she elongated the vowels, "Just go. Leave me here. Please."

I stood looking at the curled up figure of my little girl. We'd always been so close. True, Rosa had inherited, or more likely, absorbed, her father's erratic mood swings - what my mother referred to as her 'exotic' side - but even when the teenage years had kicked in and everyone warned me that things would change, they hadn't, not really. Sure, she'd started to get her own life; her own friends, and we'd started arguing about boys and homework, the usual, but it'd never taken us long to make up. But since Edson's death, things had changed. She'd become withdrawn and monosyllabic. She was out all the time, and when she was home, I tried to talk to her, about every day things, taking an interest in her school work, her friends, trying to find a point of connection, but whatever I said seemed to be the wrong thing, so eventually I stopped. It was so stupid that the one person in the world who knew how she was feeling, was the one person she couldn't, or wouldn't talk to. And it was killing me.

I picked up my bag from the bed and bent over to kiss Rosa's forehead.

"Okay, I'll let you sleep. I don't suppose I'll be more than an hour or so. Don't open the door to anyone."

"I'm not a kid, Mum."

"I know darling, but promise me?"

"Promise." Rosa yawned.

I watched her sleepy face and resisted the urge to brush away a damp hair clinging to her cheek. I hovered there a moment, thinking of the nights we used to spend together, watching films and eating popcorn in our pyjamas, whilst Edson and Gavin were out on the town. I longed for that intimacy now, that easy love we'd once had. All those years I'd stayed with Edson, sacrificing any hope of a real relationship, in order to look after the one true love of my life: this beautiful, messed up little girl, now hovering in that loneliest of places, somewhere between a child and a woman, desperately searching for her place in the world.

The sunlight hit me as I stepped out in to the square, and even with sunglasses it took a moment for my eyes to adjust. I felt conspicuous in my creased trousers and sweat-stained shirt, my pale, sun-starved skin ghost-like amongst the dark bodies and vibrant colours around me. I thought of Edson, of the last time he'd seen the sun, and had trouble imagining him here. I could only picture him in our living room at home, stuck in his wheelchair in front of the television, his right arm cowering beneath his collapsed shoulder, not a smile near his sullen face. I tried to remember his smile when we'd first met, the way it crinkled around his eyes and ran down through the muscles on the side of his neck. How he'd made me laugh and forget myself, sweeping me off my feet with his effervescent energy.

I looked at the reflection of the blushing bride in the registry office washroom and told myself I'd done the right thing.

"There you go," I said as I fastened Rosa's nappy. The little girl stood up on the counter and threw her arms around my neck as I pulled up her tights and fluffed her dress.

Edson and the others were waiting to take the official wedding photos on the steps outside. Luckily Dan had thought to bring a camera, for photographic proof of the day, and had kindly brought me a bouquet of flowers to throw for the non-existent bridesmaids.

We'd been planning this for months – so much paperwork, so many little details - and I'd started to feel quite excited about the Big Day, carried along on Edson's wave of enthusiasm. But now we'd actually done it, actually said our vows and exchanged rings, I felt suddenly deflated. I was someone's wife, but I felt more alone than I ever had.

Outside Rosa was radiant, toddling along, unaccustomed in her new dress, playing with her hair slides and proudly holding the bouquet of flowers I'd given her.

A few minutes later she held tightly to my hand as we approached the tube station.

"Are you sure you won't come back with us?" Edson asked, arm around Gavin, beaming.

"No, you're alright. You two celebrate for us, I'm shattered," I lied. It was quite obvious the two of them wanted to be alone. I smiled as I watched them float down the road on cloud nine. However much I might have given up on love and marriage for myself, I was glad I'd been able to help these two find their Happy Ever After.

That night I lay awake watching Rosa sleeping, her peaceful face oblivious to the new family forming around her. I'd never been much of a baby person – I couldn't even remember having spoken to any children before Rosa came along. I'd certainly never expected to feel so much love for a child and the feeling quite overwhelmed me. I looked forward to the nights Rosa stayed, especially now that my flat-mate Dan had moved out to go and live with a Norwegian man called Elvis, and my evenings had become rather empty.

The next morning, when Edson came to pick up Rosa, he helped me clear out Dan's old room to make a room for Rosa when she came to sleep over.

"Rosa and daddy stay?" Rosa asked.

Edson looked at me for an answer.

"You could, you know," I said.

It was as simple as that. Living together had never been part of the plan, never even been discussed, but a week later, with the 'not quite ready to come out of the closet' Gavin still dithering about letting them move in with him, Edson and Rosa moved out of their tiny rented bedsit and into my newly-decorated spare room.

The little square was littered with feet, some scurrying, some idly waiting, some dirty or dusty, others in freshly-shined shoes. The sun bore down into my bones and made my skin prickle. Feet became bodies, the bodies a swarm of activity around the edges of which I hovered. A couple sat under one of the many palm trees, snatching a moment's shelter in the shade together, before moving off in separate directions. To my right the owner of a bar was wiping down tables and shouting at an impatient customer, as his wife brought out four large plates, stacked with rice. The streets were already heaving with cars and bikes and bustling bodies. Across the road buses crowded two or three abreast around a series of bus stops, like wild animals at a fast-evaporating waterhole.

I crossed over to the pavement opposite and found myself swept along beneath the row of faded plastic sheets and tattered parasols, which served as brittle sunscreens to the street traders. Cloth-covered crates acted as makeshift stalls, adorned with phone cards, cigarettes, lighters, cards and all manner of things one might need or want on one's way to work. High above them, dust-covered workmen clung to scaffolding like flies caught in a web.

A wide-shouldered man called me over, proffering a handful of gnarled root vegetables, as his neighbour tried to entice me with a bunch of baby bananas. I was tempted to stop by the stall selling small, green oranges, which the stallholder had already cut to expose their ripe flesh, but was jostled past him. He turned and shouted something at his frizzy-haired wife peeling oranges in a wheelbarrow, a cigarette dangling from her lips, a crucifix from her neck.

Stepping carefully around the orange peel, which had been trodden into the dirt and dust on the pavement, I headed towards what looked like a central shopping street beyond. I didn't care what clothes I bought, I just needed to get out of the stale ones I'd been wearing since I left home.

In the first shop I came across I picked out a pair of white shorts, a green and yellow T-shirt and a simple dress for Rosa. There were no changing rooms so I had to duck behind a rack of World Cup football strips to try them on. The T-shirt felt a bit on the tight side but the woman behind the counter, who'd seen me from the till, grinned and gave me a big thumbs up. With no mirror to check, I had no choice but to take her word for it.

"Keep them on, they look great! It's no problem, really, just keep them on!"

In spite of her obvious enthusiasm I was unconvinced that the clothes were the right size, but embarrassed at being caught half-naked, and aware of other shoppers now looking in my direction, I shoved my dirty clothes into my bag and fumbled with a wad of unfamiliar bank notes in my haste to pay and get out of there. The woman asked me something with a smile but, not understanding, I simply nodded and turned to leave the shop as quickly as I could.

As I walked out the door I flinched as what sounded like a gunshot ricocheted in the street. No one else seemed in the least bit concerned but my heart was racing. Wembley was one thing, but this place terrified me. Another gunshot fired through the air, this time seeming to come from a passing car. A hand on my shoulder made me jump. It was the lady from the shop.

"You forgot your change," she said, handing me a couple of notes. "Don't worry," she added, seeing the terrified look on my face, "it's just the ethanol in the cars." I must have looked blank so she continued, "The ethanol, you know, the sugar cane." She smiled and turned back into her shop as another customer wandered in.

I made my way back to the bus stops. I'd asked the young chap on reception about the place in the photo and he'd told me that 'Braços Abertos' was a shelter for street kids in the city. It literally meant 'Open Arms'. He didn't know much about the place but said he knew where it was and had told me which bus to get. I was glad he had, as the rows of timetables lining the pavement were thickly plastered with fly-posters, hiding all but a few lines of the information they were supposed to be supplying.

The bus ride was long and hot and stank of sweat. The driver seemed to stop for every man, woman or child who stuck out their hand. I didn't get a seat right away but instead clung to the leather strap hanging from the rail, trying to avoid knocking into the people either side of me, as we were all swung first one way and then another. I watched, mesmerised, as a thin line of sweat trickled down the neck of the man in front of me, between his shoulder blades and disappeared under his faded orange vest. I marvelled at the muscles on his arm as it clung to the strap in front. As the bus lurched again he swivelled around and I pulled myself up just in time to avoid a face full of his thick chest hair itching to escape the vest top. He adjusted his weathered baseball cap and glanced down at my chest, a smirk tickling the corner of his mouth. I turned back towards the window, regretting my hasty choice of T-shirt. It hadn't seemed so revealing in the shop. But then I hadn't been able to look in a mirror. I tried to pretend I couldn't see him leering until the woman next to me finally got up from her seat and I was able to sink down into anonymity.

The shelter's iron gateway was a rusty hiccup in a long, crumbling wall running the length of the street. I stepped through it and found myself in a dusty red courtyard, the other side of which stood a low, drab colonial building, that may once have been pink but was now pocked with grey. Above the large wooden door hung a sign on which the words 'Braços Abertos' were still visible. It had faded since the photo had been taken and looked dank and neglected.

I knocked twice and listened. I could make out the distant murmur of voices and the clinking of cutlery. I was embarrassed to realise I was interrupting their lunchtime, but before I had time to shirk back out of the gate, a wide woman with exuberant grey curls pulled open the heavy door and beckoned me in with a smile that revealed her remaining teeth.

"Bom dia," I started, following the woman into a sombre, windowless hallway. My eyes took a moment to adjust to the darkness after the bright daylight outside. I realised the woman was gesturing at me to take a seat, as if she'd been expecting me.

"Oh, no," I said, thinking the woman must've mistaken me for another visitor, "I'm here to speak to Ricardo." I spoke in Portuguese, but my accent must've been pretty bad as the woman smiled blankly at me. "Does Ricardo still work here?"

"You've come to see Ricardo?"

"Yes, I'm sorry, I don't know his surname. He used to work here."

I pulled out the photo and showed it to the woman, who took it and went back to the door to study it in the light.

"Where did you get this?" she asked.

"Please, I really need to find him. Does he still work here?"

The woman handed back the photo, taking in her new arrival.

"Of course," she said and beckoned me through an ornately-carved archway.

We emerged into a whitewashed internal quadrant, in the centre of which grew a short twisted tree surrounded by fiery flowers and great clumps of thick cacti. Towering above them all, a palm tree shot up above the roof tiles into a rectangle of blue sky. Clearly sheltered from the sun for most of the day, it was cool and smelled of earth and damp plaster.

The woman led me around the quadrant to

the far side, where the noise from the dining room was like that of an angry beehive. More than twenty girls aged from around five to fifteen were sitting at long rectangular tables eating plates of rice and beans. The chattering stopped like an outboard motor suddenly cut as we walked in and I felt more than twenty pairs of eyes upon me.

"Sit down." The woman brought me a chair from one of the tables and brushed off some errant rice. I sat down obediently against the wall and the girls started talking amongst themselves once again.

"I'm actually just here to see Ricardo, if he's here?" I ventured again.

"I don't know. You should wait. Have you eaten?"

I hadn't but I wasn't hungry.

"Oh, yes, thank you," I lied.

I sat and watched the girls eating and felt sick with hunger. I hadn't eaten anything since leaving London and the smell of food made me wish I'd taken the woman up on her offer. I tried to focus on what I was going to say to this man Ricardo but was too nervous to concentrate. Edson had once told me that Ricardo, the man in his picture, was the person to whom he and Rosa owed everything. Without him, he'd insisted, they wouldn't have gotten out of Brazil alive. If ever anything happened, he was the one man I could count on. Only now that I was here, I felt ridiculous. What if he didn't show up? What if he couldn't help me? What then?

As the woman finished serving the dessert of fresh fruit salad and the girls started clearing their plates, a man walked in and took off his baseball cap, running his hand through his dark, dishevelled hair. He was silhouetted against the daylight.

"Anything left for me?" he grinned at the woman, who smiled back indulgently like a fond grandmother. One of the girls called over to him.

"Hey, my mum says thanks for the papers."

The man waved at her, "Tell your mother she must come back to see us."

"That's enough Marie-Lourdes, now sit down and stop your talking," chided the woman.

I was standing now, unsure whether to introduce myself. The man looked at me, one eyebrow raised, and walked over. I could see now that he was a little older than me, with the slightest hint of crow's feet around his coffee-bean eyes and a faint indentation across his forehead where his cap had been. He smiled at me and I felt suddenly bashful, stumbling over my Portuguese.

"Sorry, yes, hello, my name's Judith Summers, I've come from London. Look, I know you must be busy, I won't keep you long."

As he guided me to a table at the back of the room the girls filed past us, out into the quadrant. They all had a smile for him, a hello, a squeeze of the hand. And he, like a father, patted each of them on the head, the shoulders, the nose.

The woman brought over two plates of rice and beans.

"So what can I do for you Miss Summers?" the man asked, taking a mouthful of his beans. "Mmmm, what did you put in these beans Nenê?"

"The same as the last time you asked me," the cook said, dismissing his compliment with a wave of her hand.

"They're delicious."

Clearly flattered, she laughed and carried on clearing the other tables. I picked up my fork but couldn't bring myself to eat.

"You can speak in English if you want," the man said, taking my hesitation as a lack of vocabulary. His thick, warm accent reminded me of Edson.

"Are you Ricardo?" I asked.

"Sometimes," he said, smiling.

"It's about Edson da Silva," I said, "He told me he knew you, and that I should come to you. I think you might be able to help me."

I felt myself garbling. Close up Ricardo was striking, his dark skin soft under his stubble, his arms smooth and strong. He wore long khaki trousers, despite the heat, and a white short-sleeved shirt, open at the neck.

"Edson?" he asked. The smile had gone from his face. I was still holding the photo in my hand and gave it to him. He studied it for a while and scratched his stubble. He stared hard at the picture, as if he might crawl inside it. Then he handed it back to me.

"I'm sorry, I can't help you," he said.

"But that is you in the photo, isn't it?"

"We've had a lot of kids pass through here over the years. I can't remember them all."

"But Edson said you were his friend." I felt my voice getting smaller.

"And you are?" he asked.

"I'm his wife."

He looked up at me then, as if seeing me for the first time.

"I think you should leave." He got up and walked to the door.

"But your food, sir," the cook scolded.

"Would you see this woman out please, Nenê," he said, and walked out into the sheet of bright sunlight, leaving me holding the photo, my mouth hanging open, still formulating a response.

Back at the hotel I nodded to the man from reception, who was lounging on the sofa under the TV screen in his 'Don't worry be happy' T-shirt. He said something to me but I only understood the word 'daughter'. I hurried to the room, terrified at what might have happened. The door was unlocked. I opened it gently so as not to wake Rosa but the bed was empty.

"Rosa?" I peered behind the crumbling half-wall that separated the toilet and shower area but found nothing except the staring eyes of the gecko looking at me.

I rushed back to reception.

"Have you seen my daughter?" I asked the man, not returning his smile. He was young, beautiful and evidently amused by me.

"Rosa?"

"Yes, Rosa," I said, wondering how he knew her name.

"She went out a little while ago."

"Out?" But I'd only been gone a couple of hours.

"Nice girl," he said, grinning in a way I was unable to read as friendly or menacing.

I ran back outside and scanned the square for Rosa. She wasn't on the benches or across the street at the orange stand. I couldn't see her down at the bus stops either. A crowd had gathered towards the bottom of the square and suddenly I knew – there'd been a terrible accident and the police were on their way. Crowds like these gathered at crime scenes – gawking at the blood, the proximity to gore. I pushed my way through the jostling bodies, convinced I'd find Rosa lying injured or dead on the pavement. Instead I emerged from underneath the sweaty arm of a robust woman to find everyone laughing and applauding a group of bare-chested Capoeira dancers, who were spinning around on the ground, their trousers implausibly white in the dusty afternoon. I recognised the rhythmic music and the mix of dance and martial arts from years back, when Edson and I had seen a group performing on the South Bank. He'd grinned wickedly and run straight over to join in, always the show-off. The crowd was entranced. I looked around at the faces but saw no sign of Rosa. I turned around and stormed back to the hotel.

    The man from reception was still sprawled in front of the television and I placed myself firmly between him and the screen.

"Where is she?"

"I told you, she went out."

"What have you done with my daughter?" I hit the off button on the TV behind me.

"Look lady…"

"Don't 'lady' me. Where is she?" I could hear my voice getting shrill in my panic. He got up to move away from me, hands raised, but I grabbed him by the T-shirt, startling myself, but driven only by the fear I was feeling; the fear that something bad had happened and I was too late.

"Where's Rosa?"

"Mum?"

Looking up I saw her, loitering in the doorway, a can of drink in her hand. I let my fingers fall from the man's T-shirt and adjusted my own. He glanced at Rosa before disappearing behind the reception desk, muttering something I didn't catch.

Rosa rolled her eyes and took a swig from her can as if it were the most natural thing in the world.

"You promised me you wouldn't leave the room."

"No," said Rosa slowly, "I promised you I wouldn't open the door to anyone. And I didn't."

"You knew what I meant."

"What? I was thirsty; it's so hot here. You didn't tell me it was going to be *this* hot. And anyway, you told me not to drink the water from the tap, although come on, I bet everyone else drinks the stuff and they look fine." She finished the last drop of the drink and walked past me towards our room. I followed.

"Wait right there, young lady."

"Oh, sorry, did you want some?"

"I told you not to go out." I wanted an apology at the very least, but Rosa was either oblivious to the worry she had caused me or had decided to ignore it.

"Mum," she hissed, looking over at the receptionist, who had reappeared, and returned his charming smile, "you're embarrassing me."

I took her roughly by the arm and guided her to the room, furious.

"You can't just go walking around by

yourself. We're not at home now. It's dangerous here, don't you get it?"

"Oh, and what? London's so safe?" she was being deliberately antagonistic. I bit my tongue. "Mum, it's cool." Rosa added, "I told Tiago where I was going."

"Who the hell is Tiago?"

"The guy at the desk. Didn't he tell you?"

"No, he didn't," I said, although as I was saying it I realised this was probably what the young Tiago must have been telling me when I'd walked in and ignored him. As if to make up for the lie, I threw the bag with the clothes onto the bed.

"Thought you could do with a few things."

Rosa pulled her loose hair up into a scrunchy, before pulling out the clothes I'd chosen for her, a doubtful expression on her face.

"You bought me clothes?" she said, not with thanks but with disbelief and a certain wariness.

I didn't reply but shrugged off my own clothes and slipped behind the dividing wall to brave the cold shower again. I'd never showered this much.

As I plunged my head under the stream of water, Rosa called to me.

"So Tiago said he'd show us around, take us to the beach. He says it's the only place worth going on a day like this. He's coming over to get us later as soon as he gets off work."

I opened my eyes under the shower and let the icy cold water numb my cheeks.

BRAÇOS ABERTOS STREET PROJECT #14

Tapescript 2

Date:	**9th September 1977**
Name:	**Luciana**
Age:	**12 years**

Flavia: Why are you looking so happy?

Luciana: Mum turned up last night. I heard her arguing with Nan in the kitchen. She told us she'd met this great guy who was looking after her now, and if things worked out we could all move back to Rio.

Flavia: Is that a good thing.

Luciana: I don't know if I want to go to Rio. I don't remember it at all. Jaru says it's a really long way on the bus, two days, he says, but Mum's promised to take me shopping to buy a dress when we get there, because we'll have lots of money by then. I did this little dance with Mum because I was so excited about my new dress and that she was back, but Jaru laughed at me, not in a nice way, and said I shouldn't listen to her. Mum shouted at him and he told her to get lost and go and live in Rio if that's what she wanted, because we didn't need her or her crack-head pimp. She said Nelson wasn't a crack-head, that this time it was different, but Jaru didn't want to listen and he stormed out and slammed the gate so hard that it fell off its hinges again.

Flavia: He doesn't want to go to Rio with you and your mum?

Luciana: Dunno. He did the same thing last time Mum came back. That was a couple of months ago. He got into a fight with her old boyfriend, who pulled out a gun. He missed Jaru, but he shot a hole in Nan's picture of Jesus. Jaru was gone for days, and then he turned up one night covered in blood and with his arm bent backwards.

Flavia: Did your mum stay this time?

Luciana: She came in later to put me to bed and sang me the song she used to sing me when I was a baby. She said she'd stay the night, but when I woke up she'd already gone. She's sending her new boyfriend, Nelson, to come and get me later, and take me to a lady's house, where Mum says he's got me work, cleaning and stuff. Nan says he's not really her boyfriend but that I'm old enough to go and live with this lady. Apparently she's got this amazing house right on the beach. Jaru's going to be so jealous. So I ask Nan when we're going to Rio and she says, "Just as soon as you and your mum get enough money together." She cried when I asked her that, so I said, why didn't she come with us, but she just cried some more. Nelson's coming to fetch me later. Nan's packed my dress in a green plastic bag and she's given me her pink hairbrush with the flowers on, that her mum gave to her.

Flavia: Why today?

Luciana: It's my birthday today. I'm twelve, but we don't make a big deal about it in our family. It's not like I remember being born or anything. Jaru doesn't remember it either. He's only a year older than me, although people call us the twins because we look so alike, but I don't see it. Jaru's handsome; he's got my nan's eyes, from that other country. I don't know whose eyes I've got; I suppose they're just mine.

Flavia: Do you remember much about when you were little?

Luciana: Dunno. Valkiria says your brain doesn't grow until you're about three or four years old and then your brain grows and you can speak and walk and all those sorts of things, which little babies can't do. Jaru says he remembers his brain growing, but I don't. It probably happened when I

	was thinking about something else.
Flavia:	Is Valkiria your friend?
Luciana:	Yeah. I remember the day she came to live next door. I remember it because it was my birthday that day too. I was sitting behind our blue gate, peeling off the loose paint with my fingernails and waiting for Grandad in my best dress, the one that Nan made me especially because I was going to be six. Grandad said he was going to buy me a bottle of cola because I was a big girl now and Nan gave him some money to get it.

A bunch of men were unloading furniture off the back of a truck, only with the rain and the mud they were slipping and sliding everywhere. Valkiria's mum was shouting at them to be careful with her picture of Our Lady of Penha; her sister Wilma was whining that her clothes were soaking wet and her hair looked a mess, which it did, but no one cared; and the men were grumbling that they weren't getting paid.

I think Valkiria wanted to run away that day, because I saw her climb on to the roof of her house. She saw me watching her and I smiled and she went "shhh!" and so I didn't tell anyone when they shouted for her. She tried to climb over to our roof because from there you can climb over to the bar, but she slipped, sending a whole tile sliding down and smashing into millions of pieces, like the fireworks I saw once at the beach, only the fireworks exploded when they reached the sky, not when they hit the ground. It just missed Wilma's head, making her scream like she'd seen a huge rat, and Dona Maria went mad and sent her husband to get her. He caught her by the leg and she kicked him, cause he's not even her dad, but he grabbed her and pulled her down like a cobweb and dragged her screaming back up to the house. I could hear the shouting and the crying through the wall.

I stayed at the gate and waited but Grandad didn't come back, and Nan said we might as well go to bed, but I wouldn't come in to the house because I wanted to wait for him and I was really exited about the cola, only it got really late and I fell asleep behind the gate. He woke me up when Neginho brought him back in the middle of the night. I could smell he'd been drinking. I asked him if he had my cola and he punched me in the ear and said I was a greedy, selfish girl and that the day of my birth was not something that should be celebrated

	and I could stay outside with the dogs.
	I don't hear so well now.
Flavia:	Tell me, Luciana, who's this lady that Nelson's taking you to work for?
Luciana:	Just some rich lady, but look, I gotta go. Mum says he's not someone you want to keep waiting.

CHAPTER SEVEN

The beach at Boa Viagem

Tiago, it turned out, didn't actually work at the hotel. He'd been covering for his cousin who'd been arrested two days earlier and who was still being held at the police station. He was therefore currently without gainful employment. "But," he assured us, as he and Rosa settled back in to their plastic chairs and I brought over another round of drinks from the straw-roofed beach bar, "I have a plan."

I watched as Rosa stared in admiration at this svelte young man, naked torso glistening above his shorts, as the sun reflected off the salt water droplets still on his skin after their swim. With his smoky eyes and mischievous grin, he reminded me of the Edson I'd gone and fallen in love with when I was young and stupid and should've known better.

It took months to sort out all the necessary paperwork for the wedding, so Edson and I arranged to go out together a few times, which quickly turned into a regular event. Thursday nights Dan and I would close the restaurant and head off to meet up with Edson and Gavin. Edson's energy was on a constant spin cycle. He introduced me to a whole new London, even though he'd only been living in my city for nine months when I met him. He took me to clubs and bars I'd never even heard of. When I was out with Edson, I forgot my debts, forgot Steve, forgot my lousy job and rediscovered the live-fast-die-young teenager still hidden inside of me. Rosa was just a baby, still in nappies, and had already charmed several of Edson's female Brazilian friends into looking after her one evening a week.

It was the night before our wedding. Dan had decided he needed to take us out, and as usual we ended up at a club. We were all very drunk by this point. What's more, I'd bumped in to Steve and his new girlfriend on my way out and was feeling more than a little sorry for myself.

"I'm going to die an old maid," I told Edson.

"What you talking about, little mouse?"

"It's alright for you, you've got Gav. I come home every night to David Attenborough."

"Who?"

"It doesn't matter."

"You need to dance," he said, taking me by the hand and spinning me around the dance floor. In my memory, we rocked that dance floor. In reality, we were probably more like drunken uncles at a wedding reception. For me, though, it was just the two of us and the music. Edson pulled me to him and we danced around like nutters, until the music slowed and I lay my head on his shoulder and he held me as we swayed together like teenagers at a school disco.

"I think I love you," I whispered in to his neck.

"I love you too, my little mouse."

I looked up at him, "Why do you always call me your little mouse?"

"I could put you in my pocket."

I slipped my hands in to the back pockets of his jeans and realised I hadn't done that to a boy since I was at school. It felt good; close; together. I looked up into his impish eyes and saw that mischievous glint. Of course, I knew he was gay and that he was with Gavin, but his body was so warm, his skin so soft, his lips so near mine, so ready to lose myself in. I shut my eyes and reached up to kiss him.

"Shit Jude, you got broccoli in your hair again." Edson attempted to remove the offending vegetable, completely unaware of what I had been about to do, or at least pretending to be. I excused myself and ran to the toilets where I splashed my face with cold water and tried to pull myself together, but only succeeded in smudging my mascara. I stared in to the mirror. What had I let myself get in to? I was falling in love with the man I'd been hired to marry.

"I happen to know," Tiago was saying, explaining his grand plan for success, "that a film crew from São Paulo is coming to town to film a new soap opera about two families in the Northeast, and my cousin knows the guy who's going to be driving the camera crew around during filming. He's going to take me along." He opened his arms and lay back on his chair, a satisfied grin on his face.

"So, you want to be a driver?" I asked.

"A driver?" Tiago sat back up, looking at me in disbelief, "Hell no, woman, I'm going to be a soap star! That's where the money is - money and girls." He grinned again, his eyes lingering too long over the top of Rosa's sand-dusted breasts, exposed by the dismayingly small bikini I'd bought her earlier that afternoon, "And it's a way out of this dump. I'm going to the big city."

He was trying to impress Rosa, I knew that, but I could also see that he was utterly convinced by his own story. I smiled and sipped my juice. I looked at Rosa, who saw nothing but ambition and beauty in this boy. She didn't see the inevitable heartache, the dreams that were waiting to be shattered, just around the corner.

I let my head fall back and felt my damp hair tickle my back. It was a relief to feel the sea breeze on my face and neck, after the heat of the day. My toes played with the sand under the table, the only place it was cool enough to tread without sandals. I looked along the beach, half expecting to see a young Edson running towards me. It was strange to think that he would've sat on this beach, drunk at a bar like this one, admired boys like Tiago with his vigorous optimism. I wondered what Edson would've made of this young man. I certainly didn't trust him. He was a chancer, I could see that, and his intentions towards my daughter were clearly anything but gallant. True, his eyes were bright and fresh with the coquettishness of youth and his smile was truly dazzling. But I had seen men like him before; been hurt by men like him before, and I knew I would have to keep a close eye on this one.

We'd been swimming. Wading in to the sea

was like sinking in to a warm bath, unlike the icy water off the Sussex coast where I'd gone each summer as a child. I could feel my skin tightening as the sea salt dried all over my body in the late afternoon heat. I felt cleansed and relaxed and would've happily climbed into a hammock between the palm trees that lined the beach, and drifted off into a blissful sleep. I closed my eyes and let the sound of the waves and the people and the music from the bar drift over me. I imagined Edson here. I tried again to picture him when we'd first met, tried to remember the laugh, the sparkle. He would've been happy here. He would've been the king of the beach, at home among the tourists and the hawkers, the humming bars and the beautiful boys. I was beginning to feel I understood something about him, something vital that I hadn't seen before: the loneliness he'd felt, the great void in his heart, stuck in his wheelchair in a grey London street, when in his mind he was here, beneath this crystal sky, dancing on the burning sand, diving into the soft waves. I'd never before appreciated quite how isolating it must've been, so used as I was to London, with nothing to compare it to. I wanted to call him up and tell him that I had seen his sea and felt his sand between my toes and that I was sorry for letting him suffer his 'saudades'; his longing for home, alone for so long.

I was startled out of my daydream by the brittle voice of a young girl in my ear.

"A Senhora would like something cool and refreshing?"

The twig-like waif of a girl carried a large polystyrene box, crammed full of ice pops, three of which she was pushing into my hands, her wide brown eyes irresistible in her smooth dark skin. I reached out to accept the proffered ice pops.

"Pssst," hissed Tiago and stamped in the direction of the girl, sending her hopping off to the next table like a flea from a burning dog.

Other children came past the table as we sat and soaked up the sun, boys for the most part, fried fish strung in bundles from sticks across their shoulders, polystyrene boxes crammed with canned drinks, doughnuts and delicious smelling pastries the size of large shells. Rosa bought a bag of them on the advice of Tiago, despite my warning looks. I didn't trust the homemade food, not knowing what home they'd been made in, not wanting to imagine the bacteria we could be exposing ourselves to. I refused to taste the pastries, despite being tempted by the glorious smell.

Tiago had come by the hotel after his shift, as promised. We'd just had time to buy Rosa and myself a bikini and towel before he'd arrived and then had taken the bus to the beach.

Tiago seemed to know everybody in the city – from the bus conductors to the barmen. He'd talked incessantly, pointing out everything from the bus window, a torrent of stories and facts gushing from his grinning face. Everywhere there were posters of politicians: the suave, refined Fernando Henrique Cardoso and a funny, squat-looking chap called Lula.

"FHC is going to get Brazil out of the mess we're in," he'd said.

"Who's the other guy?" I'd asked.

"That's Lula," he'd said with a snort of a laugh, "he's just a jumped-up street kid playing at politicians, he's a joke."

From the way he spoke, I got the impression he was repeating words he'd heard elsewhere, passing them off as his own. But what did it matter? Good luck to anyone who wanted to take on this country, I thought.

"Where is everybody?" Rosa had asked, looking out at the empty city. It was true; the busy streets of the morning had become almost ghost-like. Everywhere Brazilian flags lined the half-deserted streets.

"It's the match this afternoon," he'd said, as if we'd know what he was talking about."

"What match?" Rosa had asked, more interested than me.

"Brazil against The Netherlands," he'd said, "the quarter-final," he'd added when our faces looked blank, "Everyone's either gone home or gone off to a bar to watch it. No one's going to miss that."

I could see the glow in Rosa's face as she talked to Tiago and knew it wasn't just from the sun. We'd been at the beach for just over an hour and I could already feel my skin burning. I realised I'd underestimated the strength of the sun and had been a little too cavalier in my insistence that I didn't need sun cream, that I would feel it when I'd had too much sun. I'd forgotten I wasn't in our back yard in Wembley and this wasn't the same sun. My face was fine, having bought a large-rimmed straw hat, but my shoulders and chest were starting to tingle and I was starting to feel a little light-headed.

I found myself thinking of Ricardo, of the

way the girls all greeted him like a favourite uncle, the sparkle in his eyes when we'd met, which had made me blush like a school girl. I couldn't understand why his demeanour had changed so suddenly when I'd mentioned Edson.

The night was already falling. People were arriving all along the beach, groups of youngsters carrying nothing but towels around their necks, coming in from town to spend the evening by the sea.

The match was about to start and the bar was already crowded. On the TV behind the bar the teams were filing on to the pitch. Everyone was glued to the screen. I couldn't have cared less – England hadn't even qualified as far as I knew, and even if they had, the world cup song would have undoubtedly been more successful than the actual team. But I could see that to the people crowded around the TV screen, this wasn't just a big deal; this wasn't just a football match; this was *everything*.

Although coming to the beach had been a welcome distraction, I really had no intention of staying to watch a football match. I decided I needed to go back and confront Ricardo. What other choice did I have? I'd been going over our brief meeting all afternoon and was convinced he was hiding something, although I had no idea what, or indeed why he would need to.

Rosa was less than happy about being dragged half way across the city to a shelter for street kids, when she'd been invited to spend the evening with Tiago and his friends at the beach.

"Mum, I'm nearly sixteen. I can look after

myself."

"I know you can love, but this is important."

"I don't see why you need me to come," she pouted.

"I *want* you to come. I want you to meet Ricardo. He meant a lot to Dad."

At the mention of Edson, Rosa turned her head to look out of the bus window. We hadn't talked about him. Not since the night it happened.

I'd been calling Rosa's friends all evening from the hospital but none of them knew this Darren she was supposed to be with, and I had no idea how to contact her. When I finally arrived back in the early hours, Rosa was asleep on her bed, fully clothed.

I gently shook her awake and told her what had happened, without stopping to censor what I was saying, just desperately needing to tell someone. I told her how depressed he'd been, about the empty bottle of tablets, the ambulance, the attempts at resuscitation.

Rosa half sat up and, still drunk, leant her head against the bedroom wall, hands pressed either side of her obviously pounding head, eyes resting on my shaking hands on the duvet as I told her that her dad was dead.

In the silence that followed I wondered if I ought to have lied after all, not to have told her about the pills. But I was so exhausted, so shell-shocked myself, I'd told her everything. Well, almost everything.

And still she said nothing. Instead, she threw back the duvet, bolted out the door and ran to the bathroom where I heard her throwing up in the toilet. She slammed the door shut and refused to open it. I sat down on the landing and leant against the door, talking to her through it, trying to find the words to comfort her, but too many words had already been spoken. Eventually, exhausted, we both fell asleep where we sat.

CHAPTER EIGHT

Braços Abertos

The same square woman opened the door of the shelter and shook her head as she led us to an office just off the central quadrant and its garden.

We'd taken the bus back to the hotel first to shower and change, and now the night had firmly set in. I could hear the girls' squeals of excitement accompanying the unmistakable din of the end of the football match on a TV in one of the rooms. The woman disappeared and a few moments later the noise was suddenly silenced as the television was turned off. A car drove past in the street outside, leaving a haunting stillness in its wake.

The woman returned.

"Can you tell me where the toilets are?" asked Rosa.

The woman turned back out the door, signalling Rosa to follow her.

I looked around Ricardo's office, feeling like an intruder, embarrassed and suddenly unsure whether I should be there at all. Files lined the walls, stacked on the stone floor; a broken clock leant against an uneven pile of newspapers; the fan above my head hung motionless.

Out of the window I saw the woman, Nenê, return to a couple of the younger girls, crouched on the veranda next to one of the banana trees, sorting through an enormous pile of fruit in the dull light of a naked bulb. I could make out mangoes; passion fruit; bananas; oranges. They were placing some of them carefully in crates, discarding others on a pile behind them.

A voice came from behind me.

"I told you earlier, I can't help you."

I turned to see Ricardo standing in the doorway. He looked tired, I thought. He was struggling to unknot a large Brazilian flag tied around his neck like a cape.

"I know," I stammered, caught off-guard, "I realise it was a long time ago, but I don't have anyone else to go to."

He walked over to his desk and opened a drawer, pulling out a pen, which he tried to work into the stubborn knot.

"Well," he said, as the knot slipped undone and the pen fell on the floor, "I'd suggest you ask this Edson chap again - get your facts right."

"Ed's dead."

The silence shocked us both. I saw in his eyes that he wanted to ask me more, but he said nothing. I looked at him as he carefully folded the flag. The circles under his eyes were deeper than I'd first noticed, and the crow's feet at the corners more pronounced now his eyes were half shut. I found myself wondering if he was eating properly.

Rosa came in, shaking her hands dry, not seeing Ricardo by the desk.

"God, the toilets here are disgusting. Can we go now?"

Ricardo looked up sharply and Rosa started, embarrassed, looking suddenly younger and so much more vulnerable than she had a few hours ago at the beach.

Ricardo stared at her.

I broke the silence.

"This is Edson's daughter," I said.

"Rosa." His voice was almost inaudible.

"Yeah?" Rosa was immediately on the defensive.

"You look so like your mother," Ricardo said.

Rosa laughed, the first time I'd seen her laugh in months. Of course, she had taken him to mean she looked like me, which couldn't have been further from the truth.

"So you knew my dad?" she asked, to my surprise.

"Your dad?"

"Edson."

"Oh yes. I mean, no. Not much, not really. It was a long time ago."

Rosa pressed her lips together and nodded, quickly averting her eyes from him, instead surveying the photos around his walls. I watched her and longed to hold her, to let her know it was all right to cry. But Ricardo had already sensed her distress and deftly steered the conversation in another direction.

"That was taken at the São João festival last year. The girls made their own costumes." He walked over and looked at the photos with her, "We teach them to sew and to cook. We give them an education and the basic skills they need to get off the streets. It's not much, but *you* try getting funding for anything more."

"How many girls are here?" Rosa asked.

"Twenty-three at the moment, although the

numbers are quite fluid, depending on family circumstance. We do our best, but in some cases, they're the main earner in the family. Not everyone manages to stay."

I realised it was him now who was embarrassed, garbling, maybe not wanting us to leave after all.

"Do some of them have families then?" I realised as I looked at Rosa that now Ed was dead, she was, to all intents and purposes, an orphan herself, without even knowing it.

"Usually. Some live with their mothers, some with their grandparents, or older siblings, others on the street. The notion of family is pretty fluid here too." He looked at me and then lowered his eyes in what seemed to be an apology. I could only manage a weak smile back. I was terrified he would say something about Rosa's mother, but he must have sensed my unease.

"Do you want to meet some of the girls, Rosa?" he asked.

Rosa looked at me and then back at Ricardo and shrugged, non-committedly.

"Come, I'll introduce you to some of the little ones."

"Oh, I don't know," Rosa looked embarrassed, but Ricardo was already opening the door for us to follow him.

He took us through the kitchen and out on to a veranda overlooking the garden.

"You've already met Nenê. Nenê, this is Judith Summers and her daughter, Rosa." He said my name, Judith, in such a way that the first syllable was so soft it sounded more like 'shoe', and he completely ignored the 'h' at the end. He pronounced Rosa's name like Edson had, replacing the 'R' with an 'H' so it sounded more like 'Hosa'.

"The supermarket gives us the left-over fruit they can't sell," Ricardo explained, "Nenê goes through it every week with the girls, seeing what can be saved and cooked up to help us stretch our food budget as far as possible."

Nenê the cook beckoned Rosa over.

"Go on, give her a hand, Rosa. I'm sure Vera and Vanilda will show you how it's done." Ricardo winked at the two grinning six year-olds staring wide-eyed at Rosa as if she'd walked straight out of a television set. They giggled together as Rosa took a seat on an upturned crate opposite them, which creaked and promptly collapsed. The girls burst into laughter, as if it were the funniest thing they had ever seen, and Ricardo and the cook grinned. Rosa looked cross. I knew she didn't like being made to look stupid.

"Will you be okay?" I asked, trying hard not to laugh myself.

Rosa shrugged her shoulders, her cheeks blushing, her eyes looking daggers at me, evidently not wanting to get her hands covered in over-ripe fruit. Ricardo was looking at her, as if he couldn't quite believe she was real.

"Can I speak with you?" I asked him.

"Sure, sorry," he said, "come on, we can talk in my office."

I looked across at Rosa who was being shown how to select the useful fruit from the rotten.

"Don't worry, she'll be fine here with Nenê," he said, sensing my concern.

I followed him back through the kitchen

and across the quadrant to his office, where he gathered the books off a chair and offered me a place to sit. I stayed standing as he looked for a place to put down the books and ended up replacing them on the chair. He straightened up and looked at me, his hand pulling at the back of his neck, like a reprimanded schoolboy.

"Look, there's something I ought to tell you," he said.

"It's okay, I know."

"You do?" He sounded surprised.

"Edson told me. About Rosa's mother."

"Oh."

"Only Rosa doesn't know."

"About her mother?"

"Edson and I met when she was still a baby. She thinks I'm her mother. That's why she laughed earlier, when you said how much she looked like me."

"Sorry about that, but the likeness is remarkable. Really, she's the spitting image of her mother at that age.

"You knew her?"

"I did."

"Did she work here?"

Ricardo frowned and perched on the edge of his desk.

"What did Edson tell you, exactly?"

"That she was his girlfriend, that she was young; that they were both young."

Ricardo covered his mouth with his hands and let them slide down over his chin. He got up and walked to the window where he could see Rosa undergoing instruction from the little girls.

"He didn't like to talk about her," I said.

"Are you planning on telling Rosa about her mother?"

"Well, I don't see there's much point in telling her now. She's just lost one parent, how can I tell her that her mother's dead too?"

"Luciana's not dead."

"Luciana? No, her name was Flavia. Edson said she died in childbirth."

"He said that?"

"Yes."

"That her name was Flavia?"

"Yes, the pregnant woman in the photo." I dug out the photo from my bag and handed it to Ricardo.

He looked at the picture again.

"I'm sorry, I must have been confusing her with someone else," he said eventually.

I sensed there was something he wasn't telling me.

"Why did you say Luciana?"

"No reason. I really don't know."

"Oh no, you can't just say something like that and expect me to just let it go." Who did he think he was, upsetting my world like this? Rosa's mother was dead. I didn't need him putting doubt into my mind now. I wanted to know why he'd said what he'd said, but realised that at the same time, maybe I didn't really want to know.

"Look, I... your husband, well..." he went over to the filing cabinet.

I waited; unsure whether this was my cue to leave.

"I ought to be going," I said eventually, disturbed by a feeling that whatever he was looking for, was something best left where it was.

Without looking around, Ricardo motioned to me to stay where I was.

Just then one of the little girls banged on the window.

"Ricardo!" Her face was only just visible over the window ledge.

"What?"

"Come and see, come and see!"

I looked at Ricardo.

"Come on!" the girl insisted.

"Coming," he said, then looked at me as if weighing something up in his mind.

The other girl was banging on the window now too. Ricardo slid the filing cabinet shut.

As we reached the garden we found the two girls and Rosa squashing fruit with their feet in the dim light of the veranda. Rosa was laughing and I caught a glimpse of her as a little six year-old, and suddenly missed Edson desperately – the Edson who'd come out of his room in the morning, a little sleepy girl on his back, laughing and spinning her around as she screamed with joy.

"Don't worry, we washed them first," the little girl laughed. Rosa looked up and as she saw me she stopped what she was doing and stepped out of the bucket of squashed fruit, the laughter gone from her eyes. The girls were disappointed and tried to coax her back in but she was already wiping her feet with a cloth.

My heart sank. I knew it was time to leave.

"I'm sure you're a busy man," I said. "I won't keep you any longer. It's just I really need to find Edson's family. If you could possibly give me an address?"

"I'm sorry Ms Summers, I really can't give you what you need," he said, "It was really very nice to meet you though - both of you - and I wish you all the very best." He nodded curtly and turned back to the kitchen.

"So, what did you think?" I tried to engage Rosa in conversation as the cook showed us to the gate.

Rosa shrugged, hands already in her pockets.

We walked back up to the bus stop in silence. I didn't like being in the dark, empty street, two women on their own. Down in the city I could hear the celebrations still going on for what I assumed was Brazil's qualification to the World Cup semi-final. The bus appeared around the corner before we reached the stop and I started running to catch it. Only Rosa wasn't going to be hurried. She slouched up the street, leaving me standing, breathless by the bus as the driver gave up waiting and drove off.

I didn't see the point of saying anything. Rosa was quite clearly looking for a fight, but I was tired and didn't have the strength to take the bait.

We waited in silence. I kept looking hopefully down the road for another bus, wanting to get off the streets and back to the hotel as soon as possible. Rosa leant casually against the bus stop as if she had all night. I could see she was angry. I was angry with myself for having given up so easily. I told myself I should have stuck to my guns, should have pressed Ricardo further, but the truth was I was intimidated by him. Something about him made me feel inadequate.

At the same time I knew he was hiding something and that he knew more than he was letting on. I looked back down the street, trying to build up the courage to go back, to march in and demand he tell us what we needed to know, but I was just so tired, the jet-lag really starting to kick in. What was the point anyway? Edson's ashes were still missing, and even if they did turn up, I had no idea how to reach his family. It looked more and more like I'd failed before I'd even begun. It seemed Rosa had been right to doubt me after all.

A car pulled up alongside us. I stiffened, fear gripping my chest. A head stuck out. It was Ricardo.

"I've got to go into town, can I give you a lift?"

"It's okay," I said, immediately on the defensive, "we'll get the bus."

"There won't be another one for at least half an hour now," he said, raising his eyebrows in a 'well, what about it?' way, which I decided to take as his way of apologising.

"Mum," Rosa hissed, fed up of waiting there in the dark. I acquiesced.

"Thank you," I said, without smiling, and opened the passenger door. Rosa got in the back.

As we drove off I watched Ricardo trying to organise a wad of papers on his lap, whilst driving slowly to the end of the road, expertly swerving to avoid the multitude of enormous potholes. He must've been in his early to mid forties, his hair ever so slightly starting to recede, thick and so brown it was almost black. His eyes were the same colour as his hair, deep and tired, his skin like smooth caramel. I wanted to reach out and stroke his arm, to see if his skin was really as soft as it looked, but I remembered I was still angry with him and instead tried to think of a way to get him to tell me about Edson.

"Have you always worked here?" I asked.

"Oh no, well, yes. I don't work here, officially, I sort of help out, keep an eye on things. My wife started the shelter years ago. I'm a lawyer, so I go where I'm needed." He shrugged his shoulders and then added, "Why did you come to me? What did your husband tell you?"

"He told me that if anything happened, then you were the man to go to. I think you meant a lot to him. He said if it hadn't been for you he'd be dead by now." I realised what I'd said and felt my cheeks redden even more than they already were from the sun at the beach. The car had no air conditioning. Even with the windows open the breeze was warm and dirty, and the dust from the tyres stuck in my hair. The humidity clung to the air around us, heavy with the stench of the drains.

"Please tell me where Edson's family lives," I said, watching his lips for an answer.

He glanced at me and then looked back at the papers on his lap.

"I told you, I can't help you."

Distracted by his papers he didn't see the boy running towards the car, waving his arms wildly.

"Stop!" I shouted, afraid he was going to hit him. Ricardo slammed on the brakes. I looked at the boy through the windscreen. He must've been no more than twelve years old and was running up to Ricardo's window. I was sure we were going to be car-jacked.

Between his gasps for breath I only managed to understand the words, "They're back…"

"Get in," Ricardo reached behind and opened the back door for the boy, who clambered in. Rosa shuffled along to give him room, pushing herself right up against the opposite window.

"How long ago?" Ricardo asked, already driving off.

"Dana called the garage – then I ran here as soon as I got the message. I don't know."

"How many are there?"

"Too many. Dana just said go get the lawyer."

Ricardo went silent. The papers had fallen off his lap and were getting crumpled by the pedals.

"What is it?" I asked.

"His family, their neighbours. He lives in a favela – a shantytown being targeted by developers. They pay squads to carry out random raids on the place to scare away the people who live there, to make way for their new luxury apartments." He hit the steering wheel with the palm of his hand, making me jump. "It must've taken him at least ten, fifteen minutes to get here, maybe more."

"Why didn't he go to the police?"

The boy spoke, but not to me, "Who's this? Why are you bringing her?"

"She's a friend, Leo. Tell me, is anyone hurt?"

"I told you, she just said to come and get you. Can you do anything? Dana said you could do something."

"I'll speak to Dana. I don't think it's a mystery who sent them but we need to get back, make sure everyone's alright."

"Shit." The boy thumped the back of Ricardo's seat hard with his fist.

Ricardo said nothing but I was scared by the look on his face. He was driving fast now, his knuckles pale as he gripped the wheel.

"I'll have to drop you off at the corner," he said to me, without slowing down.

I didn't like the look of the boy and wasn't sure what sort of thing they were headed towards, but I knew that if I left now, I might never get the information I needed; I might never get to take Edson home.

"No, not until you tell me about Edson," I said, decidedly.

Ricardo glared out of the windscreen.

"Fine," he said, passing the corner and taking a side road that swept down the hill and joined the main road along the river, past the bridge. What seemed like millions of city lights reflected in the water, as the residents celebrated the match. Beyond them somewhere lay the sea, thousands of miles across which lay home: normality; peace; a new bottle of gin in the cupboard waiting patiently for my return.

Eventually we turned off down a dirt road. I held on to the roof of the car to steady myself as we tore over the uneven ground. Wires were tangled around the lampposts, which cast their light on a makeshift muddle of half-built houses, concrete electricity pylons and forgotten brick walls. Debris of broken cement blocks were strewn along the side of the road as if they'd rained down.

We drove past a woman perched on the edge of a great pile of rubbish holding her head and crying. Behind her a dog foraged for food.

"You want to know where your husband lived when I met him?" Ricardo said.

I looked at him and nodded.

"Well, welcome to hell." He pulled over and the boy jumped out of the back of the car.

"But Ed lived in a house by the beach," I said, "his father was a surgeon…"

"Stay in the car," Ricardo interrupted me as he leapt out. He poked his head back in and added, "I'll be right back. Shut the windows and stay in the car." He threw me the keys and ran after the boy who was already turning the corner.

I watched them disappear past the row of shacks and into the shadows beyond the last light. I saw Rosa in the rear view mirror, terrified. I turned around but her expression immediately changed. I realised she was trying to look cool.

"It's okay love," I said, "he'll be right back. They've got stuff to do, that's all."

Rosa glared at me. I wound up the window as Ricardo had told me to, despite the heat. There was no one around. I guessed they were all recounting events to Ricardo. I wasn't clear about what had happened, but it seemed that Ricardo was used to it, whatever it was.

We waited.

Eventually, unable to bear neither the humidity nor the tension in the car, I wound down my window and put my head out to try and cool my face. Instead, I inhaled the stench of rotting waste from a pile of rubbish seeping into the ground. I covered my mouth and nose and quickly closed the window again but the stench was already in the car.

"Oh, that's disgusting!" yelled Rosa. "Why did you open the window?"

"I didn't know it was going to stink like that."

"Well, you could've guessed by looking around you."

"Look, I didn't bring us here," I said.

"You might as well have done."

"What's that supposed to mean?"

"I didn't even want to come to this disgusting country. You're the one who thinks it's going to make any difference."

"You know I had to come for Dad."

"Yeah, so this is *your* guilt trip. You didn't have to bring me."

"This was his home."

"This? You think this was his home? He lived in a mansion by the beach, Mum. His dad was a surgeon. You think he would've wanted me to come here?"

A knock on the window startled us both. We'd been so intent on our argument that neither of us had noticed the woman approaching the car. Now she stood, hand on my window, a thin child perched on what little hip she had. He had a dummy in his mouth and his face was marked with patches of white.

I opened the window.

"Mum!" Rosa started to protest. I shot her a look that shut her up.

"Please, you have to bring the car," the woman said, out of breath.

"What?" I said.

"The lawyer said you have to bring the car. He needs it now." I noticed that there was blood on the woman's T-shirt.

"But I can't drive," I said, looking blankly at the woman.

"You have to bring the car now," she said, starting to walk back in the direction she'd come.

"Shit." I shuffled across to the driver's seat.

"Mum, he said to stay here," Rosa said, plainly scared.

I ignored her. The woman was beckoning us to hurry up and I fumbled with the keys, trying to get them into the ignition. I tapped my feet on the pedals, first the left and then the right, checking which was the brake and which was the accelerator. I thought I could remember but then had a sudden panic and my mind went blank. Did left-hand drive cars have the same pedals as in the UK or were they all back to front? It was no use asking Rosa, she was too young to drive. I'd only driven a handful of times myself and had never passed my test. Living in London I'd never seen the need. The last time I'd driven had been when my then-boyfriend told me to drive a drunken customer home from his pub, and he wasn't someone you argued with. That had been nearly twenty years earlier, and the steering wheel had been on the other side.

I revved the engine far too aggressively, then nervously pressed down the clutch and put it into first gear. 'Yes,' I thought, but as I pulled away I immediately stalled it and the car juddered like a cat coughing up a fur ball.

"Mum, just forget it, he'll come back if he needs the car."

"He's asked me to take it over to wherever he is, I can't just ignore him," I snapped, angry with myself for having got us into this situation.

"You don't even know if she's telling the truth, it could be a trap."

"We're not in one of your films, Rosa. Look at her, for God's sake, does she look like she's lying?"

I restarted the engine and eased up the clutch once more. This time it purred and I followed the woman the same way as Ricardo had gone.

Turning the corner the road was full of holes and the improvised street lamps shed only a dim light. I had to drive over piles of rubble and wire to avoid the deep holes in the middle of the dirt street. I didn't fancy getting stuck in a pothole here at this time of night. Parts of the street looked practically finished; brick houses painted blue and pink. But right next door it was like a building site, bricks thrown up against each other, some painted white; others covered in graffiti; windows with no glass; doors blocked with wood. An expressionless face watched us pass from a hole in a door.

As I pulled into the street the woman was indicating, I saw a group of people gathered outside one of the houses, far up on the left. This road was different than the last. They weren't so much houses as shacks, haphazardly constructed from wooden planks and mud and straw and goodness knows what else. Somehow they were being held together, but there was no glass in the windows and the corrugated iron sheets on the roofs seemed ready to slide off at any moment.

The woman was waving her arms in a wide circle and I wound down the window.

"Reverse!" she was saying, "You won't get out that way."

I'd never done a three point turn in my life and I made a hash of it, first misjudging the front of the car, which rode up a concrete block and back down again, crunching the underside of the bumper, then having to break suddenly as a dog scampered out of a gate and across my path.

"Mum," Rosa whined.

"Well, you could help," I snapped, angry at myself and embarrassed as I realised the group of people had now turned their attention to me and my atrocious attempt at the manoeuvre.

"Don't have a go at me, it's not my fault you can't drive," she said.

As I reversed I could see the people pulling apart and making way for the car. A group of kids were kicking a semi-deflated ball opposite. Ripped pieces of green and yellow plastic bags had been strung along the front of the houses as improvised World Cup bunting. The woman who had come to get us was already pushing her way past the people. They saw her coming and made room for her to get through.

In the rear-view mirror, I saw Ricardo walking towards us, carrying a boy, limp in his arms, a small woman hurrying behind him.

"I told you, we've got to get him to hospital," he was saying to the woman, who was tugging at his shirt as they arrived at the car.

The woman, the boy's mother, I presumed, was pleading Ricardo not to take him, fearing that he would be killed by the men who had done this.

"He has no choice," Ricardo was saying to her, "Stay here and he'll die, do you want that? Do you want to lose another son?"

She didn't answer but barked at a group of neighbours watching them and followed Ricardo as he opened the back door and got in. Rosa leapt into the front seat next to me as the mother followed Ricardo into the back seat and they lay the boy across their laps.

"Come on, let's go," Ricardo said. I'd left the engine running. I pulled off jerkily and heard the boy groan. At least he was alive, I thought, but I had no idea where I was going. The bumps were awful and the mother started praying behind me. I swore at the gear stick as I struggled to find second gear.

"Stop the car," Ricardo ordered.

I broke too quickly and felt the boy lurch against my seat.

"Sorry," I said.

Ricardo was already shuffling from underneath the boy and out the passenger door.

"Come on, let me drive," he said, opening the driver's door and waiting impatiently for me to get out.

"I'm sorry," I said again, getting out, but Ricardo was already in the driver's seat and I realised that if I didn't get in there and then I would be spending the night in the shantytown.

I clambered in to where he'd been sitting, lifting the boy's limp legs and laying them on my own lap. He was bleeding from his side. His mother held his head. I tried to avoid touching any blood whilst equally trying not to offend the mother. But the mother couldn't have cared less about my presence. She was stroking her boy's hair and mumbling prayers. He wore red shorts, his torso bare, other than a rather ineffective makeshift bandage wrapped around his midriff.

I looked at his face, his eyes shut, the pain visible, the low moaning of someone giving up hope of being heard. I shut my own eyes and held on to the door handle as Ricardo careered through the streets. I didn't want to think of Edson but I couldn't help myself. I felt the boy's legs on my lap and felt the weight of Ed in my arms again; saw his face. I'd held him tight as he'd shouted, then moaned, then looked at me with such terror in his eyes. He hadn't slipped away peacefully like I'd told Rosa, he'd fought; he'd struggled; at the last moment he wanted urgently, desperately, to cling on to life. And I'd held him and told him everything would be all right as we waited for the ambulance, already knowing it was too late. His lifeless eyes never left me. I saw them every day, couldn't shake them from my thoughts. I knew the only way of closing his eyes, of letting him go, was to bring him home, to lay him to rest where he had once been happy, had once run along the beach, swum in the sea, fallen in love and had his heart broken to the sounds of Samba and the taste of fresh coconut milk, as he watched the boys go by.

CHAPTER NINE

Recife hospital

In the drab, dimly-lit hospital corridor Rosa refused to sit down. Instead, she perched against the windowsill, body turned towards the exit, trying not to interact with anyone or anything.

I sat on the plastic bench, which ran the length of the wall, leaning back, blinking into the fluorescent light bulb above me, trying to synchronise my blinking with the bulb's erratic flickering, until my eyes started to water and I could no longer see the light but just a fuzzy haze. I bent my head back down to focus on the floor between my aching feet and my ankles that still felt swollen and tingly from the flight. My upper back, where I'd stayed too long in the sun, was starting to feel taut. I wished I'd thought of bringing cream, but then dismissed the thought as useless. What would be the point of even the best cream in the world, without someone who cared enough to rub it on?

I closed my eyes and they stung, making my ears buzz with exhaustion. Hospitals were the same the world over: the smell of disinfectant hiding death behind closed doors; of wilting flowers and dwindling hope. I thought of Edson, after the attack, and felt tears prick the inside of my eyelids.

I'd brought flowers, although as I walked in I felt ridiculous and stood there feeling hopelessly inadequate. Rosa had brought her panda bear and propped it up against Ed's pillow as she clambered up on to his bed. He'd been asleep and shouted out as he woke up, scaring her. She scrambled to the foot of the bed and held out her arms for me to pick her up.

"It's alright my love, daddy just had a bad dream, that's all."

It had been a week since what the police were calling the 'incident' and it was the first time I'd brought Rosa to see him.

"Hey, baby girl," Ed held out his uninjured arm and Rosa hesitantly nuzzled up to him, handing him her panda bear.

"The doctor says they're moving you to the ward this afternoon," I said, trying to make conversation.

"The police were here again this morning."

"Have they found them?"

"Have they fuck. They haven't got a clue, I can tell. No tape in the camera; obscured view of assailants; racially motivated crime. Shit. Race had nothing to do with it."

Edson had been leaving a gay nightclub with Gavin. Gavin had stopped to relieve himself behind a bin and Ed had gone on ahead, down into the underpass. The group had followed him. He heard the names they hurled before they caught up with him, but by then it had been too late to run.

Rosa leant on his stomach and he winced in pain.

"Sorry Daddy."

"Não é nada, querida. It's nothing, my love. Just a bit sore there." He spoke Portuguese to Rosa, as always.

"Mummy says your legs don't work."

Ed looked at me.

"Yeah, well, they're just hurt, that's all. They'll be better soon," I said cheerfully to hide the devastation I felt. We both knew that wasn't true.

"Has he called?" he asked me, as he had every day that week.

I shook my head and looked away.

He turned to the wall. I put my flowers on the bedside table. Another bouquet was there. I picked out the card and read it.

'Thinking of you - Gav.'

The truth was, I already knew what it said – I'd dictated the words to the florist myself. It was only a white lie, I told myself. I just couldn't bear to see the hope in Ed's face every morning when he asked if I'd had a message from Gavin, his eyes pleading with me to tell him that today was the day he was coming to visit.

Gavin hadn't been in to see him since the attack. I'd rung him to tell him how he was doing, but he'd been caught up at work and had promised to go to visit as soon as he could. I'd phoned again the next day but only got his answering machine. When I finally managed to speak to him, he'd actually said, "The thing is, I'm no good around sick people," as if Edson had put on a new suit that wasn't to his taste and he was going to wait for him to change back into something more suitable. I knew it would be up to me to break it to Ed, I just couldn't bring myself to do it yet.

I looked at Rosa, perched on the end of the

bed, panda clutched to her chest, behind her Edson turned to the wall, and I knew that I would never leave them. They needed me. I was all they had now. We were a family.

"Come on darling, we'll leave Daddy to sleep now."

I heard a raised voice and looked up. Ricardo had been on the phone almost constantly since we'd arrived at the hospital and was becoming irate with whoever was on the other end. I watched him, half way up the eternal corridor, the receiver tucked under his chin, his hands gesticulating as if the person on the other end could see him. Every now and then he would take the receiver and hold it against the wall as he, too, leant his forehead against the wall and took several long, deep breaths, before putting the receiver once again to his ear.

Eventually he slammed the phone back on to its hook, stood a moment staring at the wall and then came back to stand next to me, hands deep in the pockets of his trousers, his body rigid with frustration.

"How is he?" I asked.

"Not good."

"Was it drugs related?" I was still not quite sure what had happened at the favela.

"Drugs related? No, it wasn't drugs related," Ricardo said, tersely.

"I just thought..." I started, but Ricardo cut me off.

"You know, there's more to life in a favela than drugs. Of course, that's what people like to believe though, isn't it? Favelas are dark, dank, evil places, crammed to bursting with gangs and crime and hate." He was getting more and more wound up. "You know how much the kids who work for the drug traffickers earn?"

I shook my head.

"Less than a hairdresser, and they get next to nothing. It's not well paid at the bottom, you know. Young people, they want jobs, they want professions, they want to work. There's a whole new generation of entrepreneurs in those favelas, like you wouldn't believe. You should see what some of these kids achieve out of next to nothing. The rest of us could learn so much if we just harnessed that energy instead of constantly trying to squash it. You kick people enough, they're going to kick back at some point. And then everyone points the finger."

He was talking *at* me now, not *to* me. I could've been anyone. I engendered 'the other'. I felt a need to defend myself but Ricardo hadn't finished.

"No, this wasn't drugs related, Ms Summers. This was purely about money; this is a developer trying to build on the land they live on. Everyone knows who he is, but he's got money, and apparently money is more important than the lives of kids like Raphael."

I didn't know what to say. I was embarrassed that I hadn't even thought to ask the boy's name. I was out of my depth already but felt I ought to make some comment, some remark to show Ricardo that I wasn't just some ignorant tourist, however much I felt like one.

"I suppose he was just in the wrong place at the wrong time," I said, attempting to diffuse the palpable tension.

"That's just it, isn't it?" Ricardo spun around so abruptly that I jerked my head back instinctively and smacked it against the wall. He seemed not to notice. His tired eyes were livid, his hand now tugging at his hair, "It's always the child's fault, isn't it?"

I shrank into my seat, not daring to take my eyes away from his as he continued.

"Clean up the streets, send them home, restore childhood to the children."

I couldn't see why he was so angry. Surely that was what he was working towards every day at the shelter.

"Nowhere do we hear the question 'Why are these kids on the street?' No one wants to tackle the real issue here, which is not just getting children off the street, but looking at what is so fundamentally wrong with this country that the street becomes their preferred rock to the hard place they're supposed to call home. In the 'wrong place'? This is his country. We should be making it safe for him, not shoving him somewhere where the world can no longer see him."

I found it hard to hide my confusion, as he continued.

"What? You think kids are safer at home than on the streets? He *was* at home. An hour ago he was at home with his family, and now he's hanging on to his life by a thread, and for what? For being at home!" He stopped talking but kept looking at me. I wasn't sure if he'd finished, so said nothing. I was afraid to open my mouth and be subjected to another onslaught. He rubbed his face with his hands and slid down on to the bench next to me.

"I'm sorry," he said, speaking quietly now, "What do you know? You're just a tourist."

He was right. I didn't belong there. I should've stayed in London. At least I knew who I was there, even if I didn't necessarily like who I was. He wanted to explain though.

"We're an old country, but a young democracy. You know, we've only just created our bill of human rights, that's how behind we are. We're fledglings, afraid of falling out of the nest, however stagnant that nest might be. And whilst the country is obsessed by the World Cup, attention is deflected away from those with the money and the power, and the politicians in their pockets, who swan through the elections like puppets, with big words and hollow promises. You know what? Go back to the beach, Judith Summers. Go for a swim, buy a big hat, take photos of the bare-foot kids to show your friends, and go back home. Forget your husband. Bury him and move on. This isn't your fight."

We sat in silence after that, until it was time to go. Even Rosa relinquished her stand and came to sit with us.

Raphael's mother stayed, refusing to leave the hospital, even though she was only allowed to stay in the corridor. I understood. I wouldn't have left either, despite the fact that I hated hospitals. Even if she wasn't allowed in, the boy would know she was there. I could think of nothing worse than fighting for your life in a hospital bed with no one by your side.

Ricardo didn't speak in the car. He dropped us a

block from the hotel, at my insistence. Even though it was late there were still hundreds of people milling around the streets; lights still on; bars still heaving with the post-match celebrations. I needed to get some air, even the still, heavy air of this city, after the claustrophobic corridor of the hospital.

"Come on, I'll get us something to eat," I said to Rosa as Ricardo drove off, reaching my arm around her shoulders. She immediately pulled away as if my touch were poison.

"I'm going to go meet Tiago," she said.

"Since when?"

"Since he asked me to," said Rosa, starting to walk in the other direction towards the bus stop.

"No way," I said, following her, "you're staying with me. Don't you get how dangerous it is here? You don't even know this boy."

"He's not a boy, he's almost twenty. And anyway, there's a whole group of us. You saw for yourself, Tiago knows everyone. It's totally cool, Mum. Stop acting so middle-aged."

"But didn't you see that boy back there at the hospital?"

"That was about the land, I heard what Ricardo said. It's got nothing to do with me or Tiago."

"How can you say that?"

"How can you always want to spoil everything?"

"I'm just looking out for you. This isn't London."

"No Mum, this isn't London, and whose fault is that? You're the one who made me come. Sal's going to be getting off with Darren behind my back now I'm not around."

"Is that all you care about? Who's getting off with who?"

"You wouldn't understand."

"No, you're right, I don't understand. I don't understand what I've done to make you so angry at me."

"What you've done? You don't understand what you've done? And you think *I'm* the one who needs to wake up?"

"Tell me then. Tell me what it is so I can make it better."

"Like you made Dad better?"

"I beg your pardon?"

"Dad was fine when you weren't around."

"That's not true."

"You didn't give a shit about him. You were always out working, leaving him there on his own. You didn't even sleep in the same room."

"It was complicated."

"Was it, Mum? Was it? Or was it you who drove him to it?"

"Rosa!"

"No Mum, you want to know what the matter is? You want to know what you've done?"

"What? Tell me."

"It was you, Mum."

"What was me?"

"You. You, you, you, you, you." Rosa was shouting now.

"What did I do?"

"You killed him."

Silence.

I heard a glass smash on the pavement somewhere behind us, followed by laughter and drunken applause. My mind was swimming. Rosa was shaking with anger, seething hatred.

"Rosa, Dad was very ill; he was clinically depressed."

"No Mum, he just needed you to love him."

"I *did* love him."

"He needed you and you let him die. And I'll never forgive you for that. Never."

"I did love him."

"Yeah? Then how come I never saw you kiss him; hold him? Dad needed you."

"It wasn't me he needed."

"Then who Mum? Who did he need? Who are you going to put the blame on this time?"

I shook my head, the tears pricking my eyes,

"Who Mum? Tell me, who did he need so badly, who left him there to die on his own?" She was in my face now, practically spitting at me. She was becoming hysterical. People were looking at us. I didn't know what to do so I said the first thing that came to mind; the last thing I should've said,

"Gavin."

Rosa pulled back.

"You remember Gavin, don't you?" I could feel my heart pounding under my T-shirt and tried to keep my voice steady, "Rosa, I loved your dad."

She looked up at the trees above us as if she didn't want to hear what I was about to say, but she had to hear it.

"I loved him, but he was in love with Gavin. We couldn't tell you, you were just a baby..." How I wished I could take back the past ten seconds, rewind, go back to the beginning and the lie that had served me so well until then, but it was too late. There was no going back.

"Rosa, Dad was gay."

The minute I said it I felt a burden lift from me, only to be replaced by a gut-churning dread. I'd gone too far. I'd sworn I would never tell her. But it was for the best, wasn't it? Oh God, what had I done?

Rosa made a deep guttural noise, which I took as her attempt at a cruel scoff of disbelief, astounded that her mother would make up such a hurtful lie to get herself off the hook. But my face couldn't hide my horror at what I'd just said. Rosa stumbled back, looking hard into my eyes, searching for something that would tell her it wasn't true, but I could see that a part of her already knew it was.

She pulled at her hair and bit her lip. I could see she wanted to say something but couldn't find the words. I hated Edson at that moment, and I hated the sweaty, fucked-up country he'd made us come to.

A bus pulled up alongside us. Rosa was still looking at me. She nodded her head slowly and walked backwards into the line of people waiting to board the bus.

"Rosa," I began, but stopped. There were already a lot of people staring at us, undoubtedly intrigued to hear us arguing in English. I didn't want to call any more attention to ourselves, I certainly didn't want to make a scene. Rosa was at the back end of the bus, where people were now filing on, working their way through the turnstile, handing their prepaid tickets to the conductor, who perched on his stool just inside the back door, as others sidled down the aisle and filed out of the door at the front. As the bus started to pull away, Rosa grabbed the pole and jumped on and the doors closed behind her. She didn't look back.

I was left blinking through the dust from the bus wheels as my little girl disappeared in to the Brazilian night.

CHAPTER TEN

Rosa

What the guidebook says:

- 92% of new cars in Brazil use ethanol (produced from sugar cane) as fuel.
- Brazil's homicide rate is 25 per 100,000 people – four times higher than in the US.
- Homosexuality hasn't been illegal in Brazil since 1830.
- Around 20% of men in Rio de Janeiro are gay or bisexual.

So Dad's gay, apparently. Whatever. I'm on a bus in this messed up country, heading to the beach to get drunk with a boy I've only just met and I don't care. What's the point of any of this life if we're not having fun? We might as well be dead. So that's what I'm planning on doing from now on: having fun. Sod Mum; sod Dad; Sod this Gavin or whatever other imaginary guy Dad's supposed to have been in love with. This is a new low, even for Mum. Talk about dodging responsibility. I think I'd have known if my own dad was gay.

I was going to send a postcard to Darren, but forget that. I couldn't write 'wish you were here' because that wouldn't be true. I don't wish he were here. In spite of Mum's efforts to put a downer on everything, I've actually been having a good time with Tiago. He's cool, he makes me laugh – plus he's got an amazing body. I couldn't keep my eyes off him at the beach earlier. He's got this way of looking at me, with his hooded eyes and crooked grin, that makes me feel like I'm the most beautiful girl on the planet. Which of course, I'm not, but I don't care when I'm with him. It makes a change to be with someone who's falling over himself to please me, as if my happiness is his sole goal in life. Of course, I know it's probably all just an act, I'm not stupid. All men are the same, aren't they? And let's face it, anyone who thinks I'm anything to write home about has to be a nutter, right? But being with Tiago makes me forget my shitty little life for a while. Plus it feels like sticking two fingers up at Darren. And what harm can it do, a bit of a holiday romance? Doesn't everyone do that?

Mum can't hide her disgust when I talk about Darren. I shouldn't have told her I was moving in with him, but I couldn't help it. He's a shit, but it'd be nice if she would just trust me to make my own decisions, without constantly judging me. I didn't tell her, but the night Dad died, the night me and her had that fight, and she slapped me and I walked out, that's when I saw them together, Darren and Sal, snogging, Darren with his hand up Sal's skirt. I didn't say anything, they didn't even know I'd seen them, I just walked around the streets for hours until I couldn't walk any more and went and sat in a bus shelter until some weirdo came over and asked if I was 'looking to party'.

So I went round Darren's house and asked

him about Sal, and he denied it. Course he did. Then, when he saw I wasn't buying any of it, he starts crying, like real tears, and telling me how sorry he is, and that she came on to him, and that I'm the one he wants to be with, and I stupidly wanted to believe him. He was pretty convincing. I still told him to get lost though. Then I got back home and crashed on my bed until Mum woke me up and told me Dad was dead, and everything just fell apart around me. I needed someone to hold me, someone to tell me it was going to be alright, so I called Darren. I told myself that nothing he'd done or hadn't done with Sal mattered any more; not after that. Sometimes you just need someone and you take who you can get.

CHAPTER ELEVEN

Ricardo

Outside Ricardo's open window the music of the city celebrations still blared from the bars and houses, filling the streets. Brazil was through to the World Cup semi-finals. He had enjoyed the match, watching it with the girls, who he expected were more excited by the occasion than by the football itself. The whole country was wrapped in a blanket of Bebeto, Romário, Dunga, Taffarel, and of course, the new young hope, Ronaldo. The hope of a nation was on their shoulders. The country needed them to win, and it wasn't just about football.

He thought of Raphael, the boy in the favela, one minute kicking a ball around with his cousins, the next being beaten like a dog and left to die. They'd deliberately taken advantage of the match to attack. He'd called everyone he could think of but almost everyone was out celebrating – no one wanted to hear bad news tonight.

He knew who was responsible; everyone knew who was responsible: the same man he'd been pursuing since he was a young man: Coutran. Only nothing would stick on him. No one would ever testify, and if they looked like they might, they disappeared and no questions were asked. They just ceased to exist. Not even their families would press charges.

He sat alone in the half darkness, the coolness of the bottle held against his forehead, keeping him from sleep. He prised it away for a moment to top up his glass, then swilled the clear liquid languorously around his mouth before letting it slip down his throat and under his skin.

He looked around the walls: the photos of the girls; the newspaper articles; the press cuttings; the pile of files on his desk threatening to topple over; the leads that led nowhere.

The file for Senhor Coutran lay open in front of him. Sixteen years he'd been working on it. Each time he thought he was getting somewhere something like this happened. He was running out of influence, running out of motivational speeches to make to the people of the favelas. How long could he ask them to have faith in him, to resist violence and retaliation?

But it wasn't just for the attacks on the favelas that he wanted Coutran. Behind the public fight lay something even more sinister, something he couldn't, no matter how he approached it, find a way through. And now Coutran was running for Governor, and no one seemed to care about any of the rest.

He took another swig of cachaça. His thoughts turned to Judith Summers, the beautiful mouse of a woman appearing like that out of nowhere, speaking of Edson, her husband, in her far away accent that sounded like snow. Despite himself, he liked her. He'd promised himself never to get involved, but then he'd seen Rosa and he'd been hurled back to 1978, into the fear and the dark and the light that had come back into his life as he'd held her in his arms, that new-born baby, that child with no future. There in the kitchen he had promised himself that he would never let her feel fear like that. He would not let her grow up to give birth on a dirty kitchen floor to a child she didn't want.

And then there she was, standing in front of him, talking like an English girl, like she'd never been there with him. He thought of her father; of Edson, so young to die. He longed to ask Judith Summers about him, about how he'd died; how he'd lived, but he knew he had to keep his distance. He couldn't get involved now.

And inevitably, thinking of Rosa made him think of his wife. He remembered the first time he'd met her, all those years ago, when the military still ruled the country and people were afraid, and he thought of the boy who had brought them together.

It was her perfume he noticed first: the smell of her. In the crowded bus, bodies tight against each other, sweating and tired, aching to get home, she brushed past him. His head turned in time to see only the back of hers, dark curls bouncing playfully as she negotiated her way past the lady with the washing in her lap into the seat by the window. Newly out of university, he was carrying his books; research for the case he was working on at the law firm, full of plans to travel to America, to see the world. With his free hand he held on to the leather hoop as the bus shuddered back on its way. The night was creeping in between the buildings and he tried to make out her face from its reflection in the window.

They were leaving the centre when a boy pushed past him. He instinctively put his hand into his pocket and checked his wallet was still there. It was. He looked back at the girl. The woman with the washing pulled herself up to standing, adjusting the weight of the large sheet carrying her clothes. The boy slipped in behind her before anyone else could take her place. Ricardo thought how he would like to be that boy, to be that close to her and smell her neck, her hair. It was only then that he saw the glint of the knife and her eyes as she looked around at the other passengers and then straight at him.

He pushed past the two girls busy checking each other's teeth for lipstick stains, and saw the knife nudge her lower ribs, where the soft brown skin of her back was exposed above her shorts. He hesitated, not quite knowing what to do.

"Your watch." The words came out of the boy's mouth without his head turning in her direction. It wasn't so much a request as a statement of fact.

Instinctively she reached for the metal clasp against her wrist, ready to hand it over. Behind Ricardo the two girls giggled shyly, teasing each other about a boy. A woman stood applying lipstick without a mirror, one hand clinging on to the seat by her side. Had no one else seen? He looked at the boy who was twisting the knife deeper into her side. A bus stop was coming up. The boy clearly wanted to get what he had come for and get off quick.

And then he heard her voice, clear, loud and sure, "Get your own watch."

The bus fell silent. Ricardo found himself holding his breath.

All eyes turned in disbelief, the only sound, the lone humming of an old lady somewhere towards the back of the bus, echoing easily around the other passengers' stiffened bodies. The boy stared at his chosen victim, unsure what his next move should be.

"He's got a knife!" squealed one of the previously giggling girls behind Ricardo.

Ricardo stepped forward and spoke to the boy.

"Excuse me, I think this is your stop."

No one breathed. Ricardo held his nerve, feeling her eyes on him.

A large mustached man, his skin covered in the fine film of white dust, which was the trademark of those working on the construction of the new hotels, pushed his way over to the boy, and stood over him like a storm cloud over a buttercup.

The bus shuddered to a halt, clumsily catching the curb as the driver, overly eager to be rid of the unwanted passenger, misjudged his speed. The sudden jerk made the boy start and his knife slip. Men and women were now jostling to get off, terrified of what might happen. The big mustached man and his temporary entourage stood strong.

"Take your knife and get off the bus." Ricardo spoke softly. The boy knew he was outnumbered. He knew he had lost this time

and Ricardo could see he was afraid. But he wasn't afraid of these men. His fear was undoubtedly that of going back empty handed and how he would be made to suffer. Ricardo knew what could happen to him, but he wasn't going to be held responsible. It wasn't his fault what the boy had got himself into.

With a final frustrated nudge the boy removed the knife from the woman's side, sliding it back into his shorts as he stood up. His hole-ridden T-shirt was drenched in sweat, the foul odour making Ricardo nauseous. As he squeezed out of the seat the mustached man grabbed him like he might a week-old bag of putrefied rubbish, throwing him to the next man, who threw him with equal disgust to the man down from him. As such he was passed down the aisle like a condemned man to the gallows, everyone wanting to be part of this triumph against aggression.

Ricardo watched him go. As the boy reached the door he looked back and found him. Lifting his right hand like a gun, with a soulless smile, he pulled the imaginary trigger and 'shot' him between the eyes. And then he was gone, disappearing immediately amongst the crowd of irritable passengers, waiting impatiently to get on, oblivious to how close they had come to the blade of his knife.

Ricardo's legs went weak. He sat down in the seat next to the woman. It was almost dark now. They rode the bus down to the central square, around which all the city's buses converged.

He didn't know what to say to her, although he needn't have worried.

"That was brave," she said.

"It was nothing."

"It was something." *She smiled and then added,* "You spoke so softly to him."

Ricardo was embarrassed, taking it as a criticism.

"There was good in his eyes."

She looked at him as if seeing him differently and her eyes moved down to the books in his lap.

"You're a lawyer?" *she said, surprised.*

"Yes."

"Are you doing anything right now?"

He was supposed to be meeting friends, but even if he'd been invited to take tea with Pelé himself he would've cancelled on the spot for this woman.

"No, not right now," *he said.*

The bus shuddered to a halt at the next stop and she got up.

"Come with me," *she said, pushing past the people in front.*

"Where are we going?" *he asked.*

"I think you could be the very person I need."

Ricardo missed his wife. She would've known

what to do. She'd always been the strong one, the one who dove into things without looking. He'd been the one who held back, who thought things over, who weighed up all the options before making a decision. Some said they'd complimented each other but he'd always taken this to mean that he was the weaker one. What would she have done now? She would've just told this woman Judith the truth, he was sure, but then what? No, he instinctively wanted to protect both Judith and Rosa. They were so fresh, so full of belief in the world. And Rosa had clearly loved Edson.

He thought again of the night he'd got off the bus with his future wife. She'd explained about the shelter for street children where she worked and their desperate need for a lawyer. They'd arranged to meet up the following day and she'd taken him to the shelter, which he'd heard of but had never been in.

She nodded hello to the security guard at the door and lead him through to a courtyard where a group of boys were playing football. On his own, sitting against the wall in the shadows, was a familiar figure. She called him over.

"Hey, you, come here."

The boy looked up and slunk over to them. As his face came into the light Ricardo saw it was the boy from the bus; the boy who had held a knife to her side. He realised that he was older than he'd looked on the bus, probably in his late teens; only a few years younger than Ricardo himself, although more wiry and clearly malnourished. Ricardo tensed up, but his future wife remained calm.

"Tell this man your name," she said.

"Junior – Francisco de Assis Cabral Junior." His voice was surprisingly small.

"Do you have anything you'd like to say to this man, Francisco de Assis Cabral Junior?"

The boy shrugged his shoulders.

"Junior?" she repeated.

"Sorry, sir," he eventually mumbled.

Ricardo, who'd never before been referred to as 'sir', nodded in acceptance and looked at this tiny yet formidable young woman, who he knew he would spend the rest of his life trying to impress.

CHAPTER TWELVE

Looking for Rosa

I leant my head back against the peeling plaster wall of the hotel room and watched as the gecko ventured cautiously over the shower wall, before scurrying out the metal grill. It had been well over an hour since Rosa had stormed off onto the bus and I'd half expected her back by now. I'd wanted to follow her but I hadn't even seen the number of the bus or the direction it had driven after turning the corner. I'd been convinced that, however big the shock she'd had, Rosa would come back to the hotel eventually and we would finally be able to talk.

I didn't know what to do. I didn't dare leave the room, for fear Rosa might come back and find me gone. She was so nearly a woman and yet still so young. Edson would've told me I needed to trust her, to let her make her own mistakes, but this was not somewhere I wanted her making mistakes.

However hard I tried to shake it off, I couldn't get what she'd said out of my head. Rosa blamed me for Edson's death and maybe she was right, I ought to have been there for him. I blamed myself too; I'd been a terrible friend. I could've done so much more, made more of an effort to understand him, his country, his language, but instead I'd let the gradually building resentment over being his carer cloud the love I'd felt for him, and instead of spending time listening to his stories of the past, I'd hidden myself away in the bottom of a glass and in a series of sad affairs with unsuitable men.

I looked again at the photo of Edson, Ricardo and Flavia. It was strange looking at the photo now, having met Ricardo in person. He looked more tired in the flesh; older. I wondered what he'd made of me turning up like that, claiming to be the wife of someone so clearly not the marrying type. No wonder he'd mistrusted me.

I looked back up at the ceiling and the cosmos of florescent fungus seeping out of every corner. I thought of Ricardo and the way the girls at the centre had all been so happy to see him. I thought of the families he had tried to help and wondered what kind of life he had, so foreign to mine. I'd taken on one child; he and his wife must have taken on hundreds.

In my fingers I held the piece of paper with the shelter's number on. I'd folded and unfolded it again and again, telling myself I needed to be strong, that I needed to sort out my own problems instead of involving a stranger, but Ricardo didn't feel like a stranger. Despite his evident distrust of me, despite the fact that he was clearly hiding something, I felt comfortable with him, as I had once done with Edson. There was that same familiarity; a feeling of security, as if when I was with him, no one could touch me, I was safe.

It was getting late. The noises of the night were humming around the square outside. The celebrations from Brazil's victory were in full swing. Everyone, it seemed, was out tonight. I had walked down every street between the bus stops and the hotel. I'd got lost and found my bearings again; I'd stopped to look in every bar, on every street I passed, ignoring the stares and the whistles, ignoring the panic in my chest, just searching for my little girl, but it was hopeless. Rosa didn't want to be found.

I unfolded the piece of paper one last time and stared at the number. I knew Ricardo had more important things to worry about but I didn't have anyone else to call. Grabbing my bag I slid off the bed and out the door. There was a phone across the square; I'd seen it earlier. I crossed the busy street, dodging two buses fighting to pull out in to the traffic, and ran to the phone. I had to wait an agonising few minutes while a young girl kissed goodbye to her distant lover through the receiver, and then I was dialling.

Ricardo's battered yellow car swerved to avoid a barefoot boy darting out from behind a gaggle of women, before he brought it to an abrupt halt in front of the bus stop. He leant over and opened the passenger door and I jumped in, only just pulling the door shut as he took off again, avoiding a bus by a whisker.

"Thank you for coming..." I started.

"Where have you looked?" Ricardo interrupted, concentrating on the traffic.

"All over. But I don't know where I haven't looked, and Rosa doesn't know the city at all.

The Brazilian Husband

"Where does she know?"

"Nowhere, we haven't been anywhere, except the beach this afternoon, with her new best friend, but she wouldn't know how to get there."

"She'd have found a way," he said, pulling hard on the wheel to do a U-turn. I reached my hand up to grab the handle above the door but there wasn't one. Instead, I braced my arm against the ripped roof of the car.

Down at the beach it felt as if we were walking through a photograph, with a seemingly endless string of illuminated palm trees lining the sweeping boulevard. A grand, round hotel stuck out into the water like the bulbous bow of a stranded spaceship, its hundreds of windows casting their light over the sand in wide semi-circles to either side. I had to half-run to keep up with Ricardo. We had tried to drive down along the beach, scanning the pavements, but the entire seafront had become one big street party in the time since I'd left only a matter of hours ago. A large lorry blocked half the road, it's back section transformed in to a stage, festooned with enormous loudspeakers and draped in Brazilian flags. It was blasting out the local Forró music, as around it bodies writhed; drank; danced; laughed. A pot-bellied man strolled past us sporting nothing but a pair of speedos, a wristwatch and a perfec' groomed miniature dog on a long red lead.

The whole place was smothered ir and yellow: people's clothes and baseball plastic banners adorning the beach ⱶ tied like a cape around someone's smaller version of the same wr⸝

bewildered baby; the labels on the beer bottles; the sea of painted faces and paint-smeared chests. Brazil was a country of heroes. They had made it to the World Cup semi-final.

"Mais um, Mais um!" roared the advert for beer over the music, "One more, one more!"

Salty-skinned, wide-toothed boys stood, perched or sat spread-eagled on the seafront wall beating tin cans with spoons they'd pilfered from the restaurants, as barefoot girls danced around them, their feet pounding the pavement, the road, the wall.

"So, are you a football fan?" I asked Ricardo, as much to get him to slow down as out of any real doubt.

He shrugged, "If you are Brazilian, you have no choice." He smiled, loosening up a little, and slowing down to let me catch up. He looked at my exhausted face. "We'll find her," he said.

"I know," I said, although I didn't.

I stopped and scanned the beachfront. Veiled in darkness with only pockets of lights, it seemed a completely different place to where I'd been that afternoon.

"Are you sure this is where you were earlier?" he asked.

"No." I was beginning to doubt my own memory now, "but I do remember the hotel. We weren't that far from it, so it's got to be near here somewhere."

I looked at the hotel and then back at the bars below.

"That's it." I pointed to a beach bar just behind a large man slicing off the tops of two both, green coconuts with a machete.

As we weaved our way nearer I saw that it was indeed the bar where we had sat with Tiago hours earlier, although unsurprisingly neither he nor Rosa were there now. I had run out of ideas and cursed myself for having left the hotel, convinced that Rosa would be back there by now, wondering where *I* was.

Ricardo wasn't deterred however. He pushed his way through the crowd towards the barman and spoke with him over the racket. The barman gestured with his head towards the street, continuing to serve his impatient customers.

"What did he say?" I asked as he returned.

"She was here, with her friend."

"And?"

"And then they left. He thinks they went up to dance."

"Rosa doesn't dance."

"Everyone dances," he said, smiling.

I wasn't really in a position to argue. Instead, I followed him back up on to the pavement and into the crowd. I had difficulty keeping up with him and lost sight of the back of his head as a procession of girls in flamboyant bird masks danced past between us. I stopped, spun around, frantically scanning the sea of faces, tears swelling behind my eyes, the music so loud, dizzying; bodies gyrating around me as if I didn't exist. I felt as if I'd drifted into a horrific nightmare and couldn't wake up. I was lost and alone and had no idea what to do. I'd promised Edson I'd look after Rosa. It was the last thing I said to him that night; the night everything changed.

Rebecca Powell

Gavin had taken Edson out for a romantic meal in a ridiculously over-priced restaurant up west. It was their anniversary – three years together; just over two years since the wedding. I offered to stay in and look after Rosa. I made popcorn and we snuggled up together under the blanket on the sofa and watched Chitty Chitty Bang Bang, Rosa diving behind me whenever the child-catcher came on. She fell fast asleep, well before the end, and I carried her to her room and tucked her in.

Much later, in the middle of a nightmare about the child catcher chasing Rosa, a crash woke me. It was Edson, tumbling through the front door, swearing in Portuguese as he caught his foot on the doormat and tripped his way down the hall. I fumbled to look at my clock. It was one-thirty in the morning. He'd told me he was staying at Gavin's.

"Ed?" I called out.

My bedroom door creaked open and Edson's head peered around it, "You awake?"

"It's half one in the morning, Ed. Of course I'm awake."

He came in, ignoring my sarcasm, his eyes red; his whole body drooped. His bounce had gone.

"Not staying at Gav's tonight then?"

He sunk down on to the edge of the bed and hung his head in his hands.

I sat forward, "Hey, what's the matter?"

He wiped angrily at his eyes and looked up at me, "We had a fight."

They'd had fights before. Gavin was a jealous person and Edson, a free spirit. Gavin could never seem to see just how besotted Edson was with him. Gavin was one of those beautiful people, who had both men and women falling at his feet, but who, whilst enjoying it, never quite seemed to trust the attention he got.

I rubbed Edson's back, "Hey, come on, I've got chocolate," I said, reaching into my nightstand and pulling out a half-devoured bar of Dairy Milk.

"I think that's it," he said, "It's over."

"Don't be daft," I said, "Gav adores you."

"Gav adores the fact I'm so in love with him."

I feared he was right, but I wasn't going to tell him that. "Oh, come on. You guys have been together for years. It's a hiccup, that's all. Don't worry about it."

But he was worrying about it. I'd never seen him this cut up about anything. He crawled up the bed and slipped under the covers, jeans and T-shirt and jacket and all. I was about to shout at him for not taking off his shoes, but thought better of it. He put his head on my shoulder and I stroked his hair. He smelled of aftershave and wine. I broke off a piece of chocolate and handed him the rest of the bar. As he snapped off a chunk he started to cry and I put my arm around his shoulder and pulled him to me.

"It'll be okay," I said, "You love each other, he just needs time." Even as I said it I didn't believe it. Gav was volatile to say the least. He was gorgeous and giving and charming and smart, but there was something about him I couldn't put my finger on, but which I didn't quite trust, and which stopped me from loving him the way I loved Ed.

"You're amazing," Ed told me, looking up.

"Well, you know," I said, trying to shrug off the compliment. Being this close to him, I didn't

trust myself. I wanted so badly to curl in to him and run my hands under his t-shirt and pull him to me. I hated seeing him suffering. He was such a good man; so full of life. I was furious at Gavin for hurting him, but at the same time, all I could hear in my head was my own voice saying "Ed's in my bed, Ed's in bed."

I stroked his hair and we looked at each other and then he leant in to me and put his hand on my cheek, "You're my rock," he said, his speech slurred by drink and choked-back tears.

"You're drunk," I said, smiling to hide my arousal. And then he leaned in, and before I could figure out what he was doing, his lips were on mine and we were kissing. He tasted of chocolate and daiquiris and I had never wanted him so badly as I did right then.

Then the phone rang.

He pulled away.

"Oh my God, I'm so sorry, fuck, that was not supposed to happen." He rolled towards the edge of the bed and fumbled for the phone, as it was clear I was in no state to answer it.

As it turned out, it was for him anyway. When he eventually hung up, he jumped off the bed like an excited puppy on hearing the word 'walkies'.

"That was Gav," he said, "He says he's sorry. He wants me to go back. He's still at the club."

"But it's the middle of the night," I said.

"Jude, "he hung his head and rubbed the back of his neck, trying to figure out what to say to me that would make this all less embarrassing.

"It's okay, Ed."

"I love you, little mouse," he said, taking my hand in both of his and looking up at me with those

big brown eyes of his, red-rimmed and still glistening with tears.

"I love you too," I said.

"I should go."

"Yes, of course," I said, pulling myself together, "You go. It's fine, really. You're emotionally all over the place and you needed a hug. And I was here. I get it."

"Amigos?"

"Friends."

As he reached the door he turned back, "I'll probably crash at Gav's tonight. You sure you don't mind looking after Rosa?"

"Don't worry about Rosa. You know I'll look after her for as long as you need. We'll be just fine, I promise. Now go have some fun."

I spun around, the throng of writhing bodies making me dizzy, "Ricardo?" I shouted into the crowd, "Ricardo!"

A hand grabbed mine and pulled me through the middle of a couple dancing. It was Ricardo. His hand was large and strong. I held tight, feeling the warmth of his skin and the shock and unexpected pleasure at the intimacy of it. How many years had it been since someone last held my hand? It was such a simple thing and yet I felt, in that moment, connected to him in a way I had failed to feel in any of my doomed liaisons over the years.

Ricardo stopped abruptly and shook hands with a couple of young men in baseball caps and T-shirts, branded with the name of the beer they were drinking. I couldn't catch what they were saying but they were pointing further up the beachfront and Ricardo started leading me in the direction they were indicating, before they'd finished speaking.

He really does know everyone, I thought. At one point he pulled me to the side of the crowd and spoke to a group of young cracked-soled boys with sores around their mouths and limp, glue-filled plastic bags dangling from their fists. They high-fived him with their knuckles and stared at me. I held tight to his hand, although there was no longer any need now we'd come out of the thick of the crowd.

"They saw them earlier," Ricardo turned to reassure me.

"How do you know it was them?" I asked.

"It was them," he said.

I didn't press him. I needed to trust him. I felt ashamed enough for having lost my daughter.

"It's okay, Judith Summers," Ricardo said, sensing my despair, "we'll find your girl. She's a teenager and there's a party. She'll be here, trust me. At least we know she's with her friend."

"That's what I'm afraid of," I said, trying to force a smile. I felt ridiculous for worrying. Of course she was here, Ricardo was right. He knew this place better than anyone and his certainty made me feel better.

"You know everyone, don't you?" I said as he waved to another group of people.

"This is my city," he said.

"And you knew Rosa's real mother."

He looked at me. We were standing at the edge of the crowd now, scanning the heads of the people dancing. I thought he was about to tell me something but then a face in the crowd caught his eye.

"There," he said, looking rather pleased with himself.

I looked. There was Rosa, dancing, arms in the air, head back, beer bottle in her hand. My heart soared. I wanted to shout to get her attention, but hesitated. She looked so free, so *happy*. I hadn't seen this fun, carefree girl for so very long that I'd started to think she had disappeared along with Edson.

"Hey," a voice beside me made me turn. It was Tiago, clutching a couple of beers in his hand, another couple in the crook of his arm. "You looking for Rosa?"

"Yes, we've just seen her. Was she with you?"

"Yeah. You want a beer?"

"No, thank you, I don't want a beer. I want my daughter."

"Hey man," he shook Ricardo's hand, ignoring my comment.

"Hey Tiago. How's your cousin?" Ricardo asked.

"Cool man, cool. Cheers, yeah."

"You know each other?" I asked.

"I helped his cousin out," Ricardo said.

"This man's a genius," Tiago called back as he weaved his way back to join Rosa. I saw him whisper something in her ear and she turned to look at me. I waved and saw the light go out of her eyes. My heart fell.

Ricardo was watching me, "Told you she'd be okay," he said.

I attempted a smile. It was impossible not to when he was smiling at me like that. He took my hand and led me through the throng to join Rosa. I tried to resist, pulling back, but he insisted and kept a firm hold of my hand.

"Are you alright?" I asked as we reached her, dabbing my eyes to rid them of the tears of relief that were threatening to make a spectacle of me.

"Why wouldn't I be?" Rosa's defences were instantly thrown back up.

"I was so worried." I leant over to give her a hug but she pulled away.

"Didn't look like it," she said, glancing behind me at Ricardo.

"Ricardo was helping me look for you," I explained, realising that I was blushing and hoping the night would hide it.

"I wasn't lost." Rosa addressed this to Ricardo, who looked uncomfortable.

The two of them stood looking at each other, neither knowing what to say or do next.

Just then someone lowered the music and it was replaced by the screech of a microphone being switched on. A scruffy man in a red T-shirt walked to the front of the stage and tapped the mic, then mumbled something I didn't catch, followed by a name: Coutran. A tall, handsome man in a cream suit and open-necked shirt bounded up the stairs on to the makeshift stage, furiously waving an enormous Brazilian flag above his head. The crowd screamed as if the Beatles themselves had just waltzed on to the stage. Everywhere, it seemed, people were blowing whistles, beating drums and cheering.

The man leaned in to the microphone, and punched his fist in the air, "Vai Brasil!"

The crowd went wild, as if he'd just scored the winning goal himself. "Go Brazil!" was clearly all you needed to say to be popular.

"Who's that?" I turned to ask Ricardo, but he was standing, hands deep in his pockets, staring, brow-furrowed at the stage, and clearly didn't hear me in the din surrounding us.

The man on the stage waved at the crowd and drew the mic towards him. He spoke slowly, deliberately, with such passion, such gravitas, that I found myself drawn in as much as everyone else.

"Today," he began, "the world has seen what all of us here have known for a long, long time: that Brazil is one of the greatest nations on Earth." He paused as the street and the beach beyond turned in to a sea of flags; the crowds stamping and hooting and cheering. This man could hold an audience. He was at least fifteen years older than me, probably more, but with a vitality, an energy, a heart-melting flash of a smile and those come-to-bed eyes that had women all around me swooning.

"Brasil é o futebol!" he cried, "Brazil is football!" The crowd roared and continued to roar and cheer as his voice echoed what they were all feeling:

"Brazil is our energy!"

"Brazil is our enterprise!"

"Brazil is our determination to never give up!" He held up the flag and waved it as he spoke.

"Brazil é você!" He pointed to a young woman in the crowd, who screamed in delight, "Brazil is you!" then moved his hand to point at another woman, and then a man, and then another, "e você, e você, e você." - "And you, and you, and you."

"Brazil is all of us; every one of us; together. I call on you all to honour your country, to work together to give Brazil the future she deserves." He was gathering momentum and his voice rose above the near-hysteria below as he roared out his message:

"Vote for our children!"

"Vote for the future!"

"Vote Brazil!"

The clamour of stamping feet, of drums and horns and whistles and screams filled the seafront. The man held a flag back up above his head, but this time, in a cunning subliminal twist, the Brazilian flag had been replaced by the flag of his political party. A young woman scrambled up on to the stage, like something from a Bruce Springsteen video, and flung herself at him. He wrapped his flag around her and the two of them danced Forró as the music swelled and the partying was turned back up to eleven.

I still had no idea who he was or what he actually stood for, but the handsome politician had cleverly aligned himself in the minds of everyone there that evening, with the image of success; of joy; of ambition and, most importantly, of hope. Whatever he was running for, he'd just secured thousands of votes. If I'd been eligible, I might well have voted for him too. People clearly adored him. As far as politicians went, I thought, the country could do a lot worse.

I jumped as Tiago grabbed my waist.

"Come on Mummy, dance with us!" He took my hand and pulled me towards him.

"I'm sorry..."

"No sorry, just dance!" He laughed and twirled me around to Rosa's reluctant amusement. He was watching her the whole time. Unable to stay away from her any longer, he waltzed me over to Ricardo, handing me over as he span around to grab Rosa again, leading her off into another drunken dance.

Ricardo took my hand, and this time his other arm slipped around my waist. In the tight space between bodies, he pulled me tight to him as he manoeuvred us between dancing feet and discarded beer bottles. I held on, feeling the strength in his back through his loose shirt, and let myself be led, my eyes still on Rosa behind us, watching her face, so happy, so light, dancing with the young dreamer.

Someone pushed me from behind and squashed me up against Ricardo. I found myself cheek to cheek with him and felt myself flush with embarrassment but not wanting to let go. And so we danced. Light-headed from too much sun and the enormous relief at having found Rosa, I let the world around me melt into a sea of colours and music and laughter. The scene, which had felt so foreign, so threatening just minutes before, now transformed in my relief into a warm, inclusive, seductive body of people of all ages, all colours, all classes. A part of them now, safe in Ricardo's arms, I was no longer a mother, a carer, a tired, failed shop assistant, but simply myself for a moment. I let the music take hold as I danced, the hypnotic beat of the drums vibrating through my body. I felt the tension beginning to melt from my shoulders and from the crease of the skin around my eyes, which had grown unaccustomed to my smile. I was with my daughter, here in Edson's world, which he had always so wanted us both to see. And I was here in the arms of Ricardo, this intriguing, impassioned man, who somehow thought me worth the trouble.

Looking at him out of the corner of my eye a calm seemed to descend upon me. I felt that everything was going to be all right. It felt like this was where I was meant to be; and this woman in Ricardo's arms, this was the woman I was meant to be. I wanted to cast off my old self like a snake casting off its skin. I knew some people would say my 'head down and get on with it' attitude was commendable, brave even, but I knew better: it was the worst kind of cowardice. It was the avoidance of making a real decision, the refusal to take action to change what had become so routine I no longer recognised it as suffering, but rather what my grandmother would have called 'my lot'. I felt now that all that was about to change.

"I'm sorry about earlier,' Ricardo shouted in my ear.

"Don't be." I could hardly hear him above the music.

"No, I was unfair."

"You had other things to worry about."

"It was not a good introduction to our country," he said, "This is what you should remember." With a wide grin he waved an arm around him, holding my waist in the other, "*This* is Brazil."

Together we danced in the steaming street, our ears pumping with the rhythm of the drums and the joyous voices of a thousand revellers drawn like a curtain around us. I looked up at the stars, felt my hair loose down my back, Ricardo's breath on my neck and I gave in to the movement of our bodies and to the possibility of joy that I had resisted for so long.

"Just out of curiosity, how were you planning on finding Edson's family?" Ricardo asked on the drive back from the beach, several hours and many cold beers later.

"I hoped you could tell us," I said, "There isn't really a plan B."

"Here," he leant down and found a piece of paper on the floor. Tearing off a slither from the bottom he scribbled something on it, without stopping the car, and handed it to me. "That's his village and the name of his family. That's all I know."

"Thank you," I said, reading the unfamiliar words, trying them out silently on my tongue. "But his surname was da Silva, not Cabral," I said, reading the name he'd written.

"That's his mother's name. That's all I know."

"Thank you," I said again, smiling. I felt I had somehow gained his confidence and felt a rush of pleasure at his trust in me. Of course, the beer helped.

Ricardo must have felt me smiling but kept his eyes firmly on the road.

"It's no life out there, mind you. Are you sure you want to go?"

"I promised I'd take him home."

"Like I said, the notion of home here is probably not quite the same as where you're from."

As he pulled up at a traffic light we sat a moment, looking at each other, neither sure what to say to the other, worlds apart, with only the ghost of Edson connecting us. I thought about the notion of home and thought of our rented house in Wembley. It hadn't felt like home since Edson died. I realised that however much I'd been wanting to go home since we'd arrived, I really wasn't looking forward to returning to an empty house.

I watched Ricardo as the lights changed and found myself smiling. I'd been hoping he'd tell me more about Edson, but at least this was a start. Rosa would be able to find out where her father had come from, which would help her feel part of this foreign land. I could finally take him home and find peace, knowing that I had kept my promise, and in doing so, maybe Rosa and I could find a way back to being close again like we always had been, and begin to build the rest of our lives, just the two of us.

CHAPTER THIRTEEN

Leaving the hotel

"You can't stay here," Ricardo said as we pulled up opposite the hotel.

"We've got to, we're still waiting for our lost bags."

He'd insisted on accompanying us to our hotel door this time, as it was so late. He got out and followed us to our room. As I opened the door, he took one look at the room and put his hand on my shoulder.

"No way, I'm definitely not letting you stay here. Get your stuff, you're coming home with me."

"No, no," I said, embarrassed, "we couldn't do that."

"Nonsense, come on, I'll go and explain to the receptionist."

As we carried our few belongings to the car I remembered that he was married.

"Won't your wife mind?" I asked.

"My wife?"

"I'm sorry, I thought you said you were married."

"I was."

Ricardo opened the passenger door and helped Rosa clamber back in.

"I'm so sorry," I said, blushing again, "I

didn't mean to..." I could feel the beer going to my head.

He smiled at Rosa as she got in to the car but I saw his fists clenched around the door, his knuckles white.

"Come on," he said, "let's get you home."

I let myself relax in the jet stream of warm water. What a pleasure to have a real shower. I let the water run over my face and massage my shoulders. I could've stayed there all night. The relief of having found Rosa, the warmth and the euphoria still buzzing on my skin from dancing so close to Ricardo, spread a smile over my face. But as I turned off the water and dried myself, the feeling of disquiet returned. What was Ricardo hiding? Why did he seem to suddenly clam up and throw a wall up around himself whenever I mentioned Edson?

Rosa was already asleep in the spare room. She'd excused herself as soon as Ricardo had made up her bed. She hadn't said much but something had changed. When she'd blamed me for Edson's death, I'd instinctively defended myself. How I wished I hadn't, but I had; it was done. Once I'd told her the truth about Edson, I'd thought there would be no coming back. I thought of Rosa dancing, how free she looked. I'd seen a glimpse of my little girl again. And as we'd all danced together with our newfound friends, side-by-side in this strange, glorious, terrifying city, I could have sworn Rosa had smiled at me. Maybe it was just the fact that I'd said it; that it was out in the open instead of churning up inside me, but I felt the ice between us might just be starting to melt. It wasn't much, a smile, and I knew it would take time, but I'd wait. I was sure now that my little girl would come back to me, eventually.

I slipped on the T-shirt Ricardo had leant me to sleep in and towel-dried my hair. I went to clip it up as always but decided to leave it hanging loose for once so that it would dry before I went to bed. I'd often wished I'd had hair like Rosa: long and dark with gentle curls. My straight, mousey-blond hair was always tied back these days. It was so much more practical that way. Besides, I never really knew what to do with it when I let it down. Back when I'd been dating the owner of a nightclub, and again in the restaurant, I'd permed it and dyed it blond and had loved the way it bounced as I flitted between tables, enjoying the admiring looks of the male customers. But it had been years since I'd bothered about such things and I couldn't kid myself I was young enough to pull it off anymore.

I was thirsty. I popped my head around the living room door, hoping Ricardo had already gone to bed for the night.

"Feeling better?" He was in the kitchen, making a drink.

"Wonderful, thank you," I said.

"Can I get you anything to drink?"

"You read my mind."

He held up a jug of clear liquid with slices of lime floating in it. I nodded, "Yes please."

I put it to my lips. Full of crushed ice it was beautifully refreshing, but as I swallowed it, it almost burnt my throat.

"What is this?" I asked.

"Caipirinha," he said, smiling, "a mixture of

sugar cane alcohol and lime. Warms you up, doesn't it?"

"I can't say I was cold," I said, taking another sip of the irresistibly sweet drink.

"Oh there are many kinds of cold. This warms them all, believe me," he said.

I watched him drink and saw in him a reflection of myself back at home, sitting alone in the kitchen late at night in the light of the oven hob, drinking gin from a tea cup. I guessed that he, too, was a lone drinker - the way he held the glass, like it held the answer to something he couldn't bring himself to ask.

We moved through to the living room and sat in silence for a while whilst we drank, listening to the sounds of the night through the open window and the playful clink of ice on glass. The drink relaxed me and quietened the niggling voice in my head that wanted answers.

I looked around the room. The small house was minimalist. Ricardo sat on the only chair; me on the sofa. On the wooden coffee table between us lay various files and piles of paper, from under one of which stuck out the handle of a fork. The bookshelf by the door was a mess of half-opened books, large ones on small, maps next to magazines, law books with novels. In the corner by the window a pile of newspapers threatened to topple over.

Ricardo got up and looked out at the night.

A photo on the bookshelf caught my eye. It was a young woman, laughing, looking over her shoulder, straight into the lens. I thought I recognised the face.

"That's Flavia isn't it?" I asked Ricardo,

shocked by the sound my voice made in the still room. He looked around.

"Yes. That was taken a long time ago," he said, walking over to the bookshelf and picking up the photo as if he had forgotten it was there.

"But I don't understand. When I showed you the photo before I thought you said you didn't know her very well."

"Didn't know her? Of course I knew her. Flavia was my wife." He took another sip of his drink and replaced the photo.

I tried to understand what he was telling me.

"You said 'was'."

Without looking away from the picture he spoke, "My wife died giving birth to our daughter sixteen years ago."

"I'm so sorry, I didn't mean to..." My voice trailed off.

"It's okay. It was a long time ago."

"And your daughter...?" As soon as I'd asked the question I wished I hadn't. I felt I already knew the answer.

Ricardo's shoulders went limp. He looked at me and then looked back at the books on the shelf and shook his head.

"But," I began, trying to find a way to phrase the question I was trying to ask, "Rosa...?"

He took a book out and replaced it on a different shelf.

"I'm sorry, but there's something you're not telling me and I need to know," I continued, "Edson and your wife...?"

Ricardo took off his glasses and cupped his hand over his face, smoothing down his cheeks before walking to the window, drink in hand.

"I guess Edson had his reasons for telling you what he did." I watched his reflection in the window but couldn't read his expression. "Flavia died giving birth to our daughter: our daughter, not Rosa."

"But why would Edson lie about something like that?"

"Your husband was…" he seemed to be searching for the right words, "he needed a fresh start. I guess lying was his way of moving on."

"Moving on? He lied about his own daughter's mother. How could he not tell me?"

"Some things are best left in the past."

"But if her mother's dead, why lie about it?"

"Luciana's not dead." It was no more than a whisper.

I looked at him.

"That's what you said at the shelter." I walked over to him and pulled his shoulder to turn him to face me, the alcohol making me more daring than I would otherwise have had the nerve to be.

"Who's Luciana?"

BRAÇOS ABERTOS STREET PROJECT #14

Tapescript 3

Date:	**11th November 1977**
Name:	**Luciana**
Age:	**12 years**

Flavia: I haven't seen you down here at the beach lately. Are you still working for the lady in the big house?

Luciana: Yeah, she's good to me.

Flavia: What do you do there?

Luciana: I have to clean the house and wash up and do the laundry and all that stuff that you have to do if you want people to think you have a nice house, which she does, and I do the shopping at the market with the cook.

Flavia: Do you get any time off?

Luciana: I get to go home on Sunday afternoon and I make sure that it's when Grandad's in the bar, which isn't hard because he's always in the bar. Nan makes rice and beans and if the lady gives me some chicken then she cooks that too and we eat together with my cousins and

	sometimes my aunty. My aunty doesn't always come though; she doesn't like taking food from me. She never liked Mum in any case, and I suppose I make her think of Mum, and she hates that. My cousins don't care though - they're just happy to have the chicken. And sometimes the lady gives me her daughter's old dresses and if they're too small for me I give them to my cousin, who's six.
Flavia:	Is that one of her daughter's dresses that you're wearing?
Luciana:	Yeah, I put it on to come home so that Nan wouldn't be ashamed of me.
Flavia:	And what does your brother think about your new job?
Luciana:	Jaru doesn't live at home any more. He's in the street all the time now. I see him sometimes when I go to the market and he tries to get me to give him stuff, but I tell him I can't because I'll lose my job. He calls me names but I know that's because of the glue and stuff. He's got those sores all over his mouth and nose like the others and he's got that fungus on his arms too. I tell him, you should go home, but he says he doesn't need to get shouted at by anyone. I tell him Nan needs the

money but he says he doesn't ask her for anything and we can't all be prostituting ourselves for the rich now, can we. He's jealous I've got a good job and he's acting so cool, but he's still my brother so I give him something without the cook seeing, and he disappears. I miss sleeping next to him though. It's not the same sleeping on your own. Even dogs sleep together, it's just natural. But at least I get to sleep in a bed now. It's so good at the lady's house. She gives me necklaces sometimes and when she has people to dinner she tells me to put on a nice dress and then I get to dance for them and they clap and say that I'm beautiful. I don't think I'm beautiful. I'm ugly, I know that, and I'm ignorant, but I like dancing and it makes me feel good and I lie in my bed when I've finished clearing up and I listen to them with their music and talking and drinking and I wish Mum could see me. She would be really impressed, I know. And when I've earned enough money, I'll go find her and we'll move to Rio and work for a rich lady down there.

On Saturday the lady's having another party and she says I can wear a special dress and that there'll be a lot of important people

	there who I can dance for, so I have to be on my best behaviour and look really pretty.
Flavia:	And where does the lady live?
Luciana:	Down here by the beach. Nelson's coming, so I can ask him if he's seen Mum. Maybe he'll take me to see her, I don't know.
Flavia:	You know you don't have to stay for the party. You could come to the shelter on Saturday. You know you're always welcome. You already know Alexandra and Sandra from before, and there are lots of new girls your age.
Luciana:	Didn't you hear me lady? It's a party. What girl doesn't want to go to a party?
Flavia:	I just thought…
Luciana:	Don't think for me, okay? I can think for myself. I'm not going back to any shelter. I know what you do there, you won't let me back out, and you'll try and sell me Jesus and shit and you'll make me go back home to Grandad. Well, I'm not a kid anymore. I can look after myself.

CHAPTER FOURTEEN

The tapes

I awoke and sat bolt upright in the dark room. I'd been dreaming of Rosa; of Rosa as a child, lost in a shopping centre. I'd let go of her hand and watched as another woman led her towards the edge of a cliff. I'd shouted out and the shock must have shaken me awake.

Drenched in sweat I sat very still and tried to bring my mind into focus. I had no idea how long I'd been asleep. It felt like all night but the room was still dark, except for a crack of light seeping in from the living room, creating unfamiliar shadows, which disorientated me. I must only have been asleep a few hours, if that.

Ricardo hadn't answered my question about Luciana. Instead he'd taken the glass from my hand.

"It's late. I think it's time we went to bed."

We'd looked at each other. I hadn't wanted to go to bed; I'd wanted to know who he was talking about and why he couldn't just tell me. But something in his eyes, some sadness had made me stop myself. I saw that he needed me to leave him alone. I knew how that felt.

"Goodnight," I'd said.

He'd nodded. I'd looked back as I opened the bedroom door but he'd turned to look out of the window again, my glass still in his hand.

I looked across at Rosa in the bed next to me but she was fast asleep, her Walkman still on her ears. I lay back down next to her, not daring to stroke her hair for fear of waking her. Asleep, she was once again the little girl who had been clinging so tightly to her father's neck in the park the first time I'd met her; the little girl who'd once asked me if she was English or Brazilian; the little girl who I'd kissed goodbye at the school gates on her first day: Edson's little girl; my little girl.

At first I'd told Edson that I didn't want to be called Mummy, that it wasn't right and that we should tell Rosa, as soon as she was old enough, about her real mother, about her roots. But after the visit to the hospital, everything changed.

That night Rosa had her first nightmare. She woke up crying,

"Mummy!"

I rolled over and a little pair of shaking arms wrapped themselves around my neck and wouldn't let go, her sleepy voice whimpering,

"Mummy, Mummy, don't go, Mummy."

I'll correct her in the morning, I thought, but come morning Rosa tried to jump out of bed, laughing as her nightie caught under my still sleeping arm and shouted,

"Wake up Mummy!"

I opened my eyes and saw the love in Rosa's little, trusting face and couldn't bring myself to correct her. I'll tell her when the time's right, I thought.

But there never seemed to be a 'right' moment and so, by default, I became a mother.

I thought about what Ricardo had said. Maybe he was right; some things were best left in the past. I didn't want to know what secret he was hiding, not now that things looked like they might be starting to mend between Rosa and me.

At first I could only hear my heartbeat in my ears but then I became aware of something else: voices. There were voices coming from the living room; a woman's voice, a girl's voice. I slid out of bed and tiptoed to the scar of light that showed me the door. Gently prising it open I peered through the crack. I couldn't see anyone but could see the light on in the kitchen. I moved nearer to try and make out what was being said. The voices were speaking Portuguese. I peered around the doorway and saw Ricardo, back facing the door, elbows on the table, the jug of Caipirinha in front of him next to a cassette player. I tried to make out what was being said but only managed to catch disconnected words: "Beach, house, grandmother, job."

I tried to move closer and stubbed my toe violently on a pile of books on the floor.

"Shit!"

Ricardo looked around, clicking off the cassette player as he did so.

"Rosa?"

I showed myself, embarrassed. "No, it's

me."

"Judith," his voice was slow and deliberate from the drink, "is everything alright?"

"I'm sorry, I heard voices. But it's okay, I'll get back to bed."

Ricardo saw me looking at the cassette player. As I turned to go he stopped me. "No, stay."

"I'd better not."

"You should hear this."

He rewound the tape to the beginning as I walked over to the other side of the small kitchen table and sat down opposite this quiet, enigma of a man. I wondered what he could be listening to alone in the middle of the night.

He pressed play.

In the background of the recording cars passed, music played and people talked. I thought I could hear the sea. Could it be at the beach? I wondered. It was definitely outside. An interviewer, a woman, asked a girl to introduce herself.

"My name is Luciana,' she giggled, nervously.

"And how old are you, Luciana?" asked the woman.

"I'm eleven."

The recording paused clumsily and then restarted. This time the woman asked the girl to talk about her family and her home. The girl, Luciana, spoke about her grandmother and grandfather, her brother and her mother. I found it impossible to understand everything she was saying. It was a bad recording and the background noise made it hard to separate words, on top of which the girl's accent was strong and she was speaking fast and seemed distracted. Ricardo let the tape play, not looking at me. I watched him listening and let the girl's voice wash over me, entranced by her intonation; the excited purity of her high little voice; the openness with which she spoke and laughed.

"I don't understand," I said after a while.

Ricardo, without looking up, started translating the girl's words. She spoke of her family; of her mother; her brother who she clearly loved, and her neighbour's dog. She spoke of everything and nothing.

The tape stopped abruptly. I waited for an explanation but none came. Ricardo took out the tape, slotted in a second one and pressed play.

The same girl, this time more relaxed, was talking to the same woman about her work, about her mother's visit, about the beach. She talked about a new job and a party someone was taking her to; how excited she was, how much better things were going to be from then on. She sounded so happy.

The tape stopped. Ricardo didn't move, although there were two more tapes in front of him. I looked up, expecting him to say something but his elbows were on the table, his fists covering his face. I thought he might have fallen asleep and was about to speak but something stopped me: his shoulders, they were shaking. I realised he was crying.

I pushed a cup of coffee towards Ricardo. Embarrassed, he wiped his eyes. I'd cleared away his empty glass and had found a coffee cup in the sink. He didn't need to drink any more Caipirinha. Neither of us did.

"I'm sorry," he said, eventually.

"It's okay," I said. And then it dawned on me why he'd been crying. "The interviewer, that was your wife, Flavia, wasn't it?"

He nodded. "I haven't heard her voice in sixteen years. I never got around to listening to the tapes – they were part of her research she was doing before...but when you turned up like that, asking all these questions, I remembered the tapes and dug them out."

He took a sip of the strong coffee and winced. "You put any sugar in this?"

I shook my head. He got up and slouched over to the cupboard, where he helped himself to three heaped teaspoons of sugar. Stirring the coffee he leant back against the worktop.

"Luciana, the girl, " I started, "so you did know her then?"

"Yes, I knew her."

"So is Luciana, I mean, that voice on the tape, are you telling me that that was Rosa's mother when she was a little girl?"

"She was so little. But yes, Luciana is Rosa's mother."

"You said 'is', but Edson told me she died in childbirth."

"Judith, it's late. You need to get some sleep if you're driving to Edson's village tomorrow."

Tiago had offered to take us into the interior in the morning as he had some sort of business there, and we were going to have to make an early start.

"No, I need to get some answers."

"I can't give you the answers you're looking for," Ricardo said, surprising me with the snap in his voice, "All I can tell you is to leave the past alone."

He poured the remains of his coffee down the sink and left me sitting alone in the kitchen as he went into his room and shut the door. I reached over and poured some of the remaining Caipirinha into my coffee cup and took a swig of the warm drink. It felt good: it felt like home. My life, the last fifteen years, was crumbling around me. Nothing was what I'd thought it had been, no one had been telling me the truth about anything, it seemed. And in the middle of it all stood Rosa, this girl who had no idea who she really was, and I couldn't help her.

I drank because there didn't seem anything else to do, and because it was the one thing I could trust. I missed home and the familiarity of the lies I had lived with, and home meant drinking; drinking until I could bear it again. I drank until my head sank in to the table.

CHAPTER FIFTEEN

On the road to Boca do Canhão

Tiago slowed down and I prised open my eyes to find the steamy nostrils of a hunchbacked cow leering through the window at me. I rubbed my neck and looked out of the front window. A group of dirty white cows were nonchalantly crossing the road around the car. Rosa was laughing at something Tiago had said.

I must have fallen asleep as we were leaving the city. Now I found myself in a no-man's land, the curious cows the only company on the endless road, which stretched as far in front of us as it did behind. My head ached and the sun hurt my eyes. It was already far too hot to find any comfort - I guessed it was around midday - and there was only the mere wisp of a cloud in the startlingly blue sky.

I needed a drink. In the absence of a drink I ran my tongue over my teeth and then back over my gums and looked again out of the window. At the side of the road someone had lovingly constructed a shrine out of rocks and wood, inside of which I glimpsed the faded photo of a young man behind a meagre bunch of plastic flowers in a glass jar. I wondered who the young man had been and who on earth would come out all this way to visit his shrine.

Looking around, I was surprised by the greenery; the luscious trees and grass and plants. I'd thought it would be a barren wilderness, but the cows obviously had nothing to worry about.

As Tiago drove on, I watched the landscape change and the greenery dissolve into rock and dry earth. As the hours passed, the sun bore down ever stronger. In the front seat Rosa laughed. We still hadn't had a real conversation but that wasn't unusual. At breakfast earlier she'd smiled and said good morning to Ricardo, and had nodded a smile to me. I felt the tension dissipating. Now she'd voiced her feelings and said what she had to say, she seemed to have calmed down. Or maybe it was just the hangover. In any case, she seemed to have accepted that her dad was gay and this both surprised and worried me. I was desperate to talk to her about Edson, about what she'd said, but didn't dare provoke another fight. I didn't want to push things now that I felt this was the start of us getting back on track.

My bag had slipped on to the floor. I pulled it back up and held it against me. Our suitcases were back at Ricardo's house. He'd called the airport and driven out there before we were awake and I'd nearly tripped over them as I came out of the bedroom. When I'd thanked him he'd just shrugged and offered me a coffee. Now Edson's ashes were safely in my bag and I wasn't going to let the bag out of my sight.

After breakfast Ricardo had given us a lift down to the hotel to meet Tiago as planned. As we were heading for the car he'd called me back.

"Look, about Edson."

"Yes?"

"When he came to the city he was looking for a new start."

"What do you mean?"

"I mean, he wasn't always known as Edson. He changed his name. His family knew him as Junior: Francisco de Assis Cabral Junior."

Tiago steered the car off the highway on to a dusty carpet of sand. The landscape had changed somewhat since the encounter with the cows. With its deep golden earth and harsh brush it made me think of the western films I'd watched with my dad as a child, before he left. Indeed, as we pulled up we passed a pair of real life cowboys on horseback, complete with wide-brimmed leather hats and faded Coca-Cola T-shirts, chewing the rag with a group of leather-skinned men in the shade of a scraggy tree.

Behind the rudimentary car park, beyond the stands full of unfamiliar fruit and drinks, a long, low, white-washed wall lined a stone pathway, winding its way past a collection of basic, brightly-painted houses, before curling up the side of a rock towards some sort of chapel at the top.

"Why are we stopping here?" I asked as Tiago turned the engine off and stretched his arms behind his head.

"There's someone I need to see," he said, as if we were just popping into a neighbour instead of a lost village in the middle of nowhere, over three hours from the city.

"You know people here? But we're in the middle of nowhere," I said.

"I come this way to the festival every year. You get to know people."

He got out of the car and stretched his back. The sun was high in the sky and the air was dry. I was thirsty. Rosa leant her head out of the window.

"How long are you going to be?"

"Don't know – you guys should go see the cockerel. I'll meet you up there."

"Cockerel?" I asked, "What cockerel?"

"The one at the top of the rock – it's famous, you haven't heard of it?"

Funnily enough, no, I thought, but bit my lip and shook my head.

"People come from all over to pray and make offerings. It's like a religious thing, you know, pilgrims and stuff."

Not surprisingly Tiago's explanation didn't do much to enlighten me, but it had served it's purpose in peaking my interest enough to peel myself off the back seat of his car, where I feared I'd developed an embarrassing damp patch on my shorts from sweating so much.

In the front seat Rosa pulled down the mirror and combed her fingers through her hair. I felt the tingle of pins and needles tickle my feet. I leant out of the window and let myself out of the car, the handle on the inside of the passenger door apparently having been broken long ago. Rosa was still busy with her hair. I looked around for shade but there was none. I hadn't thought to wear a hat. I rolled back my shoulders and bent my neck forward, like I did in the mornings on getting out of bed, in an effort to work myself back to some semblance of a normal posture after so many years heaving Edson in and out of his wheelchair, his bed, the bath. The heat, and probably the humidity, seemed to be doing my muscles some good however, and I felt my body regaining a little of its suppleness.

I watched Tiago saunter over to a wooden cart with a yellow plastic sheet slung over it to protect it from the blazing sun. A young girl in denim hot pants, evidently delighted to see him, was turning the wheel of an ancient rusty contraption that appeared to be squeezing juice from shards of sugar cane. Behind her, a handful of people were making their way along the white-walled pathway to join the clumps of other visitors already climbing the immense rock, which stuck out of the flat ground like the nose of a mother whale, surrounded by similar, much smaller rocks, dotted like offspring across the landscape. At the peak of the rock I could now make out a large statue of a black cockerel, above a neat little stone chapel.

"You want to go check out the cockerel?" I asked Rosa. To my astonishment, she got out of the car.

"Okay," she said, "anything's better than sitting in this airless rust-bucket of a car."

It was the most she'd said to me all day.

The climb was gentle at first, and we walked without speaking along the path. Arriving at the lower part of the rock I stopped to rest a moment in the small circle of shade from an overhanging piece of rock jutting out over the pathway. Sitting on the low wall and leaning back against the rock, I felt the relative cool of the stone against my bare shoulders as I welcomed the shade and shut my eyes on the almost unbearable midday light. Rosa sat down next to me.

I thought of Edson, of his ashes in the back seat of this beat-up car, and wondered if he could feel the heat and feel that he was nearly home. I had come so far, and now I was nervous about meeting his family. How would Rosa react? Meeting his family would be like getting a glimpse of Edson again, would bring him back to us and keep him alive. Rosa needed that. She needed to know her roots. She was a lost soul needing answers but not even sure what questions to ask.

I opened my eyes. Rosa was looking at me.

"Hey," I said, careful not to smile too widely.

"Hey Mum," Rosa was leaning against the rock next to me and passed me the bottle of water she was carrying.

I took the bottle. "Thanks."

We sat leaning against the rock for a while, watching Tiago down below. It dawned on me that I didn't know this young man at all; that no one knew where we were. He could take us anywhere, murder me out here and take my daughter away and no one would ever know. There was no one who would miss me. I felt the vastness of the landscape echo my own loneliness.

"Sorry about what I said," Rosa said suddenly, still looking down at Tiago in the car park.

I wasn't sure what to say. "Dad was very sick, you know."

"I know."

We stood up. I sipped the water and handed it back to Rosa. I wanted so much to know what was going on in her head, but instead I started walking up the pathway.

"Come on," I said, "last one up's a potato."

The cockerel was perched a lot higher up than it had looked from the car. The pathway wove around the rock and became steeper as the sun became hotter. When we finally reached the statue Rosa stood contemplating it. I stood just behind her, contemplating my daughter.

"What're you thinking?" I asked her, concerned.

She was silent for a moment, looking at the statue, then said, "I'm thinking how you've dragged me half way around the world to look at a cock on a rock." She turned to look at me and laughed, but turned away again before I could smile back.

After a while, without turning, Rosa spoke, more seriously this time.

"I remember once seeing dad kiss a man. They were arguing and then he just kissed him. He didn't know I was there, I was supposed to be in bed, but I was thirsty so I'd come out of the bedroom to get a glass of water and I saw them. I don't know how old I was – he wasn't in his wheelchair, so I can't have been that old. I just remember knowing that it wasn't something you talked about. I didn't think about it much at the time. I think I supposed that that was how Brazilian men said sorry."

I reached to take Rosa's hand. She moved away.

"God, I need a cigarette." She pulled out a half-smoked packet from her back pocket.

"What, you smoke now?"

"Oh, like you didn't know."

"I didn't."

"Shit, I need a light."

Rosa looked around and found Tiago someway down the path, weaving his way up through the groups of tourists to join us as promised.

"Back in a minute," she said as she skipped down the rocks to the path. She turned back as she walked away, holding a cigarette in one hand and stuffing the packet into her pocket with the other.

"And Mum," I looked up, "The word you were looking for is 'bi-sexual'."

I watched Rosa's back as she walked toward Tiago, then shut my eyes. After all this time I'd told Rosa what we'd tried so hard to hide from her and she was fine. She still hadn't quite understood the nature of my marriage to Edson, but there was no need to go into details. It felt like we'd come closer, that this had somehow made sense to Rosa; explained things like nothing else could ever have done. I felt a lightness and knew it was not just the heat but also the relief of a burden removed. I smiled and let myself slide down the rock to sit on the dusty earth. Far below a lone pair of sunscorched trees stretched up from the arid earth like the gnarled hands of a sinking witch. Looking out at the haze of the horizon far behind the cactus-covered rocks, I felt so very far away from London, but strangely so much closer to Edson than I'd ever been in that sullen house in Wembley. If only he could see me now, I thought. If only he could see his little girl back where she belonged and know that she loved him, no matter what. He would always be her father and nothing would ever change that.

A Japanese couple in matching 'I love Copacabana' baseball caps stepped up behind me and asked me to take a photo of them by the venerated cockerel.

As I levelled their grinning faces up below the painted statue in the viewfinder, trying to avoid the glare of the sun, I heard raised voices behind me and looked around. Further down the pathway, stopped by the little flower-robed chapel, stood Rosa, cigarette in hand, arguing with Tiago. Her back was turned to me but I could tell from the expression on Tiago's face that he had said something to upset her.

The Japanese lady called my attention and I swung back around and took the photo. When I looked back Rosa was still standing in front of Tiago, taking angry drags of her cigarette. Tiago held out his hands. Rosa shouted something at him. He leant towards her and tried to hold her shoulders but she wriggled free and turned, storming towards me.

"Mum, tell Tiago he's an idiot."

"Sorry darling, what?" I could see Rosa was worked up but hadn't a clue what they'd been arguing about. Tiago wasn't coming any closer. He was leaning against the rock, sucking on his cigarette and looking back down the pathway towards the car.

"I went and told him about Dad," she started.

"Rosa, I told you that in confidence," I said, disappointed. I hadn't meant it to be public knowledge.

"And then," Rosa continued, ignoring me, "he goes,'shit, your dad's gay', and laughs, and I tell him it's not funny."

"No, it's not funny," I reiterated, scowling down at the thoughtless Tiago, although he still wasn't looking in our direction.

"But then, you know what he asks me?"

"What?"

"He asks me, 'so, have you found your real mum yet?'" She laughed, incredulous.

My limbs went limp. Everything seemed to swim around me, as if I'd fallen into the sea.

"What?" I managed.

"My *real* mum. He said he heard you talking to Ricardo down at the beach last night. I told him he must've misheard you, it was so noisy down there, but he said no, he'd heard you just fine."

"What, what do you mean?" I was stumbling over my words, trying to recover and smooth over this boulder that had shot up from beneath us.

"Why would he say that, Mum?" There was still a nervous laugh to her voice.

"I, uh, pfff, I don't know. Like you said, he's an idiot, what can I tell you? I didn't like him from the word go." My voice was gathering confidence as I spoke and I was almost beginning to believe my own denial. Rosa's words had come as too big a surprise and I hadn't been prepared. I knew I'd fumbled, I knew I was looking guilty and I tried to cover up by talking fast, only the more I tried to sound sincere, the worse it became.

"It's hot, isn't it?" I said at last, fanning myself with my hand. "We should probably get back to the car." The more I wanted to shut up, the more I spoke, unable to stop myself. I realised that Rosa hadn't moved a muscle. She was standing stock still, looking at me, watching as I dug a pit for myself. The smile had gone.

"What the fuck, Mum?"

She was looking at me, waiting for me to tell her she'd got it wrong; that Tiago had got the wrong end of the stick. And I was about to tell her this, but looking at her there, alone on a rock in the middle of the immense landscape of her father's life, I knew it was too late. Whatever I said now I was damned. Just when I thought I'd won back her trust, Rosa was being ripped away from me before my eyes and there was nothing I could do but watch.

Rosa calmly drained the last of the water from the bottle and scrunched it up. The noise of the folding plastic sounded so loud in the silence between us. She threw it over the wall, turned away from me and started up the last part of the pathway towards the cockerel.

"Rosa," I called after her. She didn't take any notice and continued walking. "Rosa, come back," I called. She stopped, turned towards me and looked me straight in the eye.

"Mum...?"

This was the moment, the moment I had promised myself I would face one day when the time was right, but had never thought I would ever really have to say the words.

"Rosa," I started.

"Mum..." it was a plea for a truth she knew no longer existed.

"Tiago's not an idiot. Well, he probably is,

but not about this."

"Mum, no." Rosa was shaking her head, all the time looking in my eyes for another answer.

"Rosa, I'm not the woman who gave birth to you."

Time didn't make sense after the words had left my mouth. They seemed to float across the rock and out over the plains, sending their echo careering from boulder to boulder, intensifying with every second. I could hear my heart beating in my ears and bile rising in the back of my throat. I took a step towards Rosa as if I could somehow catch the words as they floated towards her and pull them back. But instead I watched as they reached her ears and worked their way down to her heart, which I stood and watched breaking. There was nothing I could do. I'd let it out and I couldn't take it back. But then after all, she had a right to know. I stood and listened to the people around us. Another couple were standing next to Rosa now, grinning inanely for their photo with the cockerel. All the words I could've, should've said came swimming through my mind. I wanted to turn back the clock and start over.

Rosa stood, her eyes seeking another answer; still willing me to tell her everything would be all right. Her left leg was starting to shake as it did when she was worried about something. I watched as the shadow of realisation fell over her face, pulling down her eyes, her lips. I watched as my daughter crumbled away and at that moment I hated Edson: his lies; his charming smile; his wicked laugh; the years I'd suffered and the promise I'd made as I'd watched him die. And for what? To break this girl's heart?

I took a step toward Rosa, my hand outstretched.

"Come here," I said, wanting to comfort her; the only person who could; the last person she wanted. She stepped back, shaking her head. I stepped closer. Rosa, still shaking, stepped back again.

"Don't fuck with me, Mum," she whispered.

"Come here, my love." I tried to calm her.

"Get away from me." Her voice was louder now, anger masking pain.

"Rosa," I took another step towards her.

"Go away," she spat, without making eye contact. She turned and started to climb the rock up to the statue, using the 'no climbing' sign as a foothold.

"Rosa!" I called after her but she didn't react. We were so high up and there was no wall, just a sheer drop down to the tiny houses below.

"It's not safe," I tried to warn her, but she was determined. I knew it was higher than it seemed and was scared that Rosa, in the state she was in, would lose her footing and fall. I started climbing behind her, to the horror of the tourists wanting their photos taken without two crazy women on top of the statue behind them.

Rosa flicked her cigarette butt and it fell on to the dry earth far below, ricocheting off a jagged elbow of rock before landing next to a group of boulders, clustered together in the sea of sand.

I watched her climb, her feet in flimsy flip-flops, searching for footholds in the rough stone as she tried to get as far away as possible from me and Tiago. I was so angry at that jumped-up little shit, who'd stranded us in the middle of nowhere and ruined everything just when we were starting to get on again. I looked up at the fast-retreating figure of my daughter and my heart sank.

Up high next to the cockerel there was a faint breeze, enough to feel the sweat on my neck cooling me down.

Rosa was standing like the figurehead on a ship, too close to the edge, holding on to the statue with one hand, the car a distant blotch on the landscape below.

"Come down from there," I ventured, trying to sound breezy, although I was completely out of breath from the climb, "you know what you're like with heights."

"Don't pretend you know me," seethed Rosa, edging even closer to the sheer drop.

"Rosa, get away from there, it's dangerous, I'm not kidding."

"Back off, Mum."

I stepped back to the other side of the statue.

"I really think we ought to be getting back to the car now. It's getting hot out here and we're out of water."

Rosa spun around to face me but she was too close to the edge. Her shaking leg lost its grip on the edge of the rock as it crumbled away beneath her and she slipped. Her leg disappeared, her body behind it. Her right knee somehow managed to wedge itself against the ledge and one hand clung to the hard rock. She screamed. I lunged forward but was too far away.

"Don't touch me!" Rosa yelled, her knee slipping from the edge. The jagged rock stuck out below. I knew that even if that didn't tear her apart, the fall would kill her. Her knee started to slide off and she screamed again. I froze. I watched as my daughter hung by one hand, unable to move, the world turning to slow motion as she slipped away from me.

A figure shot past me. It was Tiago. He didn't hesitate. His bare torso lunged over the edge of the rock and he grabbed Rosa's wrists just as her grip slipped. For a moment I thought he was going over too and I threw myself on to his legs, using all my weight to hold him steady as his hands worked their way down Rosa's arms and dragged her far enough up that she could get one foot up, then another.

With Tiago helping her, Rosa crawled up and away from the cliff edge, falling limp on to the warm rock where she lay without moving, face down in the dirt. After a moment she tried to pull herself up on to her knees but fell back onto her stomach and threw up, retching again and again. I moved to help her but Tiago motioned for me to stay where I was. He pulled out a cigarette and handed one to Rosa, who took it and let him light it as she knelt, head bent beside him.

I watched and tried to bring my breathing back to normal. My chest was so tight I felt I was going to faint, but I didn't. I sat and stared at Rosa's back as it moved in and out with each drag of the cigarette. Tiago held out the packet to me and I shook my head. He pushed it towards me.

"Go on," he said.

I took one, my first since Edson had come out of hospital, all those years ago. I put it between my lips and leant towards Tiago, who was holding out a lighter with a picture of a bikini-clad woman on it. I leant back and inhaled the smoke, letting it open my lungs and calm my shaking hands. I watched as the smoke stole out from between my lips and lingered over Rosa's back, veiling her dirt-covered hair.

Gradually my breath returned to normal, but I was still trembling from the shock: the shock that my daughter had been about to fall to her death and I had frozen, incapable of helping her. I looked at her, shivering, curled up like a baby, nuzzled into Tiago's smooth chest. I had done this to her. I had forced her over the edge and someone else had had to step in and save her, whilst I'd stood there and let it happen. I knew she would never forgive me - not for the lies, not for this. I'd never forgive myself. Sure, she was all right now, wrapped in the arms of the man who had saved her, but I knew that everything had changed. Rosa hadn't fallen, but she was broken - irreparably broken.

BRAÇOS ABERTOS STREET PROJECT #14

Tapescript 4

Date:	**18th January 1978**
Name:	**Luciana**
Age:	**12 years**

Flavia: It's Wednesday, why aren't you at work?
Luciana: I don't work there any more.
Flavia: What happened?
Luciana: Nothing.
Flavia: Have you got another job?
Luciana: Not really.
Flavia: So why did you leave the lady's house?
Luciana: 'Cos I felt like it. I can do what I like, can't I? I'm not a kid anymore.
Flavia: Did something happen?
Luciana: Like what?
Flavia: Did anything happen to you at the lady's house?
Luciana: Are you just gonna ask stupid questions all day or what? 'Cos I don't have to be here, you know.
Flavia: Are you living with your Nan again?
Luciana: Nan's dead.
Flavia: Oh, Luciana, I'm so sorry. How? When?
Luciana: Cooking the rice.
Flavia: Cooking the rice?
Luciana: I went home after the party at the

lady's house because the man told me to and because I didn't have anywhere else to go. I really wanted to see Nan and live at home again like when I was little, but when I got there Grandad said, 'Hey, go make me dinner.' and I said, 'Where's Nan?" and he said, 'Nan's dead and I'm hungry.'

I thought he was just drunk, so I went into the house but she wasn't there and her dress was hanging up in the bedroom. I took her headscarf, which was on the end of the bed, and I was about to go back outside to ask Grandad what had happened but then I saw that the bus from town had just arrived. I knew because Neginho was coming down the street, covered in white dust from the worksite.

And then through the window I see a man coming and it's Nelson. He's walking like he's balancing a football on his chest. He's wearing new trainers and two gold chains and behind him there's a girl, who's running to keep up. I don't recognise her. She looks younger than me and her eyes are all red and puffy. I think he's come to get me, 'cos that's what the lady said he would do, but he stops next door and I think he's got the wrong house, but then Valkiria's step-dad comes out and shouts for Valkiria. I see her climbing up on to the roof, but I don't say anything. This time she's careful not to knock any tiles loose and she makes it on to our roof, but then Grandad shouts and Nelson looks up and sees her. He calls her to come down but she legs it like a cockroach, over to the roof of the bar on the corner. Nelson doesn't move, he just shouts to the two men at the bar and they go to get her down. Valkiria manages to kick one of them in the face, but this just makes him really angry and he grabs her leg and pulls her down like a spider. He drags her to Nelson, who bends down, brushes her hair from her neck with his finger and whispers something in her ear. She stopped screaming then but I saw the terror in her eyes.

Nelson looks over at our house. I crouch down under the window, 'cos he doesn't know I'm there, and I don't want him to see me. Only Grandad tells him and he calls me to come out. Nelson takes my face in his hand and I want to bite him, but I think of what happened to Neginho's dog and I keep my mouth shut. He lets me go and says he'll come find me later. I want to run back into the house and bury my face in Nan's dress, which

	smells of rice and blue soap, but instead I stand and watch as he walks off and Valkiria has to run to catch up with him. She looks back at me, like I'm supposed to do something, I don't know. I just hope he doesn't take her to the lady's house, that's all.
Flavia:	Why not?
Luciana:	Dunno.
Flavia:	So did Nelson come back for you?
Luciana:	No. Well, I don't know, probably. But I wasn't going to stick around to find out. Grandad's shouting at me and saying where's his dinner and so I spit at him, really spit at him, you know, like Jaru taught me to do, and then I turn and walk down the street and leave him sitting there on his own on the bricks outside the house. He keeps shouting at me but he can't run after me, can he? And I don't turn around. Then, as I go round the corner of our street I can still hear him, but I'm not listening anymore because I'm thinking of Mum and of Rio and of going shopping together. I'm thinking I'll buy that new dress Mum promised me and a pair of trainers for Jaru; real ones, like the football players wear, and I'll keep them for when he comes to live with us in Rio, just as

soon as we've got enough money together.

CHAPTER SIXTEEN

Boca do Canhão

The red dust from Tiago's tyres settled to reveal a row of crooked painted houses held loosely together by the deserted dirt street. A handful of similar streets fanned out like afterthoughts from the fenced-off stone monolith in the square behind us.

I needed a drink. The air was dry. I wanted to get rid of the taste of earth in my mouth – it felt as if I'd eaten great handfuls of cobwebs. The dry, metallic taste on my tongue made me not want to swallow, and the lack of saliva meant I almost couldn't.

Rosa wasn't talking to me. She hadn't said a word to me since the rock. Overly affectionate to Tiago the rest of the journey, she had ignored me, deliberately putting on a show of reckless disregard, whilst avoiding eye contact. Now she stood apart from me, her bag slung over her shoulder as if waiting for a bus back home, but I could see the clenched jaw under the hair that tried to hide her face, and the tension in her back, deliberately turned to me.

I looked up each of the four streets, all of which eventually petered out like those in the old westerns, minus the brothels or saloons.

A flea-bitten rat of a dog snarled at us from

below a rusting pick-up truck across the square, before settling sluggishly back to sleep, like a sherry-mellowed great-aunt after Christmas dinner. It was early afternoon. Tiago had wanted to get to the festival in the nearby town to set up his stall and had arranged to meet us there later.

"But how are we going to get to the town?" I'd asked him.

"Oh someone'll give you a lift. Everyone goes there," he'd answered casually. I couldn't believe he was just leaving us there, stranded. Surely that hadn't been the arrangement. What if we couldn't find Edson's family? What if no one had heard of his mother and this was a wild goose chase? I'd be stranded in the middle of nowhere with a daughter who hated me, and my dead husband stuffed in my bag.

Ricardo had referred to Boca do Canhão as Edson's hometown. 'Home' it may have been, but 'town'? From what I could make out even the term 'village' would have seemed a wild exaggeration. The air was perfectly still and smelled of the upturned flowerpots in my grandfather's shed. I thought I heard the occasional muffled voice but saw no one. It was still siesta time, I supposed.

I didn't have an address and by the look of the place an address wouldn't have been much use. Ricardo had suggested I go to the local bar or shop, if there was one, which there wasn't, at least not that I could see.

I looked at Rosa. I'd still only told her half the truth. I wasn't her mother and now she knew. But there was one more question to come, to which I didn't yet know the answer. If I wasn't her mother, then who was? There was something else too, which I couldn't put my finger on. There was something Ricardo wasn't telling me, something I wasn't sure I wanted to know, but which was niggling me and wouldn't go away. Edson had never told me why he'd left his country, this country he'd professed to love so much, which he'd been so desperate for Rosa to visit. I'd always assumed it had something to do with Rosa's mother – the pain of losing her like he did and the memories that must still have been there, too entwined with his notion of home. But the little he had told me about Rosa's mother had now turned out to be nothing but lies. So what was it that had driven him to leave his home, too scared to return? How did the girl Luciana come into it? And why had he changed his name?

I hoped that meeting his family would give me some answers. Things would become clearer; I would find out who Edson really was and then I would be able to move on, get on with my life and with rebuilding Rosa's trust, although I feared I had already lost that for good.

To our left the shutters of a house, which must once have been orange, but had long since been battered back to grey, opened like those of a haunted house. A stout, wrinkled woman, hair tucked into a scarf, used a broom handle to nudge the shutters flush against the wall and squinted suspiciously at the mother and daughter lingering in the square, before disappearing back into the darkness of her home.

"I say we ask her," I said to Rosa's still unmoving back. Rosa took her Walkman from her bag and put the headphones over her ears.

"Right then," I said, pulling out the piece of

paper Ricardo had written the family name on, "here goes."

The woman didn't appear at once. On her windowsill were a selection of baskets with penny sweets in plastic bags; marshmallows; cheap plastic toy guns and naked dolls with blue eyes and blond hair. When she eventually appeared I asked her for a packet of the biscuits and a bottle of water, hoping that it really was bottled water but fearing it was from the lady's own tap. As the woman handed me the change I asked her if she knew Edson's family.

"Eh?" replied the woman.

I repeated the family name and showed her the piece of paper in the likely event that I'd mispronounced it. The woman looked at the paper without reading the name.

"Eh, Josemar!" she shouted into the darkness behind her.

"What?" came the sleepy reply from within.

The woman squawked something, of which I understood only the words 'blond woman asking questions.'

Rosa hadn't moved and looked like a bored celebrity waiting for a film shoot.

Eventually a dishevelled man in flip-flops and grey shorts, over which he'd slung his belly, shuffled through from the back of the house, placed his hand on top of the window frame and leant forward, his armpit alarmingly close to my face. I knew better than to recoil. I needed him to help us.

"Cabral you want, is it?"

"Yes, please, I need to find Mrs Cabral. Do you know if she still lives around here?"

"If you can call it living," he said. His wife shook her head solemnly and looked at the floor.

"So she does live here?"

"What do you want with her?" the man asked, eyeing me suspiciously.

"Well, it's sort of private," I stammered, not wanting to aggravate this man, but certainly not wanting to share my life with him.

He leant on the windowsill and took a good look at me and then his eyes came to rest on Rosa behind me. He looked her up and down with a smutty sneer and his eyes lit up. "She with you?"

"She's my daughter," I said in what I hoped was a warning voice.

"Hey," he shouted to Rosa, "You don't want to be standing out there in the sun."

Rosa, with her headphones on, was oblivious, or at least pretended to be. It was hard to tell.

I mimed headphones and music, unsure if he understood. A young woman called the man from the back of the house.

"Shut up, I'm with a customer!" he shouted back, still looking at Rosa.

"So, Mrs Cabral?" I asked again, trying to pull his focus back to me.

"Oh yeah," he said, looking at me again. He leant forward and pointed down the road, "down there – lot 23 – blue house with bricks in the garden."

"Thank you," I said, following his finger, without seeing either a blue house or any garden with bricks.

I was aware of the man and the woman watching us as we walked down the street. I tried to give off an air of calm. I found myself thinking of Ricardo and wishing he were there with us. I knew I'd feel safe with him. There was something about him that was so grounded and sure, as if nothing in the world could rattle him.

A young girl, not much older than eight or nine, came out of a gate, a dirty-kneed baby on her not-yet-formed hip. The baby wore what looked like a tea towel in place of a nappy and sucked on a dummy tied on a frayed piece of material around its neck. The girl watched us as we walked past. I smiled, but her face remained impassive as she continued staring at us, bouncing the baby as we passed.

Further down the road another girl came to her gate and stood watching us. Without taking her eyes off us she called her mother, who came out holding a large bed sheet, which her daughter helped her fold.

I saw the blue house beyond the sheet.

"Hey, there it is." I turned to Rosa. Rosa glared back but continued to follow me. I knew that if it weren't for the fact that we were here to meet Edson's family, she would've left with Tiago.

Behind us a group of children had emerged and were following us, not daring to speak. Then one boy plucked up the courage.

"Hey, lady, are you going to convert us?"

I struggled to understand.

"Are you from the land of the Mormons?"

"Mum!" Rosa was getting pawed by a group of adoring girls. She realised what she'd called me and shoved her Walkman into her bag, as if she'd said nothing.

I looked around and clapped my hands at

the girls, who obediently let go of their new best friend but continued to walk along side her, gazing admiringly at her handbag; her clothes; her shiny gold flip-flops. I went to take Rosa's hand, but she pulled it away, making out she was adjusting the strap of her handbag.

I spoke to one of the older girls, "Do you know Mrs Cabral?"

The girls giggled at my accent.

"Mrs Cabral, Marilede?" I repeated.

"Ah, Marilede? She means old white eyes," one of the boys shouted.

"Can you show me her house?" I asked the boy.

"It'll cost you," he said, his hand held out.

I shook my head. "It's okay, I'll find it myself."

The boy shrugged then ran ahead, shouting,

"Hey, Dolores, there's a foreign lady here, come to take your mother away at last!"

I followed him to the blue house and through a small wooden gate, held open by one of the girls, and waited in front of the open door. There was only one window, with no glass in it, a tenacious shutter somehow hanging from it.

Rosa had stopped at the gate and as I looked back at her I realised suddenly that these strangers, who we were about to meet, were technically more family to my daughter than I was myself. And I could see that Rosa realised this too, and that it scared her. Despite her bravado she didn't know how to react. I had always been there for her but now I'd ripped that support away, just at the moment she needed it most.

"Hello?"

I turned to see a slight woman about my age, her grey-flecked, frizzy hair itching to escape the loose knot she'd tied it in.

"Bom dia, I'm looking for Mrs Cabral, Marilede. Is this the right house?"

It was only then that I saw the old woman, sitting as still as a shadow on the narrow terrace. Her greasy grey hair fell wildly around her sunken face; her withered, shapeless body, loosely covered in a crumpled pink dress, spread on the wooden bench like bread dough in the sun. Her eyes were shut and she leaned on a cane. The woman with frizzy hair nodded over at her.

"You sure you've got the right house?"

"I'm looking for Edson's mother."

"Edson who?"

"Sorry, I mean Junior," I said, remembering what Ricardo had told me, "I need to speak to the mother of Francisco de Assis Cabral Junior."

The children by this point were playing what seemed to be a favourite game of waking the old lady. The frizzy-haired woman hissed at them and shooed them away. They duly scattered like mice and took refuge behind the wall, eyes peeping over so as not to miss out on the entertainment.

The woman shouted into the darkness of the house, "Dalva!"

There was no answer so she went back in. I stayed put, unsure what to do. I looked at the old woman; eyes shut to the world, sinking into her bench, her face like worn leather, the skin on her arms slowly melting over diminished bones. She mumbled something and made me jump.

"I'm sorry?" I said, unsure if she was still

asleep. I took a couple of steps towards her, bent down and looked closer at her face. Her eyes flicked open, startling me. The children had called her old white eyes and I now saw why. Her eyes were veiled with cataracts, a ghostly grey, almost white. I recoiled without meaning to and felt embarrassed at my rudeness.

The woman mouthed something that I didn't understand, revealing her gums, devoid of all but two of their teeth. Her lower jaw stuck out and her lips seemed to have collapsed into her face.

The frizzy-haired woman reappeared in the doorway and motioned for me to come in.

"Is she with you?" she asked, looking at Rosa.

Rosa heard and quickly followed us, clearly not wishing to be left outside alone.

Entering the house my eyes took a moment to adjust to the lack of light. The contrast from the glaring sun outside was too strong for my eyes. I was aware of several people around me and others through a doorway at the back of the room, but I couldn't make out their faces. I felt claustrophobic and wanted to run back outside and keep running. Again I felt a rush of anger towards Edson.

The woman shut the door behind us, shooing the children who had tried to advance on the house.

"Why are you looking for Junior? What's he done?" She asked in a lowered voice. She spoke quickly with a thick accent that I found hard to follow. She too was missing more than one of her teeth.

"He hasn't done anything," I answered, "I'm

just looking for his family."

"And you are?"

"I'm Judith Summers, sorry, I'm his wife."

"What did she say?" asked a man sitting on the sofa, who I could now see as my eyes grew accustomed to the diminished light.

"She said she's his wife," said the man next to him.

"Whose wife?"

"Junior's."

"You're Junior's wife?" The first man asked me.

"That's right."

The men roared with laughter and sat back.

"Oh, that's a good one, that's a good one!" They laughed and banged their legs.

"Shut your mouth José," the woman said, kicking him.

"His wife! And I suppose this is his daughter!"

"I told you to zip it," warned the woman.

The men wiped their eyes.

"I'm sorry my dear, I think you've got the wrong house here," the woman said apologetically.

"Actually, he was right, this is Junior's daughter, Rosa," I said.

Rosa studied the cement floor and rubbed at an imaginary spot with the toe of her flip-flop. I pulled out the photo of Edson as a young man with Ricardo and Flavia and showed it to the woman.

A car hooted outside and the two men got up.

"Hey, you should get yourself a real man!" They joked as they went out to a pick up truck waiting on the road.

Their sudden absence left a hole in the air. The woman was looking at the photo.

"What has the idiot done now?" she said.

"Nothing, really, he's not in trouble."

"But married? Are you serious?"

"Yes, we met in London."

The woman looked confused.

"In England," I clarified.

"He went to England?"

"Yes. Sixteen years ago, you didn't know?"

"We haven't seen Junior for... God, I don't even know. He was younger than this," she gave me back the photo. "I remember the night he left; the fight. It was ugly; it didn't surprise me when he never came back. I wouldn't have come back either."

"So you didn't know he'd left Brazil?"

The woman shrugged, "What difference if he's in England or Recife? He's not here."

She took Rosa by the shoulders and held her at arms length, looking her up and down.

"Well now, may the angels come down and hit me on the head, a kid? You serious? My little brother is your dad?"

Rosa nodded but said nothing. The woman pulled her towards her and hugged her close. "So that makes you family. Bloody hell, who'd have thought it, Junior's got a kid."

The woman wiped the crumbs from the sofa, which despite its obvious age was still covered in its plastic film, and beckoned us to sit down.

"There any more of you out there?" she asked.

"No," I said, "just us."

The woman pulled a chair from under the table and perched on the edge of it, crumbs from the sofa still in her hands. We looked at each other, no one quite knowing what to say next. Eventually the woman leant forward and spoke in a lowered voice. "I'm glad he got away. He wouldn't have survived long here, Junior," she said, "he was 'different'." I saw that she was choosing her words carefully. She went to the door and threw the crumbs out on to the ground. "But you know that, right?"

I nodded.

"I'm Dolores, his sister."

"And is that his mother, outside?" I asked.

"That's Mum."

"Is she blind?"

"Good as, but she hears everything, sly old cow. Mad as a cactus though." She straightened the plastic covering on the sofa around us.

"Here, I'll get you something to drink."

She disappeared through the door at the back of the house just as another two women appeared at the front door. They looked at Rosa and me sitting like frightened rabbits, sticky in the heat.

"You the one that says she's Junior's wife?" the flat-faced one said without introducing herself.

"Yes," I said, standing up, "I'm Judith." I held out a hand as if to shake theirs but they ignored it and went over to the kitchen where they spoke in loud voices with Dolores.

I leant forward, my head in my hands.

"I'm so sorry, my love," I whispered to Rosa, "I'm so sorry."

Rosa said nothing but I could see her leg

shaking and knew that she was trying not to cry. I knew what she was thinking. This was so very far from the stories he'd told us of his home and family. Where was the surgeon father; the politician mother; the house on the beach?

The women were arguing in the kitchen. I could hardly breathe in the airless, stifling heat.

"Sod this," I said and got up and walked over to the open door.

"Where're you going?" Rosa asked, getting up.

"Come on," I nodded for her to follow and led her out on to the terrace where the old woman was still sleeping.

"Hello?" I ventured. When a polite cough failed to wake the woman I leant over and shook her gently on the shoulder. She almost toppled off the bench.

"Hello," I said again, "my name's Judith Summers. I'm Junior's wife."

The woman reached out her hand and touched my face, patting first one cheek, then the other.

"Junior? My Junior? Oh thanks be to the Lord, my little boy is alive. I knew he wouldn't leave this world without saying goodbye to his old mother. Come here."

I moved closer and let her feel my face in her wrinkled hands.

"I knew he would choose a good one," she said with a toothless grin. "They told me I was mad, but I knew."

"This is Rosa, Junior's daughter." I motioned for Rosa to approach the woman, which she did, nervously, bending down like me, to crouch at the level of the old woman's face. She took Rosa's hand in both of her trembling hands and felt her face, her hair.

"You have his nose," she said, "So where is my boy?"

"He's in England, Mum," said Dolores coming out of the house, the two other women peering over her shoulders.

"What's he doing there? When's he coming home?"

No one answered. She turned to me and her milky eyes glistened. "You tell him to come home, my dear. You tell him his mother is waiting for him and I've made his favourite for dinner."

I looked at Dolores, who shrugged and shook her head.

"I'll tell him," I said at last.

"You tell him to hurry up now," said the old woman, "his dinner's getting cold."

"I'll tell him," I said again. What else could I say?

"He's a good boy, my Junior. Always takes care of his mother, always there for me."

"Was he your youngest?" I asked, biting my lip as I realised I'd used the past tense. The woman appeared not to have noticed.

"Oh no dear, but the rest were no good. Twenty-three children, that's something. Twenty-three, but the rest were no good; no good at all."

"She's been like this for years now," Dolores explained, as we drank the thick sweet orange papaya juice she'd prepared for us.

"She talks about him, you know. You'd think she'd have given up by now but she's still waiting for him to come home, especially since Dad fucked off and left us. He was always her favourite, the little bugger. He could get away with murder, he could, whereas us girls were never good enough, oh no. Whatever we do, we're never going to be him."

"Why did she say twenty-three children?"

"Because that's how many she had, if you count the ones that didn't make it. It's better now, but back then it was worse than shit. A child got ill; it died. Some died little, some died a bit bigger. We're five of us left now – plus Junior.

"Dolores, about Junior…" I began.

"He's dead isn't he?" she said.

"I'm afraid so. How did you…?"

"Look, I may be ignorant of a lot of things but I'm not stupid. Two girls like you – you'd never have come here if you'd had the choice. I'm right, aren't I?"

I looked at the floor, embarrassed. I reached for my bag and unzipped it, pulling out the urn.

"I've brought Junior's ashes with me. It was his last wish. He wanted to come home and I promised I'd bring him. Here, I want you to have them."

I handed the urn to Dolores but she pushed it away.

"What am I going to do with that?" she asked.

"But he wanted to come home."

Dolores shook her head and then said quickly with a lowered voice, glancing at the door, "You can't tell her."

"I know."

"And I can't take this."

"Please."

"This wasn't his home. Wherever he was talking about, dear, it wasn't here. His life started the day he left. You didn't know our dad. Junior wasn't the son he wanted and he let him know it, every day."

"How old was he when he left home?"

"God, I don't know. I was about seventeen, it was just before I got pregnant with Maria, so he must've been, what? Fourteen? Fifteen?"

I hadn't realised he'd been so young when he'd left home.

"Where did he go?"

"Who knows? We only saw him once after that. He came back for the São João festival one year. He was what, eighteen maybe? He brought meat and beer. Mum thought he'd come back to stay but he had another fight with dad, as always. Dad near killed him. Well, we never saw him again after that."

She took our glasses and went back into the little kitchen. Rosa had gone back outside and was sitting on the terrace with the old woman: her grandmother. That felt strange. I still couldn't get my head around the image of the two of them sitting together, both from such different worlds, both desperately clutching at this chance to bring Edson back to life in a few moments of shared memories.

Gradually the woman nodded off and I watched as Rosa sat a while, staring at her. Dolores appeared from the kitchen with two new glasses of freshly squeezed juice.

"Passion fruit, that's all we've got."

"Perfect," I said, taking one of the glasses. Dolores went to the door and called Rosa.

"Hey Rosa, come and have some juice with your aunty and your mother."

"She's not my real mother," Rosa said as she came in.

Before Dolores had time to react, Rosa spoke again.

"You don't happen to know if my dad had any girlfriends before he left, do you?"

"Rosa!" I said, horrified. They both ignored me.

"Well, yeah, there was Vera, but then that was when we were all young," said Dolores.

"Vera? And she was his girlfriend?" asked Rosa.

"Yeah, I suppose."

I could tell what Rosa was thinking and wanted to warn her against getting these people involved.

"What do you think you're doing?" I whispered in English.

"What do you care?"

"But she's just told us that he left here years before you were born."

"So?"

"So don't go talking about our lives to complete strangers."

"They're not strangers, they're my family."

What could I say?

"Hang on, I'll call her," said Dolores.

"Who?" I asked.

"Vera."

"Oh, look, there's no need to go to the phone box…" I started, but Dolores had already walked out onto the terrace and was shouting down the street.

"Oh, safada! Vera!"

After a moment a scrawny woman came out of the house three doors up across the street.

"What?"

"You went with Junior, didn't you?"

"Your brother? Little Junior? My God woman, what do you want to be talking about him for all of a sudden?"

"So, you ever do it with him?"

"You're kidding, right?"

"Seriously. You did – that time behind the bar, everyone saw you."

"He lied, safado. He told me if I didn't tell everyone we'd done it, he'd leave me."

"What did you care if he left you? You had a whole bunch of others on the go."

"Yeah, but Junior was special, he wasn't like the others, was he?"

"So you guys weren't doing it?"

"Oh, like you didn't know. He was too busy trying to snog my brother if you remember!" She cackled, amused at her own joke.

I looked at Rosa who was looking intently at the floor. Had she really thought it would be that easy?

A couple of ladies from the other houses had appeared at their doorways and were listening with amusement. One was pretending to hang out her washing; the other didn't even make an effort to hide her eavesdropping.

Dolores shouted at them, "Oi, you'd be better off spying on your husbands than on your neighbours." She laughed as the women went back into their houses and slammed their doors. She turned to me and Rosa.

"Come back inside and drink your juice." She went back in.

I paused a moment next to the old woman and looked at her. She still seemed to be asleep. Had she heard? I wondered.

"Don't be worrying about her, she doesn't know what's going on," called Dolores from within. Rosa went in but I lingered on the terrace, looking around at the dirt street that Edson must've seen every day growing up; the home he'd left for the uncertainty of the city. How lonely he must've been, how scared. But Dolores was right. This couldn't have been the home he'd meant. This wasn't Edson; this wasn't where he would've been happy. Hadn't Ricardo told me that he'd changed his name to escape this part of himself?

Walking in I spoke to Dolores.

"Thank you so much for the juice."

"Any time," she said, as if England were just down the road and we would pop in again any time soon.

"I'm sorry, but we'd better be going. Is there a bus from here to the town?"

Rosa interrupted before Dolores could reply. "I'm not going."

"What do you mean?" I asked.

"They've asked us to stay."

"But we've got to get back."

"You go, I'm staying."

"Not on your own."

"You can't tell me what to do any more, I'm sixteen."

"Not until tomorrow you're not," I said,

realising that I'd completely forgotten about Rosa's birthday, "Come tomorrow you can do as you please but until then you do as I say."

"Well, I'm not going."

"Yes you are, now stop embarrassing me."

"I'm staying."

"Why would you want to stay here?"

"They're my family."

She didn't have to add "and you're not", the silence said it all.

Supper was served at the cloth-covered table in the corner of the room, under the pictures of TV stars and footballers and a fading photo of Edson's parents, identical to the one I'd found in his shoebox under the bed.

I realised I was starving. Whatever was cooking in the saucepans on the hob smelled delicious. Dolores' children and grandchildren had appeared whilst she'd been cooking and they sat perched on the sofa or cross-legged on the cement floor. The eldest girl brought out their dishes and they shovelled the rice and beans into their mouths, their eyes glued to their two visitors, watching our every move, laughing as we ate politely at the small table. Everyone had the tiniest morsel of chicken, which looked delicious, but Dolores had saved the best part for her guests. I picked up the chicken foot between my fingers and followed Dolores' instructions as she mimed sucking. Forcing a smile I put the foot into my mouth and sucked as if it were an ice-pop, the jelly-like meat slipping down my throat like frogspawn. I smiled, tight-lipped and the children burst into laughter. Rosa followed suit and again the children laughed to see us two women making such a fuss over the best bit of the chicken. They questioned Rosa continuously:

"Have you got any kids?"
"No."
"Are you rich?"
"No."
"Have you got a telephone in your house?"
"Yes."
"Then you must be rich!"
"How did you get here?"
"In an aeroplane."
"Do they have swimming pools in aeroplanes?"
"No."
"I heard that they did. They're so big that you get swimming pools in them."

And so the questions kept coming. After the meal the men came back from work at the factory. Whilst the men ate, the women moved outside with the children to sit in the street. They took it in turns to plait each other's hair, checking for lice as they did so. The little ones clung to Rosa, playing with her hair and her necklace. Teenage boys started loitering across the street, eyeing Rosa, which amused the women and enraged the teenage girls. Rosa was evidently enjoying the attention; all the more for seeing that I was not.

By the time the men had finished eating and the air had cooled down, quite a crowd had gathered.

"So why did he leave when he did?" I asked Dolores.

A herd of children sat, stood and perched

around Rosa, the girls holding her hand proudly, stroking her hair like a favourite doll, showing off by dancing Samba and Forró. A group of young boys played football with a can, looking over to check if the guests were watching their display of expertise.

"He was going with Vera," Dolores explained.

"The lady from down the road?"

"Yeah, he was best friends with her brother, Chico. They were always hanging out together."

"But he preferred Chico to Vera?"

"We all took the piss, of course we did, they were asking for it, but bloody hell, no one guessed he was actually a real, proper shirt-lifter."

One of the boys piped up. "Uncle Junior went to the city to prostitute himself."

"Shut up, you faggot," Dolores called over and the boy put one hand on his hip and the other hand in the air like a teapot and minced up and down just out of her reach. Dolores threw a dried mango stone at him and he scampered back to his football game, laughing.

"Are you surprised he left?" she asked.

I shook my head. Edson had never once spoken of his real childhood and now I finally understood why.

Later, when the women had gone back inside and we were left alone on the street with just the children, Rosa spoke, without looking up. It was the question I'd been dreading.

"So, if you're not my mum, who is?"

"I don't know," I said.

"What, and you think I'm going to believe

you?"

"I know, I know, and you're right to be angry, you are, but I'm going to find out for you, I promise."

"Oh, you promise? Oh well, that's okay then."

"That's all I can do my love, I'm so sorry."

"Oh you're sorry? Oh, okay then, that makes everything all right. Forget about the whole thing, what was I thinking?"

"Rosa…"

"You lied to me."

"It wasn't like that."

"I want to know who my real mother is."

"I'll find out for you, I promise. "

"Whatever." Rosa stood up and walked up the street with the children clinging to her. I called after her, "Rosa, I promise you, I'll find her."

She didn't look back.

CHAPTER SEVENTEEN

Rosa

What the guidebook says:

- Life expectancy in Brazil is around 62 years.
- Rio has the world's largest landfill: the size of 247 football pitches.
- Between the 16th & 19th centuries, four million slaves came from Africa to Brazil.
- In 1958, a rhinoceros was a candidate in council elections in São Paulo.

Why didn't Dad ever tell me? I want to call him; ask him what the hell he was thinking; ask him why he never thought to tell me I had a real mother out there. No wonder I never felt like I fitted in. Turns out I don't even fit in to my own life anymore, let alone anyone else's. But I can't call him; I can't ask him anything. Dad's gone, and now, for all intents and purposes, so has Mum. Darren's up his own arse and Sal's a two-faced cow. I've literally got no-one left.

And even putting aside the whole 'I'm not your real Mum' thing, why did Dad lie about his family?

There's no surgeon dad, no politician mum. From what I can see, he escaped a living purgatory and moved in to hell. But why lie? Did he assume I'd think less of him? Why didn't he trust us with the truth? Or maybe Mum knew all along and she just wasn't telling me, like she neglected to tell me Dad was gay. Not that it matters. It's kind of obvious now, looking back. What do they call that? The Black Swan effect? How, when you find out something you hadn't even considered, it suddenly seems to make sense after all, in retrospect. I get that. What I don't get is why they lied to me about Mum not being my real mum. That's major. That's made everything I've ever known mean nothing at all. How did she think I was going to react? Did she think I was going to say, "oh, gee Mum, thanks for the heads up. Who cares, let's move on?" Is that why Mum is so hard on me? Because she doesn't really think of me as her own daughter? And if I'm not her real daughter, then whose daughter am I?

I should be more like Tiago. He's on his own and he's just fine. He lives in the here and now. He doesn't sit around feeling sorry for himself, he just gets up every day and gets on with it. He's totally carefree; no ties; no worries. That's what I'm going to be from now on: carefree. I don't belong to anyone anymore. No-one can tell me what to do. I'm going to have the time of my life and I don't care what anyone thinks or says. Maybe this is a good thing. Maybe not belonging is exactly what I needed all along - stop trying to fit in with everyone else's expectations and just live for myself. Maybe Darren was right all along; maybe my expectations have always been too high.

Everyone lies. Everyone cheats. In the end, we're all on our own. Tough shit. Get on with it. So tonight I'm going to party like there's no tomorrow – and when tomorrow finally comes, I'm going to go out and find my real mum.

BRAÇOS ABERTOS STREET PROJECT #14

Tapescript 5

Date:	**12th May 1978**
Name:	**Luciana**
Age:	**12 years**

Flavia: How many months gone are you?
Luciana: Five or six, I don't know. I didn't even know I was pregnant. Valkiria said you couldn't get pregnant until you were thirteen and I'm only twelve, so looks like something went wrong somewhere, I don't know. And now I don't know what to do. I have to get rid of it, but Jaru tried already, only it didn't work.
Flavia: He tried to get rid of the baby?
Luciana: Yeah, of course. He said his mate got a girl pregnant and he made sure she didn't have it and so Jaru tried to help me, only this baby is a stubborn little shit and doesn't want to go away.
Flavia: How did he try to get rid of it?
Luciana: Well, I was all crazy about it and panicking about it and stuff, and I knew I couldn't go home to Grandad or my aunty, 'cause she hates me anyway, so he gives me Rohypnol and glue and I'm off my face by now and I'm thinking 'this is nice, I could

	have the baby and live in a big house like the lady and she would help me and everything, seeing as how it's her fault in the first place', then Jaru stands me against the wall down there and he gets his foot and he kicks me, bang in the stomach. He's good at kicking 'cos he's always dancing Capoeira. He kept kicking and then he stopped and I was sick and I bled some and I thought that was it, but the baby didn't come out like it was supposed to and it's still growing, and now I don't want Jaru to kick me any more because I don't care how much it's supposed to work, it hurts too much. So now I don't know what to do. What are you going to do with yours?
Flavia:	I'm six months pregnant and I'm keeping my baby.
Luciana:	Yeah, but you're with it's dad, right?
Flavia:	Does that make a difference?
Luciana:	It's better if you're with the dad, right?
Flavia:	I don't know, what do you think?
Luciana:	I think it depends on the dad.
Flavia:	I think you're probably right.
Luciana:	What do you want, a girl or a boy?
Flavia:	I'm hoping it'll be a girl. What about you?
Luciana:	I don't care. I just want it to go away.

CHAPTER EIGHTEEN

Campina Grande

We drove for miles without seeing anything but the stars and the white lines in the centre of the road, driving without end, driving past emptiness into nothingness. The truck radio blared out the local accordion-heavy Frevo and Forró music in honour of what they called the São João festival. I sat in the front of the truck with two of Edson's cousins, or second cousins, I wasn't entirely sure of the family connection. The others, whose names I had immediately forgotten, were singing in the back of the truck, excited about their trip into the town for the festival. Dolores had suggested, or rather insisted, that they give Rosa and me a lift into Campina Grande and we'd finally set off around nine o'clock. Rosa had opted to sit out the back with the other cousins and I hadn't argued.

"So is this like Carnival or something?" I asked the taller of Edson's cousins, the one who wasn't driving. I had heard of Carnival in Brazil of course, who hadn't? Edson used to make fun of the English version of Mardi Gras – pancake day – he could never get over how the English could take something so wonderful, so full of joy and life, and transform it into the forced consumption of yet more white and yellow fatty carbohydrates, as if we didn't have enough of that all year round.

"It's tradition," I'd told him, insisting on pancakes each year for Rosa's sake. But he wanted colour and laughter. When I'd first met him he'd been full of colour and laughter.

"Carnival?" the cousin replied, "This is better than Carnival. This is São João. This is our festival, a month-long festival, now that's something, isn't it? Not even Rio does it better than us here in Campina Grande."

As we neared the centre of the city we could hear the music before we could make out any of the festivities. The colourful lights of the big city were a welcome sign of life after the darkness of the road. Edson's cousin drove us into the very centre, where he parked the truck on a curb in a side street, which was already crammed with cars and trucks. There were eight of us, besides me and Rosa: young cousins and their various boyfriends and girlfriends – their 'namorados' as they called them, all excitedly adjusting their dresses and suits as they dismounted from the back of the truck. They were dressed, from what I understood, as guests at a pretend wedding, which they celebrated every year at the festival. The girls wore identical yellow and gold ruffled skirts and off-the-shoulder matching tops, hair all done the same, or as near as they could get. The men wore their best and I guessed only suits, ready for the dance. I hadn't quite understood why they were dancing – if it was a show or a competition of some sort, but it was obviously the biggest event of the year and they were bubbling with anticipation. As I stepped out of the truck I saw groups of other men and women, dressed in similar attire, making their way to the lights beyond. I could make out the top of a large stage and street vendors spilling out from a central square.

Arranging to meet back at the truck at five o'clock in the morning, if for whatever reason we hadn't managed to find Tiago before then, we followed Edson's cousins up the road to the central square, where the whole group skipped off to join their friends, who they were dancing with later. Suddenly alone, Rosa and I stood awkwardly apart, neither one of us knowing what to say to the other.

We wound our way through stalls and past bars and dance floors, carried along by the heaving crowds. There was already a band playing and people dancing everywhere. Eventually Rosa spotted Tiago, standing behind his little makeshift stall to the right of the stage. She waved but he didn't see her, so she ran over, eager to escape me. I followed her. I didn't have anywhere else to go.

Tiago was taking money from a young girl clasping a cassette tape in her hand. His stall was no more that an old wooden table piled high with illegally copied cassette tapes of all the big Forró bands, surrounded by an eclectic collection of plastic toys, key-rings, pens and wallets.

Rosa ignored my attempts to enter into a conversation with her or Tiago and, conscious that Tiago was getting embarrassed in front of his customers, I left Rosa helping him and went to look for Ricardo. He'd told me he'd be manning a stall at some point during the evening, but there were so many stalls, so many rows of snack stands, temporary beer tents, street sellers and dancing bodies that I gave up hope of finding him. Instead, I made my way through the crowds of people to see if I could find Edson's cousins in their dance show.

I found a sort of straw barn constructed for the occasion, where a line of men stood opposite a line of women, awaiting the music from the band. I didn't recognise any of them but lingered to watch them all the same. I wondered if Edson had ever danced at the festival or if they had even had one when he lived here, given that the country had been under military rule at the time.

I watched a while but couldn't help worrying about Rosa, alone with that boy Tiago. He might have saved her life but I still didn't trust him. I decided to go check on her and made my way back to the stand where Tiago was charming some elderly woman into buying a key ring she probably didn't need, and Rosa was flirting unashamedly with a group of boys drinking beer at a table near by. I watched her from a distance. She was clearly loving the attention, perfectly aware of the affect she was having on her testosterone-fuelled audience, yet at the same time so utterly naïve. Tiago was obviously unimpressed and kept looking over at her as his elderly customer tried to decide whether or not to purchase the key ring. She eventually gave in to Tiago's insistent charm and went away happy with her purchase. Tiago was not so happy and pulled Rosa over to him. I couldn't hear what he was saying but I didn't need to, it was quite obvious from the look on his face. The group of lads took their cue and wandered off, one of them blowing Rosa a kiss as he went. I didn't like the look of them. They were already drunk and Rosa was leading them on shamelessly. I knew Rosa was bored, angry and looking to get back at me however she could and she knew her flirting would enrage me and make Tiago jealous. It was all attention seeking; it was all a game to her. I moved nearer.

"Hey, Judith," Tiago saw me and called me over, "Ricardo was looking for you."

"You've seen him?"

"Yeah, of course. He's on the stand over behind the beer tent there. You know, with his political stuff."

I made my way over to the tent Tiago had indicated and squeezed through the gap between the canvas sheet and the stall beside it, surprised at how excited I felt at the prospect of seeing Ricardo again.

The other side was just as busy as Tiago's side. Another temporary barn had been constructed there too, with hundreds of young couples dressed up ready to dance to yet another band. I saw Ricardo's stand: a long table spread with posters and flyers and pamphlets of 'Lula: Brazil's next president' blazoned across them. Ricardo didn't see me at first – I watched him, deep in conversation with a young couple until eventually I caught his eye.

"So, who's Lula?" I asked, surveying his stand.

"The next president of Brazil," he said, smiling, apparently pleased to see me. I wasn't sure how we had left it between us and had been a little worried he would be irritated by my presence. He handed me a leaflet.

"So I see."

"Lula started out as a street seller, worked his way up through the unions in São Paulo and now he's the favourite to take Brazil into the twenty-first century."

"Is Lula his real name?"

"No, it's his nickname. It literally translates as 'squid'.

"Seriously?"

"It's a long story, but he's the man, I'm telling you."

"So is this part of your job?"

"Not really. This is just something I believe is worth fighting for."

"I wish I had your strength," I said.

"I wouldn't say I was particularly strong."

"But you fight for what matters to you. You don't just stand by and hope others will sort it out - you put yourself out there. I've never been any good at that."

"We all have different strengths Judith."

"Yeah, well I'm not feeling very strong at the moment, I have to be honest."

He put the pamphlets down on the table and turned to me.

"Fancy a drink?"

There was such enthusiasm about Ricardo. Like Edson when I'd first met him, he was able to motivate people, bring out the best in them. But unlike Edson, he didn't do it through his bubbling, frenetic energy. Ricardo's was a different energy; there was a sureness, a stillness about him, which drew you in and made you feel safe.

I sat down and he brought over a cold beer and offered me a 'churro' – a long, thin, greasy affair, not unlike a stretched-out doughnut. We sat in silence a while, allowing the music to wash over us. I licked the churro's sugar from my lips and watched the mesmerising array of costumes, hats, flags and faces flooding around and about us. I felt the cold beer flow through my body.

"Tell me about Rosa," Ricardo said, breaking the silence, "What's she like?"

"Like any teenager, I suppose: stubborn, angry." I realised I was probably being unfair. "No, she's a wonderful girl, she really is. This last year's been hard, especially when Edson...you know, Junior, when he...well she blames me."

"She blames you for his death?"

"She's probably right. I should've been there for him, I should've understood."

"Was he ill?"

Of course, Ricardo had no idea what had happened. He'd pretended he hadn't known Edson.

"He was seriously depressed. He was attacked on the underground about ten years ago and that left him paralysed from the chest down. And well, that changed him, sort of changed his personality overnight. The doctors said it wasn't unusual to see some personality changes, but it knocked all the energy out of him. You knew him; you knew what he was like. You can't dance Forró in a wheelchair."

"Did he have anyone?" Ricardo phrased the question carefully, clearly still unsure what my relationship with Edson had been.

"His boyfriend paid for our wedding, to keep him in the country, but then buggered off after the attack. That was it for Edson. After that he just withered away."

I took another swig of beer and watched a

group of dancers run past, late for their show. I realised that Ricardo was still looking at me. I guessed that despite his denials he'd been close to Edson and would want to know what had happened. But I hadn't talked about it to anyone, not really, not after I'd told Rosa that night. I'd told white lies, wanting to protect his dignity. He wouldn't have wanted everyone knowing that he'd given up – that he'd taken his own life. Or maybe it wasn't giving up. Maybe it was his way of taking control.

Ricardo was still looking at me, searchingly. Embarrassed, feeling my cheeks redden with the beer, the heat and the closeness of him, I played with my bottle on the table and spoke, still watching the dancers.

"Until the call from his ex. That was a couple of weeks before he died. We were in the bathroom. I was giving Ed his bath, so we let the machine get it. When I played it back and heard Gavin's voice, after all those years, I was going to erase the message. How dare he? He was leaving a message telling Edson he really needed to see him, that he was sorry for everything and that he would call back. And like I said, I was about to erase the message. I should've done. I mean, how thoughtless, how cruel, to call like that after leaving him to suffer alone for all those years. He'd been completely and utterly in love with Gavin. They'd been talking about getting a place together. Gavin was something big in the city – he was always flashing his cash around, but he hadn't 'come out' at work. It was the seventies, the early eighties. Being gay may not have been illegal anymore but it wasn't exactly welcomed by everyone either. He kept promising Ed that they'd get a place soon and I remember wishing they wouldn't, because I couldn't bear the idea of living alone again after sharing my life with him and Rosa for so long. We'd always meant it to be temporary, but I was scared of losing them. I suppose I was more than a little in love with Edson myself, if truth be told."

I took another swig of beer, embarrassed at the confession. This I had never, ever told anyone. I hadn't even wanted to admit it to myself, not really. I carried on, not turning to look to see if Ricardo was listening.

"You don't know how much I hate myself for wishing that. 'Be careful what you wish for', isn't that what they say?" I laughed nervously, "Well, I got what I wished for alright, and a lot more besides." I snuck a glance at Ricardo. He was looking at me and nodded. I felt I could tell him anything.

"I was so in love with him, or so I thought. He embodied everything that I wasn't and everything I wished I could be: confidant; charming; so sure of himself; so funny; energetic; charismatic, the centre of any situation he found himself in. And I suppose, although I knew he was gay - of course I knew, I'd known from the very start, he'd never lied to me - but I suppose I thought that if he had fathered a child, if he had had Rosa, then, however vague it was, there was surely still hope that he would feel the same way about me, and that eventually we would become a real family, just the three of us. And again, I should have been careful what I wished for, shouldn't I? I got what I wished for, only I hadn't been specific in the details. And look how it ended up."

"And Rosa?"

"She never knew anything. Until this morning she thought I was her mother and that Edson was straight – or at least bi-sexual, I don't know. We hadn't planned on hiding it, it was just that after the attack, with all the carer's allowance and everything, and he didn't have any boyfriends after Gavin, and well, we thought it best if she didn't know, that way she couldn't tell anyone about the fake marriage. We didn't want to put her in that position - she was still only little."

"But why stay all those years?"

"Edson wasn't the only one to have gone into our marriage wanting to escape the past. I'd had some bad experiences of my own. I'd given up on men. And then he came along and we were great together, really we were. We became best friends. But then I became his carer. You can't just leave your best friend to wither away alone, can you? And I couldn't leave Rosa. By then it was as if she were mine. I did think of leaving, of course I did. Some days I just didn't know how I was going to cope. But the longer I left it, the more scared I became of leaving. I don't think it was until I heard that voice on the machine – Gavin's voice from ten years ago - that I actually realised how long we'd been living like shadows of ourselves. Our lives had been reduced to emotion-numbing routine – everything was on automatic pilot; practicalities providing us with an easy shield from real relationships. The day became something to get through so that I could sleep. We became invisible to each other. And now, all of a sudden, I feel as if I'm waking up and that I didn't know him at all. How lonely must that've been, can you imagine? To have no one understand who you really are? And I never took the time to really know him. All he ever wanted was to go back home – to come back here."

"So why didn't he? Why not come back home?"

"After the attack we knew that flying wasn't practical or advised, and without him working we couldn't have afforded it anyway. But still he talked about going home, about showing Rosa where he came from, showing her her roots. He so wanted to bring her here. He'd had plans to go back with Gavin, years ago, they'd planned on coming back just as soon as the military government were thrown out, but then he was attacked and Gavin buggered off, the little shit. If only he'd stayed away."

The knock startled me. I thought at first it must be Rosa, then remembered I'd heard her come back in the early hours. The funeral seemed so long ago now, although it was less than twelve hours since I'd shut the door on the last guest. I'd crawled out of bed and was still in my pyjamas, a blanket from the sofa wrapped around me, freezing, although it was the first day of April. The sun hadn't bothered rising and neither had Rosa.

The door shuddered as an aeroplane thundered overhead. I opened it to find Gavin standing there, a shoebox in his hand, a wide, forced grin spread deliberately across his face.

"Hi," he said, as if it'd only been a matter of days since we'd last seen each other instead of a

decade, "Sorry to bother you like this. I tried calling but then I thought, why not just pop 'round. I'm only a couple of stops away."

'A couple of stops?' I thought. All this time he's been living just a couple of stops away and he hasn't found the time to 'pop 'round'? Rosa had asked for him for months after he'd left. He'd been like an uncle to her and he'd never thought to call. Not once.

He was looking over my shoulder.

"Edson around?" He waved the box at me as if in explanation.

I felt goose bumps crawl up my back to my shoulders and down both arms.

He didn't know.

I shook my head, suddenly unable to speak, the lump in my throat so big.

"Damn. Thought I was bound to catch him on a Sunday morning. Still, I only wanted to give him this. I found it when we were packing up our things and, well, it didn't seem right to chuck it." He held out the box. "I forgot to bring it last week."

I found my voice. "You were here last week?"

"Yeah, on Wednesday. Didn't he tell you? I told him to say hi."

I shook my head. Wednesday. The day I came home and found him; the day he died.

"I was going 'round saying bye to everyone and thought it only right that I come and say sorry – you know, for what happened. All water under the bridge now, I know, but I'm just in such a happy place right now, I wanted to get rid of all the old baggage. You know, clean slate and all that."

"Happy place?" I heard myself saying.

"Oh yes, I'm finally 'settling down'." He tried

to make bunny ears with his hands but realised too late that he was still holding the box and it became one bunny ear.

I couldn't speak but must've looked confused.

"I met someone: Paulo. Brazilian too, what are the chances, right? And we're going back to Brazil to live together. His family has a house right on the beach. That's why we're packing up our things. That's how come I found this old box."

I stared down at the box as he handed it to me.

"Look, I can see this is a bad time. Tell Edson I said hi – and bye, yeah?"

He turned, hunched his shoulders and tucked his chin into his thick winter coat as he stepped out of the gate. I watched as he crossed the road and met up with another man, Paulo no doubt, and they walked shoulder to shoulder until they turned the corner to the bridge that led to the station. I closed the door and stood leaning against it, slowly sliding down until I was crumpled on the doormat.

So, he'd been over on Wednesday. He'd told Edson, who'd been stupidly waiting for him to come over and tell him he'd made a huge mistake, that he loved him and couldn't live without him, he'd come to tell him he was 'settling down' and moving to Brazil – doing all the things he'd planned to do with Edson all those years ago; doing what Edson had still, somehow believed he might do one day. And in coming he had pushed the knife in and twisted it. Edson had given up; it had been the last straw – the reality of never being with Gavin, or anyone else; the reality of never going home.

I held the box in my arms, hugging it to my chest, and cried for my husband, my best friend, for the man who had lost everything, whilst I'd stood by and watched.

A procession of young men and women rolled past; the men in suits, the women in elaborate white wedding dresses.

"Ah, the happy couples," said Ricardo, changing the subject.

"Great costumes," I said.

"Oh, they're not costumes," Ricardo told me, "These guys are actually getting married."

"But there must be twenty couples."

"More, probably. It's a big thing at the festival – the mass wedding."

I watched the young faces full of joy as they filed by, oozing hope and certainty in the future, which I already knew would never live up to their expectations of this night. I looked at Ricardo and tried to imagine him with his wife and his little girl. I couldn't help thinking what a wonderful father he would've made. He caught me watching him and changed the subject again.

"Well, what would Junior, I mean, Edson, sorry, what would he be doing if he were here with us tonight?"

"Dancing with you, if you'd have him, no doubt," I said laughing, realising how much Edson must have loved this man and starting to understand why.

"Then what are we waiting for?" said Ricardo, standing up and offering me his hand.

"Oh God, no, you know I can't dance."

"Everyone dances." He smiled.

I stretched out my hand to take his and let him lead me through the maze of plastic chairs, past the kiosks and towards the throng of dancing couples. I tried to make nervous small talk but the music was so loud he couldn't hear what I was saying, so I gave up and let myself be led.

Near the stage there was hardly space to move, but he held me close to him; so close I could smell him. He smelled good: of sunshine and beer and ink from the flyers. I laughed as he spun me around. I'd had a few beers by then and was feeling a little dizzy. My back was better than it had been in years. So much heavy lifting with Edson had left me with a tendency to hunch over, but in Ricardo's arms I was unfurling like a butterfly from a cocoon. I looked up into his face and found him looking down at me, smiling. His smile transformed his face, the tiredness evaporating. I wanted to kiss his lips, to discover if they were as warm and soft as I imagined, but I simply smiled back, closed my eyes, and gave in to the dance.

The music swelled around us. We bumped into other couples like dodgem cars, laughing and smiling at each other. Everyone was there to have fun. There was a powerful feeling of camaraderie: we were all in it together and it felt wonderful. I felt like Cinderella and wanted to dance all night. I flung my head back and thought of Edson, of how much he'd loved to dance. I remembered his face in the hospital bed. The doctor had taken me to one side and asked me if he had insurance, before telling me he'd never walk again and leaving it to me to break the news to him. I would never forgive the doctor for that. The way Edson had looked at me when I'd told him; the way the hope drained out of his eyes as I stood by, powerless. Nothing prepares you for that moment.

I brought my head up to lean against Ricardo's shoulder, my eyes still closed. My memories merged with the music; the lights; the movement. I lifted my head without opening my eyes and leant my forehead against Ricardo's. I felt his breath on my lips and then his lips brush against mine, as soft and warm as I had imagined. His touch gave me goose bumps, even in the heat of the night. Suddenly my body ached to be touched; longed to be joined with his. I opened my eyes and found him smiling back at me. I wrapped my arms around his neck and he squeezed me tight around the waist as our lips came together, at first hesitant, then with an urgency that shocked and excited me all at once, as if we were both making up for all the years we had wasted apart. I closed my eyes and let the music fill my head; the music and the closeness of him; the smell of him; the taste of him. I stroked the nape of his neck as his hand worked its way under my t-shirt and stroked my lower back, sending shivers of pleasure up to my ears. How had I lived for so long without this? It felt so real; so right.

And then, so perfectly complete there in his arms, I started to cry.

I didn't understand. I was happy at last, happier than I ever remembered being, and yet still the tears came. I pulled away. Ricardo took my face in his hands.

"Hey," he said, wiping my tears.

"I'm sorry," I spluttered, but he couldn't hear me.

Instead he put his arm around my shoulders and led me back to the edge of the crowd.

"I'm sorry," I said again, embarrassed and confused at having spoiled what had been such a wonderful moment.

"Hey, it's okay. Don't be sorry."

"No, I'm an idiot, I'm so sorry."

"Honestly, it's fine, I understand."

I cried despite myself, unable to stop. He sat me down on an upturned crate and pulled another next to it for himself.

When I was finally able to control my sobs he spoke. "I cried in the supermarket once."

I looked up at him.

"A baby was crying behind me and I looked around and saw the mother pick it up and cuddle it and...well," he paused, "it was such a beautiful moment. Sometimes they are the hardest to bear."

He pulled me to him and my tears soaked through his T-shirt. I listened to the beat of his heart and gradually it calmed me. He understood. I never thought I would find anyone who understood and it came as such a relief.

"Do you know much about Tiago?" I asked after a while, not wanting to talk about myself any more.

"Not really, but I know his cousin. I represented him on a few occasions. He's a petty thief – a bit of a con artist, but he's not violent, just a bit, well, lost I guess. I knew his mother and promised her I'd keep an eye on him."

"And Tiago?"

"Tiago I don't know so well. What can I tell you? He's a bit of a chancer but he doesn't seem so bad. He's no criminal. He's a worker and a dreamer. But look around, he's not the only one."

"I don't trust him," I said.

"What makes you say that?"

"I see the way he looks at Rosa."

"I see the way she looks at him," he said.

"Touché," I laughed, lifting my head and looking back out at the people dancing and at Rosa and Tiago at the stand in the distance. Ricardo made me relax. Rosa had always been a terrible flirt. She was just having fun - a holiday romance. So what if I didn't trust Tiago? I'd just have to make sure I didn't leave them on their own, that was all.

I could see from where we were sitting that Rosa was getting bored with hanging around the stand, watching Tiago serve his customers. The gang of drunken boys were back and calling out to her from their seats at the bar, and she was doing a bad job of pretending she hadn't heard them. The boys were coaxing one of their friends to go up and talk to her, which he eventually did. I could tell he was extremely drunk but Rosa didn't seem to care, delighted by the attention. Tiago on the other hand was not at all happy, but he was in the middle of a sale and Rosa took advantage of the fact to flirt outrageously.

The boy invited Rosa to dance and she took his hand and let herself be led away on to the makeshift dance floor. Tiago called out to her but she waved at him and shouted something I couldn't make out. As they walked towards the other dancers, I saw the boy making some sort of hand gesture, clearly designed to insult Tiago without Rosa seeing. I resisted the urge to chase after them and bring Rosa back.

Ricardo had to go back to his stand.

"Are going to be alright?" he asked me.

"Yeah, thanks. I think I'll just sit here a while. I'll come over in a bit."

I watched him weave his way back through the people and chairs and disappear down the side of the tent. I thought I saw a spring in his step that hadn't been there before, and I smiled. I turned back to the dance floor and watched the hips of the girl dancing directly in front of me as her partner whirled her around. I started to relax again. I felt somehow closer to Edson now, the real Edson.

Through the constant ebb and flow of dancers I could see Tiago finishing his sale. As soon as he'd pocketed the cash he made his way through the crowds of dancers towards Rosa. The other boy was getting a little too friendly and I was rather pleased that Tiago was going in to break it up. Although I couldn't make out what they were saying, I could see quite clearly that Rosa was telling Tiago he was embarrassing her. As he turned back to his stand to serve a waiting customer the other boy pulled a face and Rosa flung her head back provocatively and laughed.

What Rosa didn't appreciate was that I had been young myself once too. Admittedly, it felt like another life, but I'd been where Rosa was now, lapping up the attention, glowing in the adoration of young men. It had taken me the best part of a decade to learn that not everyone who told you that you were beautiful was your soul mate, and that sleeping with boys didn't make them love you, or stop them leaving you. Edson had been my ticket out of that cycle and for that I would be eternally grateful. What was so upsetting to see now was Rosa, thinking she could somehow smother her pain in the arms of a stranger. But then again, wasn't that exactly what I was doing?

I looked back up at where Rosa had been dancing but couldn't find her. I stood up and peered over the hundreds of moving heads, but couldn't make out Rosa or the boy. Worried, I grabbed a chair from the bar and stood up on it and looked again. I still couldn't see them but I spotted Tiago pushing his way through the crowds towards the stage and followed his gaze to where Rosa was being led by the boy, off behind the straw-covered stage. A man from the bar shouted at me to get down and I realised people were looking at me. I didn't care. I couldn't lose Rosa. It didn't matter whether Rosa never spoke to me again; her safety was all that mattered. This wasn't a game.

Jumping off the chair I pushed my way through the dancers, keeping my eyes on Tiago's red baseball cap.

Rounding the stage I thought I'd lost them but I caught sight of Tiago disappearing around a corner up the street. I followed him as fast as I could, weaving my way through the dark alleys, away from the noise and the lights until I was no longer in the festival itself but in the deserted back streets. It was like being in another city altogether and I remembered Ricardo's warning, that this was the biggest festival of its kind in the world and that there was no more danger here than anywhere else, as long as you stayed with the crowds, stayed in the lights and the party. But the music was growing fainter and the lights a distant glow. Where the hell was Rosa?

I stumbled over the uneven pavements, not so much cracked as shattered, great chunks of concrete debris lying ready to trip up passers by. The handful of small shops were closed and the houses were empty. Everyone was at the festival.

At the end of the road loomed an impressive white Baroque church, its twin towers and yellow-bordered façade lit to join in the festivities, although half the building was still hidden behind scaffolding. I saw Tiago disappearing down the side of the church between two palm trees. Across the street a sign in a hotel window blinked 'no vacancies' and in its sporadic light I could just make out Rosa, under the scaffolding, pressed against the wall of the church, the boy against her, kissing her fiercely as his hands clumsily ran up her skirt. I felt embarrassed. I could hear Rosa's voice in my head telling me she wasn't a kid any more, that she didn't need my help, she could look after herself. She'd told me so on more than one occasion. I slowed my step. I wanted to make sure she was all right, but I didn't want to embarrass her. Tiago on the other hand had no such qualms. I heard him call her name.

"Rosa!"

"Hey baby," she laughed at him as he approached. The other boy looked around. I couldn't hear what they were saying but I could see Rosa laughing and Tiago trying to take her hand. She pulled it away and the other boy was clearly telling him to get lost. Tiago tried to insist but Rosa pulled her hand away from his. He tried one more time then, as the other boy stood between them, his chest pushed out, his fists clenched in warning, Tiago backed down and turned to leave. I felt for him. He looked genuinely wounded. The other boy laughed cruelly and started pulling Rosa's skirt back up.

I quickened my step again. I didn't trust this boy. But as I sped up I caught my foot on the crooked pavement and fell. I cried out in pain but they didn't hear me. I heard Rosa though. She was telling the boy to stop. I looked up and saw that he was trying to prove something to Tiago, showing him he could have whatever he wanted, and took no notice of Rosa's pleas to leave her alone. Tiago wasn't going to ignore her though. He spun around, ran back and lunged at the boy with his fists, smacking him squarely in the jaw, sending him stumbling back, away from Rosa. I pulled myself up using the wall to steady myself and hobbled towards the church. This was starting to look ugly and I knew I had to get Rosa out of there. The other boy pulled himself up and made a grab for Tiago's legs, pulling him down. Rosa was screaming.

"Tiago!"

But neither man was listening. The boy regained his balance and grabbed Rosa by the arm, pulling her towards him and yanking her vest top over her head. Rosa kicked him hard in the shin but with only flip-flops on she didn't hurt him, just angered him. Tiago had got to his feet again and placed a firm hand on the boy's shoulder.

"Leave her alone," he said.

What came next happened so quickly that I couldn't quite follow. One minute Tiago was standing over the other boy who was a lot shorter than him and less well built, the next he was sliding to his knees and keeling over, his hands pressed to his stomach. I saw the lights of the church reflect off the blade of a knife. I was nearly at the church now. I could hear Rosa, still against the wall, screaming. She wouldn't stop. The boy, wild now, shouted at her to shut up but she couldn't, she just kept screaming. He slapped her across the face but that made it worse and she screamed again.

"Shut the fuck up," he yelled at her, a wild look in his eyes, he was looking around now, panicking, trying to decide what to do, not seeing me as I reached the church.

"Shut up!" he shouted again, slapping Rosa across the face, sending her head banging back against the wall. She kicked him again.

I knew what he was about to do before he did it. I caught the glint of metal in his hand.

"Rosa!" I yelled, throwing myself in front of my daughter, who was still staring, petrified at Tiago's limp body lying on the ground and hadn't seen the knife coming towards her.

The boy wanted to shut her up.

I felt the knife pierce my side and drop on to the road, as the boy fled down the side of the church into the darkness.

I fell against Rosa, who tried to hold me but couldn't.

"Rosa," I gasped.

The street was fading, I could feel darkness closing in, and then I thought I heard Ricardo's voice. I turned my head on the cobbled stones and saw him running towards me up the street. As he reached me he spoke but his voice was muffled, distant. I tried to tell him what had happened but the words wouldn't come out. He tore off his T-shirt and wrapped it around his hand, pressing it against the wound I couldn't see. I couldn't look down; instead I looked into his eyes, his wonderful, beautiful eyes. He was saying something but I couldn't hear him. I just wanted to keep looking into those eyes and know that everything would be all right.

But suddenly he was being torn away. Two policemen were either side of him, yanking him up by the arms. He struggled to get free, to get back to me. He was shouting but they weren't interested. One held him whilst the other punched him in the mouth, then again in the nose. He was bleeding but still he tried to get back to me. The man holding him let him go and he fell to the ground. Before he could get up the other one was on top of him, his knee in his back, the palm of his hand spread across his cheek, pinning him down on the cobbled street. The other one was on his radio. With his free hand he grabbed Rosa and pulled her away from me. I tried to reach out for her but couldn't move. I lay on my back, eyes skyward facing the darkness and heard a van pull up and my daughter's voice drowned out by the crackling of fireworks overhead.

CHAPTER NINETEEN

Ricardo

A sharp pain shot through the back of Ricardo's head, fading to a dull, oppressive ache, as if whatever had hit him had wedged itself into his skull, prising itself tighter and tighter around the back of his head, squeezing his brain, distorting his memory, his vision, his hearing. His thoughts were confused: images of Tiago's body, the blood on his own T-shirt as he'd knelt next to Judith. He went to stand up but couldn't move. He tried to shout out but something stopped him. Instead, he tried to open his eyes, but recoiled instantly as the intensity of the electric light pierced his pupils, shooting thunderbolts through to the back of his head. He could smell vomit and wondered whether it was his. This wasn't what was supposed to be happening. They weren't supposed to bring him here. He should be at the hospital. He knew perfectly innocent people were brought to these cells or cells like them. He'd been in police stations enough times, helping those who'd been wrongly arrested. He just couldn't understand why the policemen hadn't run after the boy.

He opened his mouth but his lip, encrusted with dry blood, split like a finger on a blade of grass. Blood seeped out like lava from a too-long dormant volcano as the numbness left his jawbone and the pain hit him. He touched a hand to where it hurt. The swelling was worse than he'd thought.

Gradually he got up the strength to pull himself up on to the concrete ledge that constituted a seat. He sat there alone in the dirty, forgotten cell, nauseated by the stench of stale urine and his own vomit, and tried to focus on what had happened.

The police had been harassing him at the festival, he remembered that. They'd been trying to find a reason to shut down the stand and get rid of them. The police were no friends of his. He'd pissed off enough people in the state department to have them all watching him for the slightest mistake. He'd left the two police men standing arguing with his colleagues and popped back to check how Judith was and had seen her frantically pushing her way through the crowd. He'd pushed his way after her. The policemen must have followed him. Maybe they'd thought he was trying to run away, but that didn't make sense, as he hadn't done anything wrong to run away from. He heard them coming after him and he saw the boy stab Tiago and then Judith, but he couldn't reach them in time. The policemen must've seen it all too. So why arrest him?

He hobbled to the door of the cell, his knee buckling under his weight. He could feel the dried blood on his face and see it streaked across his bare torso.

"Hey!" he called out. No one answered. He had no idea what time it was or how long he'd been unconscious. And what about Rosa? He'd seen them take her too. Had they even called an ambulance?

He heard steps outside his cell and the key turn in the lock. A man stood in the doorway, looking at him with undisguised amusement. Ricardo looked up and instantly recognised him. It was Senhor Coutran, the property developer-turned-politician.

He knew then that he was in trouble. The police may have listened to his side of the story eventually, but with Senhor Coutran to slur his character and fuel the flames of doubt, he would be lucky to get out at all.

"Well, what do you know?" said Coutran, smirking "Who would've thought it? Top lawyer turned murderer. The stuff of headlines."

"What happened to the woman? The woman who was stabbed?" he asked, ignoring the pleasure Coutran was clearly taking in his predicament.

"Your friend, was she?"

"Tell me where she is."

"All in good time, Senhor da Silva, all in good time."

"What are you doing here?" Ricardo asked.

"A little bird told me you were here."

"You know I didn't do this."

"Oh come now, don't take it personally. You know it's just business - unfinished business."

"Tell them I didn't do it."

"Far be it for me to interfere in police business."

"You know you only have to say the word and I'm out of here."

He smiled and picked a morsel of food from his teeth.

"Now where would be the fun in that?" he

said. And then he left.

Ricardo thumped the door with his fist.

"Did they at least get the guy?" he shouted into the empty corridor, "Tell me they got him."

No one replied.

He tried to think who knew he was there, who would be coming to get him out, but the others on the stand had been students and volunteers, no one with any power to help him. They probably wouldn't even think to worry that he hadn't come back. They'd have assumed he'd gone home. He was sure Judith needed him and he was helpless. Senhor Coutran, the property developer looking to tear down the favela in Recife, had been looking for an excuse to get to him for years, and now that Ricardo had stumbled into his home territory he wasn't about to let go of this perfect opportunity to set him up.

He leant back against the wall. It was only then he heard the crying, coming from the other side of the cell wall.

It was a girl.

"Rosa?"

The crying stopped.

"Rosa? It's me, Ricardo."

For a moment he didn't think she would answer and thought maybe it wasn't her.

"Where've they taken Mum?" she asked, still sobbing.

"To the hospital. They took her in the ambulance." He tried to make the lie sound convincing.

"Is she okay?"

Ricardo leant his forehead against the wall between them.

"I don't know."

He heard a stifled sob and thought she must be covering her mouth. The wall was thin. He wanted to comfort her.

"Come closer to the wall, Rosa," he said. He heard a shuffle and pictured her sitting on the floor on the other side. "Are you there?"

"Mmmhmm."

He could hear she was up against the wall now.

"It's going to be okay," he said, "Have they hurt you?"

"No. No, I'm okay." She had stopped crying.

"They're just trying to frighten us. It's not your fault, it's not about you."

She didn't answer. Then she said, "What about Tiago?"

"I don't think he made it, my love." He wanted to hold her in his arms as he had all those years ago, and make the bad things go away. He couldn't have loved her more in that moment if she had been his own child.

"It's my birthday today," came a little voice.

Ricardo realised what the date was and thought back sixteen years. Had it really been that long ago?

"I'm sixteen," she said, unaware that he already knew only too well, "I just wanted to have a bit of fun, I just wanted to have a laugh. I wanted to piss Mum off." Her voice broke and she started crying again.

"Rosa, listen to me," said Ricardo gently, "this isn't your fault. We're going to get out of here and we're going to go see your mum and everything is going to be alright." It hurt his mouth to speak.

"Tiago's dead, isn't he?" she said.

"Yes, I'm pretty sure he is."

Ricardo slid down the wall until he was sitting on the floor. He held his damaged knee in his hands to try and stop the throbbing. The wall was cool against his bare back. He thought of his wife, of the night, sixteen years ago at the hospital, when he'd held her hand as she'd screamed in agony, the baby refusing to come out, and told her, as she gasped for breath between contractions, that everything would be all right.

"They kept asking me how I knew you," Rosa said.

"Try not to think about it."

"They kept telling me there was no other boy, that I was confused and that it was you who killed Tiago."

"Rosa, it doesn't matter. Stop thinking about it."

"They kept asking how I knew you. They kept calling you Senhor da Silva."

"That's my name, Rosa."

"They kept asking how I knew Edson da Silva."

Ricardo held his head. He should never have spoken to Judith, he should have asked her to leave the minute he had met her and told her to go back to London. It'd only been a matter of time until she'd found out his name.

"I told them, he's my dad," Rosa continued, "but they wouldn't believe me. I said he used to be Junior, Francisco de Assis Cabral Junior, and that he changed his name. And then they got this other guy, this old guy in a suit, they got him in and he got me to repeat it all and he laughed like I was telling the funniest joke. He said, 'Your dad's not dead little girl, he's sitting in the cell next door.' He said Edson da Silva was you; that you were Edson da Silva. Why would he say that?"

Ricardo's knee felt like an iron weight had been dropped on it. His kneecap was on fire.

"My name is Edson Ricardo da Silva."

There was silence from the other side of the wall as Rosa evidently tried to make sense of this information.

"So what, are you trying to tell me that you're my dad's brother or something?" she asked.

Ricardo said nothing. What could he say? He sat and tried to think of the right words, but nothing came.

Eventually Rosa must've realised how ridiculous her question had been, that something had been staring her in the face all along. He heard her voice, almost a whisper, as if she didn't really want to know the answer, but knew the question had to be asked.

"Are you my dad?"

CHAPTER TWENTY

Campina Grande hospital

I prised open my eyes, breaking through the residue of the night's tears. The starkness of the pea green walls and the silence of the early morning were disorientating. I shut my eyes but immediately saw the boy's angry face and felt the searing pain of the blade as it pierced my skin. My eyes shot open and I looked around me, panic rising in my stomach, but all I saw were the rows of other patients sleeping in their beds. There was no one to ask where I was. I looked down and saw the tubes in my arm. My mouth felt like sandpaper and my legs felt weak. A machine next to my bed beeped a steady rhythm.

"Rosa?" I heard myself say.

A nurse approached the bed and checked the monitor.

"My daughter?" I said, my mouth so dry it was hard to talk.

"Try to sleep," said the nurse, not unkindly. She touched one of the dials and I felt warm and heavy. I leant my head back against the pillow and let myself drift off.

When I woke again the silent ward had transformed. Most of the other patients were awake, many with visitors. A woman was sitting in the chair next to the bed on my left. I tried to call the nurse over but my voice wouldn't come out. I coughed to clear my throat and tried again, this time managing to make enough sound to call the nurse's attention.

"Excuse me, do you know where my daughter is?" I asked.

"You really need to rest," said the nurse, "I'm sure your daughter will be along presently."

"Please," I said, "you don't understand. The police took her. I need to know she's okay."

The nurse didn't try to hide her surprise. She tucked my sheet back in.

"I'll see what I can find out," she said, heading back out of the door.

I slid my hand under the thin, frayed nightgown I was wearing and tentatively searched for the wound. I found a neat dressing the size of a flannel over the lower half of my left side. I couldn't feel any pain but I supposed that was due to the drugs they must be pumping into me.

I thought of Edson, of the day after the attack. How scared he had still looked, how alone when Gavin hadn't turned up. I wanted Rosa, with her little panda bear, to walk though the door now, jump on my bed and wrap her arms around me.

Edson.

Edson's ashes.

They'd been in my bag.

I looked down at the side of my bed and then the other side. My bag was there, tucked under the bed, it's strap just peeking out from underneath. He was still with me.

The nurse came back with a glass of water.

"Your daughter was taken to the police station with the man they arrested for stabbing that boy," she said. I could see from her face that she was trying not to show her excitement at the sensational news she had obviously just gleaned from a colleague.

"Arrested?"

"Yes, apparently they got the man who did this to you. They took them both down to the police station. I expect they just need to question your daughter – she'll be a witness, I guess. Don't worry, she'll be back soon." I took the glass and placed it back on the table beside the bed.

"Sorry, what time is it?"

"Eleven twenty-five."

"And what time was I brought in?"

"Oh, that was before my shift." She looked at the chart at the foot of the bed. "Says here you were brought in at two-thirty this morning."

I'd been unconscious for nearly nine hours. Why would they keep Rosa in a police station for nine hours if all they wanted to do was to question her?

"How long before I can leave?"

"Another few days at least. You'll have to wait until the doctor comes round and ask her. I couldn't tell you exactly."

"When will that be?"

"Sometime this afternoon."

I thought of Tiago.

"Where's the boy who was brought in with me?"

The nurse looked around, obviously hoping a colleague would appear to take away from her the burden of what she was about to say. Looking back at me, she shook her head.

"He didn't make it, I'm afraid." She smiled a sympathetic smile and turned to the man in the next bed, pulling the curtain, which separated us.

CHAPTER TWENTY-ONE

Ricardo

"I'm not your father, Rosa." Ricardo said. How he wished he could go into her cell and sit with her. "Your dad was in trouble. I helped him out, that's all."

"You helped him out? But he took your name?"

"I gave it to him."

"What does that even mean?"

"Sixteen years ago, the night you were born, your father came to me and asked for my help."

"You knew me when I was a baby?"

"Rosa, I was the one who delivered you."

What point was there in hiding it from her now? He knew she was trying to take this all in and make sense of it. He knew he had to tell her. At the very least it would distract her from worrying about Judith. Moreover, it would distract *him* from worrying about her. He was in such pain, but the pain he could bear. It was the not knowing that he couldn't bear. Judith Summers had to be all right. He'd started all this. It was his fault they'd got into this and it was up to him to protect these two women.

"That night, the night you were born, your mother came to my office. I was at the children's shelter, where my wife worked, where I met you yesterday."

Rosa said nothing.

"I found your mother at the door."

"You knew my mother? My real mother?"

"Yes, Rosa, I did."

Rosa didn't ask the question he thought she would ask next. She didn't ask who her mother was. Instead, she kept quiet, waiting for him to continue the story. He guessed it felt wrong to her to be talking about her real mother when Judith was lying in a hospital bed somewhere. But he carried on.

"Your mother came to me because she had nowhere else to go. It was late; I was on my own. I'd just come back from the hospital where my wife," he paused, not having wanted to bring Flavia into it, "well, that doesn't matter now." He paused, thinking how sixteen years had passed in the blink of an eye, yet at the same time how that night seemed like something from another life.

"Your mother needed me. My world had collapsed, but when I saw you, when you came out into the world and I held you in my arms, I can't tell you what that meant to me, Rosa. You brought me back from the edge and gave me a reason to fight. I wasn't going to let your life collapse."

Again he paused but Rosa said nothing, so he carried on.

"Only your mum was weak," he continued, "she'd lost a lot of blood. I was about to take her back to my house, I didn't know what else to do, and that's when your father turned up. He held you whilst I saw to your mother. I can still see him now, rocking you in his arms, looking at your scrunched up face, tears streaming down his cheeks. He kept whispering, "I'm sorry, I'm sorry, I'm so sorry."

Ricardo remembered this young boy's face, tears streaming down onto the baby's arms. He'd looked terrified. He'd omitted telling Rosa that Edson had turned up covered in blood, his head split open, one shoe gone. He was barely twenty-one and looked no more than thirteen standing there in the light from the kitchen.

The girl had passed out on the kitchen floor at the shelter. She'd lost a lot of blood and was already weak from whatever beating she'd received before coming to him.

He found a wooden crate under the sink and emptied out the manioc roots that were waiting for the next day's dinner. He took off his shirt and placed the baby carefully in the crate, swaddling her in the sleeves. She was crying now, although it sounded more like the bleating of a newly born goat than a human being. She scrunched up her eyes and punched the air with her fists, furling and unfurling her tiny fingers, as if grasping for something to hold on to in this brand new, terrifying world.

He lifted the girl's head and placed it in his lap, rubbing her arms, her hands. She came around and murmured something he couldn't understand but didn't open her eyes. She curled into him, no more than a child herself, looking for someone to look after her, and he held her and stroked her hair until she drifted into a deep sleep. He knew he had to get them home. He couldn't leave them there. He settled her gently back down on the floor and set about cleaning up Dona Nenê's kitchen. It would not be right for the other girls to see the mess in the morning, and morning was not so very far away now. His head throbbed, and as he stood up he was hit by a wave of nausea. He had to lean against the cooker, eyes closed, and wait for it to pass.

He took the baby in the crate, and placed it carefully on the front seat of his car, before going back to the kitchen to get the mother. He was about to scoop up the girl in his arms when a noise startled him. He turned around to find someone standing directly behind him.

"I need your help."

It was Junior. Ricardo hadn't seen him in weeks, not since they'd had the argument about the protest Junior was organising. Ricardo had refused to help him, telling him that it wasn't the way they should fight – that people weren't ready, that it would get out of hand. His ripped, bloodstained T-shirt and split forehead told Ricardo that this was exactly what had happened.

He picked up the girl and held her against his chest.

"Turn off the light and shut the door behind you," he said, handing Junior the keys from his pocket, "Meet me in the car."

He laid the girl in the back seat. She didn't stir. As he got into the driver's seat, Junior opened the passenger door and almost sat on the baby in the crate.

"Shit, what's that?" he said. His voice woke the sleeping baby who started her bleating once again.

"Put it on your lap," Ricardo told him,

starting the engine, "and be gentle," he added as Junior took the crate.

As they left the courtyard and turned into the street Ricardo asked,

"So how much trouble are you in exactly?"

Rosa had been listening. She hadn't interrupted to ask about her real mother. She'd listened. He wondered if she'd fallen asleep.

"Rosa?" he asked.

No reply.

"Rosa?" he asked again, louder this time.

"I'm still here." Her voice sounded subdued.

He was about to continue the story when he heard the key in the lock and Senhor Coutran walked in, flanked by two police officers. The one with only half an eyebrow shut the door behind them and Coutran smiled under his moustache.

"Well now, seeing as I've got you to myself, I thought we'd have ourselves some fun."

CHAPTER TWENTY-TWO

Campina Grande hospital

The nurse had left my lunch beside my bed but I couldn't bring myself to touch it. It was gone two o'clock now and no one could tell me anything about Rosa or Ricardo. I'd seen what the policemen had done to him. He'd already told me that he had many enemies within the police and I was sure that even if Rosa were just a witness, they would be trying to get her to implicate him somehow. She was only a little girl – my little girl. My mind raced, sifting through all the hopelessness in search of a solution. One thing I was sure of was that I had to get down to the police station right away.

I went to swing myself out of bed but my legs wouldn't work. I willed them to move but they were glued to the sheet. I cupped both hands under my knees and drew them towards me, clinging on to them as I shuffled myself around and let my legs fall over the side of the bed. I adjusted my nightgown, which had wriggled its way up my back, and let myself gently down on to the floor. As I stood up and let go of the bed my legs collapsed underneath me and I fell, my face smashing against the divider curtain. The nurse pulled the curtain back.

"No, no, no," she tutted, helping me back on

to my bed and tucking my legs back under the sheet, "I told you, you need to rest. That was some shock you had there. You can't go walking around like nothing happened, you'll tear the stitches for a start."

I looked down at my gown. The nurse pulled it up and exhaled through pursed lips when she saw the blood-stained dressing.

"I'm going to have to go and redress that now," she said, resting her hands on her voluptuous hips and shaking her head.

When she finally came back with fresh bandages and started to peel off the sodden dressing I grasped hold of her arm.

"Please," I said, "I need to find my daughter."

"Well, you can't get out of bed, I already told you. You'll just have to wait like everyone else."

The nurse didn't want to hear any more and I lay back on the pillow and let her redress the wound, my mind racing as to how I was going to get out of there on my own.

The nurse had already gone when the woman visiting the man in the bed next to me got up to leave.

"I'll call Maria, let her know you'll be out tomorrow," she was whispering to the man, who by the looks of it had already fallen asleep. The woman had had her face buried in his sheet for the past few minutes, in what had looked like prayer.

"Excuse me?" I whispered to the woman, who turned in surprise that anyone had heard her. She had given me an idea.

"I'm sorry to ask you this, but if I gave you

a coin, would you be able to make a call for me?"

The woman looked around just as the nurse had done earlier, but there were no nurses in the ward.

"Please, I can't get out of bed and I need to check if my daughter is alright."

When I mentioned my daughter the woman smiled and seemed to relax. I guessed she was a mother herself.

"What's the number?" the woman asked.

"I don't know. I've been told she's at the police station. Her name's Rosa da Silva. She's with a man, Ricardo, I don't know his surname. Could you just ask if she's there and if she's okay?"

"Is she in trouble?" The woman looked down at where the blood had left a stain on my nightgown.

"No, no, nothing like that," I said, self-consciously pulling the sheet back up over my stomach.

"I don't know…" began the woman.

"Please, you don't even have to give your name or anything. Just ask if Rosa da Silva is there and if she's alright."

The woman took so long that I had given up on her, thinking she must have already used the coins I'd given her to buy her bus ticket home. Then I saw her and felt immediately guilty for having doubted this wide woman with swollen ankles and a mole on her lip, who was waddling like a mother duck up the ward towards me. She sat back down on the chair beside her husband and handed one of the coins back to me.

"So?" I asked, desperate now, "is she there?"

The lady shook her head, "They wouldn't tell me."

"But they must've said something."

"They said," and here she paused, concentrating to ensure she repeated the words exactly as she had heard them, "they are not allowed to give details of people being held in connection with an on-going investigation."

The woman kissed her husband on the forehead and got up to go. I heard the words echoing in my head, 'on-going investigation' and thought of Rosa, so alone. My little girl alone, held in connection with an on-going investigation.

And then I had a thought. It must have been the word investigation, because I suddenly knew who could help me.

Leaning across to the other side of the bed, I strained to lift my bag from the chair, where the nurse had moved it earlier, and searched inside for my passport. I found it and pulled out the business card that I'd tucked inside it on the plane on the way over from London. On the back was the number of a hotel.

The woman was already walking towards the door and I called after her.

"Please," I said.

She stopped and looked back at me.

"Could you possibly make just one more call for me?" I asked, my breath heavy from the effort of reaching for the bag, my heart pounding. The woman looked back at the door, then, adjusting the strap of her handbag on her shoulder, waddled unhurriedly back to my bed.

"Shit, what happened to you?" said Tom Porter as

he walked over to the bed. He was even taller than I remembered, with broad shoulders and a mop of dishevelled, sun-bleached hair. He was tanned now too, obviously having spent the last few days making the most of everything Brazil had to offer. We'd only spoken for a few minutes on the plane; he was, for all intents and purposes, a complete stranger, but when I looked up and saw him walk through the door there in the hospital, my heart lifted, as if I'd known him my whole life and he had come to take me home.

"The guy on reception at the hotel said it was urgent."

"You didn't speak to the lady?" I asked.

"No, she rang my hotel back in Recife, the number I wrote down for you, only I came here for the festival, like anyone who's anyone," he gestured towards me as if to include me in his group of 'anyone', "but I'd left the number of my hotel here in case anyone needed to contact me urgently." He ran his hand through his unruly hair and looked around the ward, "And I have to be honest, I never thought it would be you."

"I'm sorry," I said, "I didn't know who else to call." I felt tears prick my eyes and my face flush red. Now he was in front of me I realised how ridiculous it was to think this stranger could sweep in and save me.

"What did he tell you?" I asked, embarrassed.

"Just that Judith Summers was in hospital here and she needed my help. I thought maybe it was that whack on the chin I gave you at the airport. Thought maybe you were going to sue me after all." He smiled but his eyes didn't lose their concern. I felt suddenly aware that I was sitting in bed in nothing but a nightgown in front of a complete stranger, who looked decidedly hung over from the festival.

He took a step towards the bed, "So, Judith Summers, what the hell happened to you?"

As I finished explaining, a scowling nurse came to take away my untouched dinner. Outside the sky was already turning deep blue and the fans had been turned off. In an attempt to move out of the nurse's way, Tom managed to step on her toes, causing her to almost drop the tray of soup. He caught hold of both of her arms to steady her and apologised with wide eyes and a humble nod of the head, bending down with deliberately exaggerated concern to check her bruised toes. The nurse's scowl broke and her face brightened to a laugh as he continued to apologise and back away, head bent, hands held high in surrender. She walked away with a spring in her wounded step and allowed herself a smile as Tom winked after her.

"You seem to have a way with Brazilians," I said.

"I used to be married to one," he said.

"So did I."

He sat down and we looked at each other in silence, each acknowledging the respective memories the sentence evoked.

"You still like the country then?" I asked.

"God yeah, I love it. Never meant to, you know, but, well, it kind of has this way of getting under your skin, if you know what I mean."

I winced as a pain shot through my midriff under the bandage. I could feel it was time for another shot of whatever painkiller they had me on and looked hopefully up the ward for a nurse.

"God, I'm sorry, I didn't mean, I mean, I didn't think, you know, when I said under your skin..." Tom stumbled over his words, embarrassed at his ill-chosen metaphor.

I found myself warming to this man as he blushed under his tan.

"Look, I'll do what I can," he said, "Adriana, my ex-Brazilian, her folks were well connected, I mean, they still are, and we're still on good terms. They loved me, as it happens. You should've seen how pissed off they were when she moved back here and ran off with her childhood sweetheart. Some loser apparently, but what are you gonna do? Young love and all that. Can't help where the heart takes us, hey."

'No, you can't', I thought, watching his blue eyes dart out of the window as a bat flew past.

CHAPTER TWENTY-THREE

Ricardo

Ricardo woke up dry-mouthed and with his eyes stuck together by the crusted blood from the cut in his forehead. His nose throbbed. He knew it was broken. He was no doctor, but he had heard the crack and had felt the bone dislodge. He'd broken his leg once as a boy, falling off a neighbour's swing: a searing pain that had left him screaming. He thought of his mum, how she'd stormed up to his neighbour's house and given them what for. He smiled through the pain, imagining his mother storming into the police station, brandishing her wooden spoon, yelling at the officers and smacking him around the head for having been so stupid.

He crouched in the corner of the cell and for the first time without the aid of alcohol, he cried, each deep sob hurting him more as his broken ribs pierced him from within. He held his head in his hands and bit down hard on his already bleeding lip. As they'd left him, he'd heard Coutran say 'Thought I might pay your little girlfriend a visit next.' But as yet no sound had come from Rosa's cell.

He thought of his wife, Flavia. She'd been in a cell like this, back in Recife, years ago, the day after the raid on the party down at the beach. They'd come for her that night. She'd been working late with only the noise of the bats in the mango tree outside the window to distract her. The men had pushed past Dona Nenê at the door and grabbed hold of her. She'd kicked out and bitten them but to no avail.

They only held her overnight, Ricardo had seen to that. He'd called everyone they knew and they'd gone down to the station en masse. It wasn't the first time one of their colleagues had been arrested and it wouldn't be the last. But by the time they'd got there she'd already had a visit from Senhor Coutran. He'd walked away of course - the police knew when to turn a blind eye.

Back at home Ricardo had nursed her split lip and the bruises on her arms, and he'd asked her to tell him what had happened.

"Leave it," she'd said, and he hadn't asked again, but he'd seen the marks on her neck and wrists, and he'd lain awake that night, the possibilities racing through his mind. He'd wanted to take her in his arms but she'd turned away, curling in on her own pain.

As soon as she'd been able to, she'd gone back on the streets looking for Luciana, and had eventually found her down at the beach. She had already developed a bond with the girl but she'd wanted to do more: to help Luciana, to save her. Only Luciana hadn't wanted saving. She was making money; she was getting on with her life. She didn't trust anyone who promised to be there for her. After all, no one had been there for her the night of Nelson's party. Flavia wouldn't give up on her though, and followed her closely, interviewing her when she'd let her. Helping this girl had become an obsession for her.

When Flavia had found out she was pregnant, the bond had grown stronger. Luciana was also pregnant, almost exactly the same stage as Flavia, and the two women had talked about it together. Both Ricardo and Flavia had known who the father of Luciana's child was but now he began to wonder about the baby growing inside Flavia. He couldn't help but wonder 'why now?' After the best part of two years trying for a baby, why now? What had changed? He'd wanted her to put his mind at rest; wanted to ask her again what had happened in the cell with Coutran, but he'd known that the subject was closed and that, if Flavia hadn't told him, it was because he was better off not knowing. And so, out of respect, he'd never asked.

As the heat in the cell grew stifling, Ricardo thought of all the other women he'd known since. He remembered only fleeting images: an ankle chain catching the morning light; large lips against the skin behind his ear; arms wrapped around him and the need for a drink; a coy midriff as a dress slid over it. He'd started drinking the night he came back from the hospital, sixteen years ago. The women came after. Some stayed longer than a night – months, a year or two, on and off. But gradually the drink had been easier to get hold of and less demanding than the women, and eventually it had won. Those women he wanted to stay always left, and those who would've stayed, he'd driven away: 'too much baggage'; 'too involved in his work'; 'too many issues'. However they'd phrased it, it amounted to the same thing: he was broken.

His eyes still closed, both hands now

clasped around his throbbing knee, Ricardo thought how absurd that he'd come to dedicate his whole professional life to a cause because of the scent of a woman; the curve of her neck reflected in the window of a bus, and how now, because of the blushing cheeks and quiet determination of an English woman, he wanted to give it all up and start over. It was as if Judith Summers and Rosa were his family, come back for him at last. It was ridiculous, he knew. They'd only just met and the strength of his feelings both baffled and delighted him. After years of drifting, he'd finally found an anchor to steady him and was looking at the world straight again.

He heard the bolt slide back and the door to his cell open again and looked up to see Coutran. He was no longer smiling. He didn't come in. The officer with half an eyebrow stood holding the door.

"Looks like you and me have got a mutual friend," he said.

Ricardo didn't move. He was tired of these games. He knew there was no way out and he knew for a fact that he had no friends in high places, certainly no one who was a friend of Senhor Coutran.

"You got lucky this time, my friend," he said, "but we both know this isn't over." He turned and walked out, leaving the door open.

As Ricardo hobbled into the entrance hall of the police station, he saw Rosa perched on a chair against the wall. Coutran was holding her chin in his hands and he spoke to Ricardo without taking his eyes off Rosa's face.

"Shame, this one's even prettier than your last one. And she was good." He let Rosa's chin drop as Ricardo lunged towards him. A large, blond man grabbed him from behind and his fist only just caught Coutran's belly. He calmly brushed off a speck of dirt from his shirt, then made his fingers into a gun, pointed them between Ricardo's eyes and pretended to shoot.

Rosa looked up as he stumbled towards her. He could tell from her expression that his face looked as bad as it felt. He helped her up and she let him lean his arm around her shoulder.

As they stepped out into the night the tall blond man followed them. He came up to Ricardo, took hold of his forearm and shook his hand. Ricardo was embarrassed to find he was trembling.

"Ricardo, my name's Tom Porter. Judith Summers sent me to get you."

"Judith?"

"You know my mum?" Rosa said.

"I do now," he said.

"Is she okay? They wouldn't tell us anything."

"She'll be fine. She's at the hospital. Come on, I'll take you to see her."

Tom hailed a taxi.

Ricardo leant back on the stiff plastic seats and watched the lights of the city flash past. "You must know some very powerful people," he said to Tom.

"Let's just say I know the money," Tom said.

"What do you mean?" asked Rosa.

"The guy I called, well, there aren't many

people who'd know his name. You'd never have heard of him," he said to Ricardo, "but he's the money. He's got money and he invests – he invests in businesses, he invests in politics, he invests in people. No one gets anywhere without his nod of approval."

"But Coutran has been after me and my colleagues forever. He wouldn't have let me go for anything less than…"

"Your Senhor Coutran is running for office."

"Of course."

"And my guy is the money behind him."

"Who's your guy?"

"My ex father-in-law."

"He must love you."

"Oh, he does. Also, I have an awful lot of dirt on him and his family. He can't afford to piss me off," he grinned.

As the taxi made its way towards the hospital Ricardo looked at this large, affable man and wondered what steel he was hiding beneath his grin.

CHAPTER TWENTY-FOUR

Campina Grande hospital

"He's dead," Rosa said, sitting on her hands on the chair beside my bed. Tom had left us together to go and check on Ricardo in accident and emergency. Rosa had said nothing until he'd gone.

"I know."

"Fuck, I'm so sorry Mum."

"Forget it."

"No, I mean it. I've been a total bitch, I shouldn't have said it was your fault dad died."

"You were angry."

"I'm still angry."

"It's okay to be angry at me, I understand."

"I'm not angry at you, I'm angry at me."

"What on earth for?"

"I was there, Mum."

"Where?"

"I was upstairs the whole time."

I realised now what she was talking about.

"He wanted to talk, but I told him I had homework and went upstairs. Only I wasn't doing homework, I was listening to music, stupidly loud, just like you're always telling me not to, and I was all stressed out about Darren and Sal and all that shit. God, I was so self-involved."

"You're a teenager, you're supposed to be self-involved."

"Mum, I was the one who treated him like shit." Her voice was wavering, "I took him for granted and I take you for granted, when you're just trying to do the right thing and, fuck Mum, it's all my fault."

She let her head drop on to the bed and the tears of anger, relief and grief finally came. I reached out and stroked her hair with my free hand, the one without the drip in.

"My little Rosa," I said softly, "your dad thought you were the best thing that ever happened to him. He loved you. What happened, it wasn't about you or me. It's not your fault. Dad was haunted by things that we can't even begin to imagine. His life over here wasn't easy, despite what he'd always led us to believe. He came to England to get away from it all, to start over, but it just didn't work out like that. He escaped one hell to be thrown into another." I winced as the pain shot through my side again, "Dad died of a broken heart. He couldn't live knowing he'd never come back here. And Gavin turning up, well, that just broke him. You couldn't have done anything, neither of us could."

Rosa wiped her nose with her arm and roughly pressed her eyes with her fists to get rid of the tears.

"Do you think he knew all this would happen?" she asked, "You know, when he asked you to take him home?"

I reached for her hand. She let me take it but I could feel her freeze up. I'd been wondering the same thing myself, as I'd been lying there alone.

"I think Dad had a lot of things he wanted

to tell us, to show us. Maybe this was the only way he knew how."

As I said it I didn't know if I believed it, but I wanted to, and so did Rosa. And that would have to do.

CHAPTER TWENTY-FIVE

Rosa

What the guidebook says:

- Brazil was the first South American country to have women in its armed forces.
- Brazil is one of the world's leading producers of hydroelectric power.
- Brazil is one of the most bio-diverse countries in the world with 4 million plant and animal species and more species of monkey than any other nation.
- There are more than 180 native languages spoken in Brazil.

I'm sitting on the front steps at the children's centre. Ricardo has gone back to check on Mum but I asked if I could stay a little longer. I'm looking out on the dusty courtyard, trying to imagine my other mother, the first one, and how she must've felt the night I was born.

I felt really self-conscious walking in here this morning. Ricardo took me over to the canteen, where everyone was finishing breakfast. The two girls I was squashing fruit with last week ran straight over and hugged me – and not a casual, 'hey, how's it going?' kind of a hug, but like a real, tight, 'Oh my God, I thought I'd never see you again' kind of a hug. I hugged them back, looking up at Ricardo, who was grinning at my obvious awkwardness. The other girls swarmed around us and I thought, 'this must be what it feels like to be a movie star'. I looked back up at Ricardo but he was disappearing in to the kitchen.

A moment later, a voice came from behind me, "Hey, let the girl breathe!"

I looked around and found a girl, around my age, maybe a little younger, coming in from the kitchen. Ricardo was standing next to her. The girls scattered instantly, giggling as she shooed them away.

"Rosa, I'd like you to meet Luciclede," Ricardo said, "I've asked her to show you around, make you feel at home."

"Why? Where are you going?" I said, panicked at the thought of being left alone.

"I've got a couple of cases to work on, but I'll come back and get you after lunch. You'll be in good hands," he said, ruffling Luciclede's hair.

"Hey, mind the hair, man," the girl said, feigning annoyance, but with a smile tugging at the corner of her lips.

I stood there, in the empty canteen, smiling uncertainly at this waif of a girl. Her skin was darker than mine, her hair frizzier. She wore a pink Lycra boob tube and frayed denim miniskirt, which hung loose off her bony hips, as she looked me up and down.

"You want to see what I made?" she said.

I nodded, thankful for the distraction, and followed her across the quadrant to a classroom, where a dozen of the older girls were clustered around a handful of sewing machines.

"You know how to sew, right?" Luciclede said.

"No." I was suddenly ashamed of my lack of any useful skill. Sure, I could calculate the square root of 348, ask for directions in French, or tell you all about photosynthesis, but in front of a sewing machine, I was lost.

"Don't worry, it's easy, I'll show you." Then she turned to the girl nearest us, "Get lost, fat arse," she said, barging the younger girl out of her chair and taking her place at the machine. The girl sloped off to join another group. Luciclede grinned at me and I saw she was missing her two front teeth.

For the rest of the morning she showed me how to trace a pattern for a pair of shorts; how to cut it out, thread the machine and sew it together.

"You got a boyfriend?" she asked, guiding my hand as I tried to keep the stitches straight.

I shook my head.

"He cheat on you?" she asked.

"With my best friend."

"No shit, mine too, the bastard." She spat on the floor.

As we sewed and talked, it turned out that as well as a shared failing in finding decent boys, Luciclede also shared my love of River Phoenix, Pearl Jam and anything to do with elephants.

"I've had it with men," Luciclede told me later, as we shared a cigarette on the steps, "I'm going to be a seamstress and work for myself, so I don't ever have to rely on a man."

"What do your parents do?" I asked.

She laughed and slapped me on the back a little too hard and changed the subject. "Tell me about England. Are English boys cute? Is it true that everyone goes to films and concerts all the time? Does everyone have a washing machine and a fridge? Is there anyone like me there?"

I looked at her, "What do you mean, like you?"

Someone called from the kitchen and she jumped up, "Come on, we got something for you," she said.

As I followed her in to the canteen, I heard someone shout 'Está aqui! She's here!' followed by silence. I walked in to a semi-circle of girls singing a rendition of 'Parabéns, pra você' – 'Happy Birthday' in Portuguese.

"But it's not my birthday," I said to Luciclede, just as Nenê the cook came in from the kitchen and pushed her way through the crowd of singing girls. She was carrying a birthday cake, topped with elaborate swirls of cream and a single candle.

"I know, but Ricardo said you had a really shit birthday, and here we always celebrate birthdays, especially sixteen, you've got to celebrate that!"

Luciclede and the other girls have gone to their afternoon classes now, and I've come out here to wait for Ricardo. It doesn't feel like I'm a visitor anymore, it feels like I've been hanging out with friends. Chatting to Luciclede and the others, I started to feel for the first time in my life that I actually fitted in – not because we all come from the same background, or wear the same clothes or know the same people, but because none of that matters. And out here, listening to the birds in the mango trees and the distant buzz of the city, I can picture Dad here with his pregnant girlfriend, asking Ricardo for help. I feel connected to him and to a whole life I've never thought about before, like this is where I belong, like Dad knew that, and that's the reason he was always trying to tell me about 'home', about Brazil, like he knew, all along, that this is what I needed, that this is where I needed to be; that there was somewhere I belonged.

CHAPTER TWENTY-SIX

Recife

I lay under the thin sheet, letting the heat sit on my skin, and listened to the sounds of the street outside Ricardo's house. Rosa had gone with Ricardo to the Braços Abertos shelter that morning. She'd asked him if she could go and help out with the girls.

I'd been waiting for them to come back for lunch and was just pulling myself up to sit on the edge of my bed when I heard the front door unlock and Ricardo's footsteps walking across the living room. I saw him peer through the half-open door, checking to see if I was awake before knocking.

"Hi," I said, "come in, come in."

He opened the door and came over and sat next to me on the edge of the bed.

"Just got up? It's alright for some," he joked. I tried to smile but I was in pain.

"Can you pass me my painkillers?" I pointed to the chair in the corner of the room.

He found the bottle and I watched as he opened it and shook out two of the white tablets.

"The girls invited Rosa to stay for lunch. I didn't think you'd mind. They love her, you know. And I think she's enjoying herself." He handed me the tablets.

"Thanks."

"How long have you been waiting for me?" he asked.

"I tried to get up. I tried to get my legs to work but it hurts so much." I held my side where the bulge of the bandage showed through the T-shirt he'd given me to sleep in.

He went to the kitchen and fetched me a glass of water.

"Here," he said, coming back in.

"Thanks."

I swallowed the tablets and shut my eyes, trying to visualise the drugs already working on the pain. Ricardo went back over to the chair in the corner, took the dressing gown he'd leant me and wrapped it around my shoulders, handing me my hairbrush at the same time.

"Here," he said, "you look like you've just crawled out of bed."

He was teasing me and I liked it. It had been a long time since anyone had looked after me. I started brushing my hair as he made the bed around me and slipped my flip-flops on to my feet. I watched his strong shoulders, his gentle hands, and wondered how long it had been since he'd last had anyone to stay.

"Ready?" he asked, holding out his hand.

"Ready," I said and took his forearm with both of my hands. He placed his free arm under my shoulder and gently lifted me onto my feet. We stood chin to nose as I found my balance. He had been my rock these last few days. Goodness knows what I would've done without him. I slipped one of my arms around his waist and with the other hand held on tightly to his arm as he led me towards the living room and the chair that he'd placed by the window for me. As I lowered myself into the chair, pulling the dressing gown around my legs, I wished he would sit next to me and hold my hand, but he went into the kitchen.

"Hungry?" he asked.

"Starving," I said. It was true. I hadn't been able to eat anything for days and now that I was on the mend I was ravenous. At the hospital I'd been on fluids for the first two days and then, even when they'd offered me something to eat, I'd felt nauseous and couldn't keep anything down. Then I didn't dare eat anything as the retching hurt my stomach too much. I'd been at Ricardo's for two days now. The journey back had been horrendous. The car was hot, the seat uncomfortable, the road so very, very long. And Rosa had hardly said a word, Ricardo neither. Both had been subdued, unsurprisingly. Ricardo had horrific bruises on his face and his hands were still bandaged. I'd seen him clutching his knee several times when he thought no one was looking but he hadn't said anything and I hadn't asked. Rosa hadn't wanted to talk about the police station either. I'd asked if she was all right and she'd said she was fine. But I couldn't help hating myself for having brought her there in the first place. She'd wanted to stay with Darren back in London, but I'd made her come. I'd thought it would be good for her – for us, but it had all gone so wrong.

Ricardo came out of the kitchen with two large plates of rice covered with a thick brown casserole of beans and meat, on top of which he sprinkled some sort of dried powder. I followed his example.

"What's this?" I asked.

"You've never eaten farofa?" he said, amazed. How could you have been here all this time and not eaten farofa? It's powdered manioc flour, it's the speciality of our region – well, one of the many."

We ate without speaking for a while. I broke the silence.

"You think she'll be alright at the shelter with the girls?" I was still worried about Rosa. She'd changed so much since the festival. We still hadn't talked properly, not after the hospital. She'd gone to stay with Ricardo in a hotel on the outskirts of the town, there having been no vacancies in the central hotels. He'd taken her back to Boca do Canhão the following day to see Edson's family. She'd wanted to say goodbye. It had been very kind of him but he'd just shrugged it off like he did everything else.

"She'll be fine," Ricardo said, "She's a good girl. She's been helping Nenê in the kitchen and sitting with the girls in their class; she really wants to do something useful. They seem to be getting on pretty well. It certainly can't do any harm."

"She's devastated about Tiago," I said.

"I know."

"She blames herself."

Ricardo said nothing but I detected a slight shrug.

"What?"

"Nothing."

"You think this was her fault?" I felt myself getting angry, "This wasn't her fault. It's this stupid country's fault, that's whose fault it is."

Ricardo put his fork down and leant back in

his chair. I could see he was trying to decide how to phrase what he wanted to say.

"I don't think it was her fault, no," he said.

"But?" I could tell there was a 'but'.

"Look, just because you're on holiday, doesn't make this Disneyland. You may be in the most beautiful country in the world, with the sun, the Samba, the sea, but you're still seeing it from the outside. You take photos, get a suntan and go home. But for the rest of us, this is our life. Tiago was a good boy. He believed Rosa when she told him he should come to England, set up a Samba school. I know that for her, she was just talking, flirting, stroking his ego; she's just a kid. But he was already dreaming of a life with her in London, teaching dance, seeing the world."

"So you are saying it was her fault."

"I'm saying that what happened, it's not Brazil's fault. Look at Edson, this stuff can happen anywhere. If you respect the rules, you should be fine, but treat it like some big game, well, then you're putting yourself and others at risk, that's all."

I didn't say anything because I knew he was right. Rosa knew it too. That's why she'd been so subdued. Maybe that was why she was so keen to go and help at the shelter. Maybe it was her way of doing something good, something genuine, albeit too late for Tiago.

Ricardo took up his fork again and we continued eating in silence. I couldn't eat much. I'd been thinking about Edson all morning whilst waiting for Ricardo to come back - about Edson and Luciana. Whichever way I looked at it, I couldn't make sense of Edson, my friend Edson, getting a young girl pregnant. It just didn't fit. I'd decided to ask Ricardo about it when he came home. I watched him eat and wanted to lean over and kiss him again but knew that wasn't going to happen. In Campina Grande we'd been dancing, drinking, carried away in the moment. Now we were back to reality and we didn't have much longer together before I flew home. I needed to forget about the kiss. He clearly wasn't interested. What I needed was to find out the truth about Luciana in order to tell Rosa.

"I'm sorry to bring this up again but there's something I can't get my head around." My voice seemed loud to me as it broke the silence in the room. Ricardo looked up from his rice. I continued, "You've told me about this girl, Luciana."

"Judith…" he began, but I interrupted him.

"No, I have to ask you this." I paused, looking for the right words, "The girl on the tape…the girl who gave birth to Rosa on the kitchen floor," Ricardo had explained to me what he'd told Rosa at the police station, "Well, what I can't get my head around is how Edson could've done that to a twelve year-old girl. It just doesn't make sense."

Ricardo had obviously known the question was coming. He'd tried to skirt around her age but it had been on the tape. She'd only been a little girl when she'd given birth to Rosa. Ricardo took another forkful of rice and beans and sat back in his chair. He looked out of the window and ran his hand through his hair and then seemed to make a decision. He looked back at me.

"What I'm going to tell you…" he started,

then leant forward, his elbows on his knees, hands clasped together, "Edson was not Rosa's father."

I swallowed the morsel of food I'd been chewing and shut my eyes. It was the answer I'd been both hoping for and dreading.

"He was gay, Judith, you know that."

"I know. I'd just always assumed there was a part of him that, well, I thought, if he'd fathered a child, then..." I let my voice trail off. I didn't want to talk about myself now. "So how the hell did he end up in a pub in London with your name and someone else's baby?"

Ricardo got up and went to the drawer in his desk by the window. He pulled out a cassette and brought the cassette player over to the coffee table, stretching the cable from the wall. He put the tape in and rewound. As the tape whirred back in time I took a sip of water and looked over the top of my glass at his hand, poised over the play button. I wanted to hold it, to feel safe.

"Luciana?" I asked, although I already knew.

"She spoke to my wife the week before Rosa was born."

The tape clunked and he pressed play.

BRAÇOS ABERTOS STREET PROJECT #14

Tapescript 6

Date:	**5th July 1978**
Name:	**Luciana**
Age:	**12 years**

Flavia: How are you feeling?
Luciana: Fat.
Flavia: It's due any day, isn't it?
Luciana: Dunno.
Flavia: What are your plans?
Luciana: Dunno.
Flavia: You must have thought about what you're going to do when the baby comes.
Luciana: I saw Nelson the other day and he says that Mum wants to see me, once the baby's out, and that maybe I can go and work with her, up by the highway. He says that if I go and work there, soon we'll definitely have enough money to go to Rio, so I'm thinking, 'why not?' Have the baby, then go find Mum.
Flavia: Have you thought any more about how you'll actually look after the baby?
Luciana: Oh, it's okay, it's all sorted
Flavia: How do you mean, 'sorted'?
Luciana: I'm going to go find the father.
Flavia: You know who the father is?

Luciana: What do you take me for, some kind of slut?

Flavia: I'm sorry, Luciana, I shouldn't have said that. But do you know where he lives?

Luciana: Yeah, 'cos I was just thinking how I should do what Nelson says and go up to the highway with Mum and stuff, but then Valkiria tells me she's seen him – the father. 'Cos he doesn't live here in the city, you see, I found that out already. He lives way out in the interior, near Campina Grande, only Valkiria says she's seen him in front of the big hotel down at the beach, so I'm going to go down there tonight and see him.

Flavia: Luciana, I don't think that's a good idea.

Luciana: Not a good idea? It's a brilliant idea. He's probably been looking for me for months, thinking I don't care about him, and then he hears a knock at his door and he opens it and it's me and he'll be all like, 'hey, where've you been?' and I'll tell him and he'll look after me. He's not going to turn his back on his own child, is he? And anyway, he told me he loved me. He told me I was the most beautiful creature he had ever seen, and that he wanted to keep me forever. It was only the stupid lady who made me leave when the police

	came to the party and then wouldn't let him see me again, 'cos she was jealous I reckon. Stupid cow.
Flavia:	Come back home with me, I'll look after you.
Luciana:	I'm not going anywhere with you. I don't even know you, not really, you could be anyone.
Flavia:	Then just promise me you won't go to see him at the hotel.
Luciana:	Shut up, I can do what I like. Anyway, Jaru says I have to go because he's in real trouble now and he reckons that the man will give me loads of money and then I can help him. Jaru says he could get killed if he doesn't find some money quick, so what do you want me to do? Let him get killed? He's turned into a real bastard, I can tell you that, hand on my heart, but he's still my brother.
Flavia:	Tell Jaru to come to the shelter with you.
Luciana:	Will you stop banging on about the fucking shelter, like going there's gonna suddenly make everything alright.
Flavia:	It'd be a start.
Luciana:	I'm going to see the man at the hotel.
Flavia:	And what if he doesn't want to see you?
Luciana:	You mean what if he doesn't want to see me like this?
Flavia:	Have you thought about that?

Luciana: Of course he will. He's going to love our baby. You know what? You have no faith in people, that's your problem.

CHAPTER TWENTY-SEVEN

Recife

The tape hissed and kept turning after the two women had finished speaking. The empty noise filled the room.

"Who was he?" I asked, "The father, who was he?"

"You remember the lady told her that she was having a party? Well, she was, sort of." Ricardo looked tired. The wound on his head was starting to heal. He rubbed the stubble on his chin and continued. "Luciana's mother worked as a prostitute, up by the highway." He looked at me. I nodded. I'd guessed that much from the tapes. He continued, "She wasn't around much – hardly at all in fact. They – Luciana and her brother – they were brought up by their grandmother. Luciana's mother was only fifteen when she had her and by that time she'd already had her brother. She needed to work. She wasn't the only one from their street to be working up at the highway."

I nodded, uncomfortable.

Ricardo continued, "You heard her on the tapes. Her Nan tried to get her working with her brother, selling cakes and pastries to the tourists."

I thought of the little girl who'd offered me ice-pops at the beach when we were there with Tiago, her eyes so big, her smile so winning. It had been easy, with the sun on my face and the sound of the waves on the shore, not to question what her life was really like. But the memory inevitably led back to Tiago – Tiago sitting at the beach, laughing, his skin glowing in the sun after his swim. I had to push away the image of his face on the ground, the blood oozing from his side, as Ricardo continued.

"But her mother had other plans, or rather, the man who looked after her mother had other plans."

"The man who looked after her?"

"Nelson."

I remembered the girl talking about Nelson, her mother's boyfriend. Of course, he hadn't been her boyfriend at all.

"Her mother was high a lot of the time, Nelson made sure of that. She made the mistake of telling him about Luciana, of telling him how gorgeous her daughter was."

I wasn't sure I wanted to know what he was about to tell me but it was too late, I needed to know now.

"Nelson mentioned to a client that he had a young girl – a virgin – and the client offered him a lot of money to be the first one to have her. You can't imagine how these people's minds work. He got to thinking, he could offer her around a bit, see what price he could get."

I kept my eyes on the casserole going cold on my plate, not wanting to look Ricardo in the eye. I knew this wouldn't be easy for him to speak about.

"Then he realised there were a lot of wealthy men around who would pay a high price for a beautiful, untouched girl. So he sends her to the lady's house for grooming, on the pretext of getting her a job, and sets up an auction.

"An auction?"

"After a couple of months he got the lady to hold a party with exclusive invites to rich men. Whoever bid the highest price got to keep her."

"And then what?" I regretted the question as soon as I'd asked it. Ricardo didn't answer. He didn't need to.

"But she said on the tapes that this man was her boyfriend," I said.

"That's what she convinced herself of. A lot of the girls do that. They think these men are going to take them away, treat them well, take them to their big houses or to Holland or Germany, London or Paris. That's what they promise them, before they drop them like cigarette butts.

"So, who got to…who got Luciana?" I asked, understanding now that the answer would be the name of Rosa's father.

"A man called Coutran."

"Coutran? Why do I know that name?"

"He's a property developer, the one who ordered the attack on the favela; the politician we saw at the beach; the one who paid me a visit in the cells."

Ricardo stood up and walked to the window. I could see his mind had gone somewhere else.

It was Flavia who took the call. It was late, they'd had too much wine and had moved from the sofa to the bedroom for an early night and he rolled over and groaned when he heard the phone. She'd been working with a group of colleagues, tracking this guy Nelson for months, trying to pin something on him that would stick and hopefully get him to lead them to the bigger fish, the people with the money. But he was sly. Now finally they had a lead. She threw on some clothes.

"What is it? Where are you going?"

"They've got a lead. Nelson, you know, the one I told you about. They think they've found the place where he's having the party - at a house down by the beach. I think Luciana's there."

Ricardo jumped out of bed and pulled on his trousers and the shirt that she'd ripped playfully from him earlier that evening. "I'm coming with you."

"You don't have to. Get some sleep, you've got court in the morning." She was already heading towards the door. He scrambled to get on his shoes and ran after her.

They were too late, of course. When they arrived the police were already there with a grinning Nelson. He winked at Flavia.

"Now what do you want to go getting your knickers in a twist again for my dear," he said, "You know that I'm a law-abiding citizen and yet still you hound me. I'm making an official complaint this time."

Flavia kicked him in the shins.

"Flavia." Ricardo was behind her, pulling her away.

"You know he's lying," she said, pulling her arm free.

"Look," he said, as the soldiers came out of the house with two young girls and shoved them in the back of a military car, "they've made some arrests."

"It's not the girls we were after."
"I know, but it's something, right."
"No, Ricardo, it's nothing. It's worse than nothing. They're going to spend the night in the cells with those soldiers – shit, I should've known."

She went over to speak to her colleagues who were smoking by the walled entrance to the house. Ricardo watched the girls' faces in the back of the car as they were driven away. The one nearest the window gave him the finger.

"But where does Edson come in to all of this?" I asked, pulling him back to the here and now. He turned back around and looked at me.

"Edson came to me for help. He'd been down in São Paulo for a couple of years, working in a factory. He'd come back to Recife when he got into trouble with the police down there. He'd been inspired by Lula, the guy running for president now, but who was just a union leader at the time. And Edson was a fighter; he was passionate and believed in this Lula chap and what he was trying to do for the workers and for the poor of Brazil. But Edson was also young and didn't understand how things worked. Whilst Lula was organising the unions to strike down in São Paulo, strikes which would eventually lead to major political change, Edson wanted everything to happen faster. He wanted action, as did a lot of people. You have to understand, this was in 1978 – Brazil was still under military rule – they were imprisoning, torturing, disposing of those who stood up against them.

But Edson, once he'd found his voice, he was fearless. He thought he could change the world. He was trying to impress me, that's what Flavia said, trying to make me proud of him. We'd become close, since the day I'd first run in to him on the bus. I'd helped him get back into school, get some training, get a job. I saw the good in him. Then when I announced that I was getting married, he announced he was going to São Paulo. Flavia reckoned he was in love with me. Maybe he was. Maybe I was a father figure, I don't know.

"What happened?"

"After a while he came back up north, got involved with a group of young, angry men. They organised a protest - a demonstration. Only the military turned up, of course, guns blazing. Edson urged people to stand their ground. He really believed that a peaceful protest would be respected, would be heard."

"But it went wrong."

"They fired on the protesters. God, I wish I'd gone with him, talked him out of it. But Flavia went in to labour and I had to take her to the hospital. If I'd just been there, maybe things would've turned out differently, who knows? From what he told me, and from what I learnt afterwards, they fell like flies. It was in one of the main streets in the city. Children were on their way back from school. Edson watched as a soldier shot one of them – a schoolgirl, no more than six years old, shot in the back of the head. Her older sister kept running, holding her hand, dragging her corpse with her little backpack still on her back."

"The military knew Edson - he'd already caused a stir. They had their eyes on him; they were out for his blood – they were going to make an example of him. They pinned the girl's death on him. He wouldn't have survived even 24 hours in custody. The night he turned up at my house, that was the night Rosa was born."

He'd already told me the rest – that Edson had come to him for help. But he hadn't told me everything.

"So you gave him your passport, helped him leave the country."

"I didn't need it anymore. I told him, 'I'm going to get you out of here, but I'm going to need you to do something for me'."

"Luciana and Rosa," I said.

He nodded.

"But what about Luciana? Why didn't she leave with him?"

"They both stayed with me for the night, them and the baby. In the morning I went to register the birth. Luciana wouldn't speak, she just lay there. I left Edson with her and took the baby and Flavia's passport and the papers from the hospital and registered her as my own daughter."

"But your daughter died."

"I just didn't give them the death certificate." He shrugged. "What did I care? My wife and child had just died, I didn't care what happened to me, if I got into trouble or not, I just wanted it all to go away. I was never going to be the husband and father I thought I was going to be – so what did it matter? After that, it all just happened. It wasn't a plan so much as a sequence of events. Flavia and I had been planning to travel to London for an international conference on Human Rights. We had our visas; we had everything. We were going to take the baby and make a trip of it. I just looked at Edson and Luciana and the little baby and I thought, why not? So I gave them my identity, my family's identity.

"I booked them on a flight to London. I knew Edson had only a matter of days before they found him and killed him. And as for Luciana, that man beat her to within an inch of her life. If he'd ever found her or the baby again, he would have had them both killed. I knew I had to get her out of the country. Even if she didn't get herself killed, I didn't want her baby girl turning up on my doorstep twelve years from then, her belly swollen, her face cut up. And that's what would have happened, had she stayed. What else was there waiting for her?"

"So you gave them new identities and sent them off together." I was trying to patch together the image of Edson on the run with the girl Luciana and baby Rosa.

"I knew an artist who made a living forging documents. He owed me, so I got him to replace the photo in my passport for one of Junior - Edson. Luciana refused to have her photo taken, so I just had to cross my fingers and hope no one would notice. It was different back then; they didn't have the kind of passports they have now. Even so, I knew I was being reckless." He shrugged. "Maybe I shouldn't have done it, but in one night I'd lost everything. I just wanted to save someone."

"So how come Luciana never got to London?"

"I thought she had. I put them on the bus. I packed their cases – my cases. I waved them off.

It wasn't until a couple of months later that I saw her – Luciana – down at the beach. She looked different – all made up, touting herself to tourists. Nelson had found her again and put her to work. I bought her a drink and she asked me to forgive her."

"For what?" I asked.

"For leaving the baby with Junior – I mean Edson."

"But why didn't she go with them? How could she stay?"

"She believed herself to be in love with her 'boyfriend', Coutran. She was convinced that he'd only rejected her because of the baby and that once she'd gotten rid of the baby he'd take her back."

I was shaking my head in disbelief. Rosa's mother could've come with them; she'd had the chance to start a new life and hadn't taken it.

"I know, it's ludicrous," Ricardo said, and then continued, "So she waited until Edson had gone through customs then made some excuse about going to the toilet and made a run for it. I didn't even know if Edson had left or if he'd taken Rosa with him, or if they'd ever got on that flight, not until I saw Rosa standing in my office, looking for all the world like her mother at that age."

"And Coutran?" I asked.

"Nothing ever stuck. No one wanted to know. Who knows who else was involved? There was an investigation. Coutran was investigated, along with a few other big names, but there was a wall of silence around the whole matter. Coutran was livid. He was freed with no charge, but he doesn't forget. He couldn't believe his luck when I turned up and Rosa told him about Junior –

Edson's real identity. He was loving it. If your friend Tom hadn't turned up when he did, well..."

His voice trailed off and he looked out of the window. He was putting his weight on his good leg. I could see he was in pain. He'd hardly slept; he was exhausted. I wanted to hold him. I pushed myself up onto my feet and tried to let go of the arm of the chair to walk towards him. He turned, hearing me getting up just as I fell forward. He caught me and stumbled backwards, sitting down on the coffee table, me collapsing on to his lap, my arms around his neck. I looked at him. There were tears in his eyes. I reached out and smoothed his hair, our faces so close now I could feel his breath on my cheek.

"I'm sorry," I whispered, "I'm so sorry."

"Hey," he said, brushing my hair off my face," this is not your fault. I started this, you just got caught up in the middle, that's all."

I leant my forehead against his and closed my eyes and then felt his warm lips on mine. My eyes still closed, I kissed him back, my arms now tight around his neck, his arm strong around my back, holding me, his other hand in my hair.

"Come back with us," I said between kisses.

He said nothing but kissed me again.

I moved slightly and he shouted out in pain as his knee buckled under me. He tried to stop me falling but in doing so caught me too late and I twisted awkwardly, pain searing through my side.

He carried me to the sofa and lay me down, and then knelt down beside me, taking my hand in his. He stroked my hair and kissed me on the forehead, the nose, the chin. I felt him slowly untie the cord of my dressing gown and gently stroke the skin around my bandage. I slipped my hand under his T-shirt and he pulled it over his head. I saw the bruising on his torso and touched it carefully with my fingertips as he gently eased himself on to the sofa and lay beside me. I felt the heat of his body against mine. He kissed my neck, my shoulders, my breasts. I arched my back towards him and he sank into me, softly, gently, two broken souls healing together. And for the first time in my messed-up life, I realised what it was to make love. We knew each other, we both knew pain, we both knew loss and we knew that together we had found hope.

"Come back with me," I said again later as we lay together, our legs entwined, not wanting to leave the warmth of each other's arms. I took his hand in mine and looked into his eyes, "What do you say?"

I thought he was about to answer when someone knocked on the door.

Neither of us moved. We kept looking into each other's eyes and listened, hoping that whoever it was would think the house empty and go away, not wanting this moment to be broken.

"Hello!" came an English voice through the door.

Ricardo squeezed my hand and lifted it to his mouth. He gently kissed my fingers then slid his other arm from under my head and replaced it with a cushion. He pulled his trousers and T-shirt back on and went to the door. I pulled my dressing gown back around me.

"Hey," grinned Tom Porter as he loped into the living room, his blond hair falling in his eyes.

"Hello," I said, trying to sit myself up, pleased to see his grinning face, despite his atrocious timing. It felt like a piece of home had just walked in and reminded me of where I was from.

"I'm not interrupting, am I?" he asked, maybe sensing the energy in the room. I touched my hair and tried to suppress the wide smile I could feel lighting up my face, still glowing with the joy of what had just happened.

"Not at all," smiled Ricardo, clearing away the dinner plates.

"It's just you said to stop by after lunch."

"It's okay," I said, "we were just having a chat." I looked up at Ricardo who was standing over the kitchen table, his back to us.

"How are you feeling? Still in your pyjamas, I see."

"Not for long. I've booked our return flights. We're going back to London the day after tomorrow. The doctor said it would be fine."

"I said she should stay a bit longer," said Ricardo coming back in from the kitchen.

"Well, I can't go on pretending I live here indefinitely," I said.

"You could," said Ricardo. There was an uncomfortable silence and I tried to sit up again. Tom came over to the sofa and helped me.

"Really, I'm fine," I said, embarrassed at my ineptitude.

"So, what was it you were coming over for?" I asked Tom.

Ricardo spoke first, "Tom's writing a piece about what happened."

"What, about Tiago?" Just saying his name

was painful.

"Sort of. About it all, actually. About Luciana, about Junior, I mean Edson, about it all."

"Don't get me wrong, I love writing about football," Tom said, "but what Ricardo's told me, God, I couldn't walk away from that now, could I? Brazil – more than just football."

"I don't know what good it'll do," said Ricardo from the kitchen.

"Like I said, I've got some powerful friends. And Lula is going to change everything when he comes to power. This country is on the brink of something spectacular. If I can just get people talking, throw a spotlight into the shadows; get people asking the right questions. It's got to be worth a shot, right?"

I loved his energy. He kept surprising me - I hadn't realised he had it in him.

"But why write such a negative piece? I thought you loved Brazil."

"Brazil is probably the most vibrant, dizzying, hypnotically beautiful country in the world. And as for the Brazilians," he said, looking at Ricardo, "they are the warmest, most welcoming, electrifying, tenacious people I've ever met. And it's people like Coutran who are fucking it up for the rest of them: people like him who want to run this country with their silver tongues and hired hit men, lining their pockets with the skin of Brazil's children. Not love Brazil? It's because of my love and enormous respect for this incredible country and its people that I have to write this, to reclaim this wondrous, passionate country for the people who deserve it."

Behind him Ricardo nodded. I realised I'd

underestimated this man, having taken him for a loafing sports journalist, out for a good time. I should have known there was more to him. There was something in his eyes, I'd seen it on the plane but had brushed it off. Had that really been just the week before? I only now realised how dangerous it had been for him to have made the call to his ex-father–in-law. And yet he'd done it for me – a complete stranger. And now this. I could see that he was fired up. Under his suntan he was turning quite red. He ran his hands though his hair, now even more sun-streaked than before, as Ricardo came out of the kitchen and handed him a cachaça.

Ricardo and Tom settled down at the kitchen table and I watched them together, so animated, so focused, Tom hungry for the story, Ricardo going over all the details from the very beginning of it all, every now and again darting up to search for a newspaper article or a page in a book. My eyes were heavy. I let them close and let the sound of Ricardo's broken English and Tom's dreadful Portuguese lull me to sleep.

CHAPTER TWENTY-EIGHT

Ricardo

He'd left Judith sleeping on the sofa, and Tom at the kitchen table, writing up the piece for the paper. He knew Rosa would be waiting for him at the shelter. The other girls would all have gone by now, over to the dorms in the other building, but he'd told her to wait in his office. Why hadn't he just got on that plane with them all those years ago? Of course, he knew the answer. It had been him or Edson. He'd only had the one passport, and the boy needed a chance. Despite everything, he was a good boy. He wished he could have said goodbye. Why couldn't he stop bad things happening to the people he cared about? Rosa had come back into his life and brought with her a woman who made him feel complete again, made everything seem right. And now they were both leaving, and he didn't know how he was going to go back to how his life was, before they'd crashed into it; back to being so lonely, so spent.

In his office, he reached into the filing cabinet for the bottle of cachaça, but as he opened it, he heard footsteps in the quadrant. He knew it wasn't Rosa; she'd gone to the kitchen to get a drink, and in any case, these steps were far too heavy. He stood the open bottle back in the draw, as the door opened and a man walked in.

"You little shit." It was Coutran, his shirt hanging open at the neck, his cheeks flared, his trousers creased and dirty. His square, toned body filled the doorway. His face was half in shadow, the only light coming from the lamp on the desk.

"You happy now?" His speech was slurred. He reached out with one of his clammy hands to steady himself against the doorframe. The fingers of the other hand scratched at his neck.

Ricardo could tell he would have to tread carefully. Coutran was not someone to be underestimated, especially given the circumstances.

"What do you want?" Ricardo said, although he already knew why he had come. Tom had tipped off his former father-in-law about the imminent article. By the stunned, crazed look on Coutran's face, Ricardo guessed he'd come straight from meeting with him.

He wanted to take a step back, unable to read the other man's expression, but knowing that whatever was coming, it wasn't good. But he didn't move. He stood his ground. He was worried Rosa would come back in, and wanted to warn her, but knew he couldn't risk it. He could see Coutran was seething. His lips were moving, but no sound was coming out. He didn't need to speak though. Ricardo could see his anger in the tremble of his hand, still pulling at his neck. He was a man in shock. If he'd come in raging, Ricardo would've raged right back, unleashing the fury that had burned inside him for so long, but Coutran wasn't raging. And it was this stillness, this silence, that unnerved Ricardo more than any screaming would've done. The man was just staring, his already bulbous eyes widening as he looked Ricardo up and down. He let out a strangled laugh, and then his breathing seemed to steady, as he knew he had him cornered. He was biding his time, waiting to finish him off.

Coutran pushed himself off the doorframe and took a heavy step in to the room. Ricardo could see the flaming red of his neck, where he'd been rubbing it, as he moved into the light.

"Not so big and clever now," Coutran said. Close up, he towered above Ricardo by at least ten centimeters. And even though he was no longer a young man, with his thinning hair and the greying tufts protruding from his nostrils, Ricardo didn't want to wager who would win if he decided to take a swing at him.

Coutran's eyes darted around the room and glanced quickly back over his shoulder. Ricardo knew that the shock was already wearing off and that the reality of his downfall was beginning to seep in, along with the anger and the panic, which would be bubbling up inside him now, already reaching boiling point, ready to explode. He knew also that there was nothing so dangerous as a once-powerful man with nothing left to lose.

Coutran cast his eyes around the walls, more deliberately this time, taking in the photos of the girls. It was the first time he'd stepped foot in Ricardo's office. Until then he'd always had someone to do his dirty work for him. He stepped forward and Ricardo thought he was gong to punch him, but instead, he pushed past him, reaching up and taking down one of the photos from the wall. He smoothed a swollen finger over the faces of the girls.

"All your pretty little angels?" he said.

"Put it back, Coutran," Ricardo said, "It's over."

"Over? You've ruined me. The money's gone, you know that? Of course you do. Someone got to my sponsors. They say I'm a liability, say that it's going to be all over the papers in the morning, that Brazil is heading in another direction and that I'm a thing of the past."

He looked at the photo again, but just as Ricardo thought he was about to put it back up on the wall, he smashed it down on the corner of the filing cabinet and held up the broken frame, glass scattered all over the floor, a lopsided sneer spreading across Coutran's face.

"You break me, you little shit, I break you. If this was back in the day…"

"But we're not back in the day anymore, are we?" Ricardo said, sounding braver than he felt.

"You want to tear me down? For what? A bit of fun, twenty years ago?"

"Sixteen."

"What?"

"It was sixteen years ago."

"You think I give a shit? I was trying to run a business. I wasn't born with a silver spoon in my mouth, you know. I've had to work hard to get where I am, and when you work hard, you deserve to play hard. You'd understand if you weren't such a fucking pussy."

Still Ricardo didn't move. As much as he wanted to gouge out this man's eyes, he wasn't going to take the bait. He needed to stand strong and guard the door for fear Rosa would reappear.

"I never did any harm to anyone who didn't deserve it." Coutran continued. He looked at another photo on the wall and yanked it from its hook, letting it drop and smash on the floor, next to the first. He paced along the wall, pulling at each of the photos of the girls in turn, letting them drop one after the other on to the pile, the shattering glass punctuating his words.

"Oh yes, I know what this is about." Smash. "You need a scapegoat, and I'm an easy target." Smash. "You have no idea. I wasn't exactly on my own, you know."

Another frame shattered on the floor.

Coutran continued, "You're on a wild goose chase, boy. You have no idea how deep this goes. You dig all you want, you're never going to get to the bottom, so why waste your life trying?"

"Be more like you, you mean?"

"I should've had someone teach you a lesson long ago, but I guess now I'm just going to have to do it myself."

"What could you possibly do to me that you haven't already done?"

Coutran rifled in his pocket and pulled out a box of matches.

"Don't do anything stupid," Ricardo said. It was like trying to calm a rabid dog. If he moved, he'd strike. Coutran flicked through the files in the open drawer and slid one out.

Ricardo tried to appeal to his sense of self-interest, "I thought you wanted to run for office."

"You've made damn sure I'm not running for office anymore."

He struck a match and lit the corner of the file and held it over the open filing cabinet.

Ricardo watched.

"No, you're just running, and as long as I'm breathing, I'm going to make damn sure you never stop running."

The file was burning fast. Ricardo lunged for it, but it was too late. With a self-satisfied grin, Coutran tossed it onto the stack of newspapers on the floor, and flicked the lit match into the filing cabinet. The newspapers immediately caught light and flames were licking the walls in seconds.

"You burn me, I burn you," he sneered.

Neither of them had noticed the burning match, which had set fire to the files in the drawer, which in turn found the open bottle of cachaça. There was a roar and Ricardo watched, helpless, as hungry flames shot out of the drawer and caught in Coutran's hair.

"What...?"

The older man flayed madly at his head, screaming as he tried to extinguish the flames.

Ricardo didn't move. He stood and watched Coutran dance over the broken glass; heard it crunch beneath his feet, and smelled twenty years of work burning up around him. And yet, through the flames, all he could see was Flavia. It all came down to one, simple thing.

"You took my wife," Ricardo said.

"What are you talking about? Are you out of your mind?" Coutran stumbled towards the door, but Ricardo was already blocking it. The heat made it hard to breathe.

"You think you haven't already burned me?" Ricardo said.

"I don't take anyone who doesn't want to be taken. People love power; they respect power.

Look at you, you're nothing. She knew that, your wife. She was gagging for a real man. A man with power. Well, I am power."

Ricardo heard Rosa's footsteps coming towards the office. He pushed Coutran away and reached for the door, but Coutran pulled him back into the now-billowing smoke, tripping him up and sinking down on top of him, his knee wedged in his back, his hand pushing his face into the shards of glass on the floor. He felt the smoke in his lungs, closing his throat. Coutran was already wheezing and coughing, and as he let go with one hand to bang his chest, Ricardo managed to twist himself free and pull the desk down over the other man to stop him coming after him. He tried to get to the door but stumbled, his vision blurred, smoke now pressing against him, both inside and out, the heat creating a wall around him, sucking the air from the room. He was on the floor, smoke and flames surrounding him, and couldn't get up.

Then he felt a hand on his arm, then another, pulling him.

"Ricardo!"

It was Rosa, calling his name.

"Get up!" she shouted, "You're too heavy, I can't move you." And yet she *was* moving him, she was pulling him towards the door. He scrambled up onto his knees and crawled out in to the quadrant. Rosa grabbed his waist, and he hung his arm around her shoulders, as she led him to the front door. He stumbled down the steps and on to his knees, unable to get the air into his lungs fast enough. Rosa stood coughing beside him.

He looked up as a group of bats, disturbed by the fire, took flight and sought refuge at the far end of the courtyard. It was then that he saw them, under the cashew tree, frozen, their faces lit by the flames. Judith and Tom.

"What are you doing here?" Ricardo said to Judith through his wheezing.

"Tom wanted to show you the finished piece."

A crash came from the office as something hit the window.

"Is there anyone else in there?" Tom asked.

Ricardo looked at the window and then at Judith, who was already on her knees, cradling Rosa in her arms.

"He's a bad man," was all he could manage.

He could tell that Judith knew who he was talking about. She looked at him, her face the one still point in the mayhem around them, and calmly, she told him the truth he needed to hear. "But you're not."

He looked at her and nodded. Rising to his feet, he struggled over to the wall and picked up a large, fallen stone. He threw it up at the window, smashing the glass, sending smoke billowing into the courtyard. He found Coutran, collapsed by the window, and scrambled in and grabbed hold of his arms. Tom was right behind him, and together they pulled him out. He was barely conscious.

Ricardo dropped him on the red, dusty ground and walked away, but he just couldn't bear the knowledge that he had saved a man, who deserved so much to die. He turned and ran back to Coutran's crumpled body and kicked him square in the groin.

Coutran groaned and passed out.

Ricardo fell to his knees and started to cry.

Behind them, the door of the little hut, tucked behind the gate, opened, and Nenê, the cook, came out and stood with them, watching the empty shelter burn.

Somewhere in the distance Ricardo heard a siren, but knew it wasn't coming to help them. They were on their own. They would have to start again from scratch.

"Nenê," he said at last.

"I'm here, Senhor."

"I guess you'd better go and call the police."

She walked out of the gate and down the road to find a public payphone.

Judith stroked Rosa's hair and looked up at Ricardo.

"You could've let him burn. Why didn't you?"

Ricardo looked back at Coutran, the man who he'd been chasing for all these years; the man he'd wanted so much to wreak his revenge upon, for Flavia, for Luciana, for Raphael, and all the others like them. But now that he was lying there in front of him, helpless and broken, he knew why. He thought of his wife, of her strength and conviction, of the way things were changing for his country because of people like her, and he knew why.

"Flavia would've killed me," he said.

CHAPTER TWENTY-NINE

Cup final

Ricardo had brought us to a different part of the beach than Tiago had. For that I was grateful. It had been ten days but I still saw his lifeless face when I shut my eyes and heard the guttural cry as the knife pierced his stomach. With it I felt an echo of searing pain in my own side and the violent need to vomit.

It was tender now, my side, but the wound had healed well. I'd been lucky, the doctor had told me, although how being stabbed in a dark alley and narrowly escaping death could ever be considered lucky I hadn't quite worked out. When I'd said this to Ricardo he'd simply shrugged and said, "I guess it just depends on how you look at things."

Here across the table from me, sipping his bottle of beer and watching the Brazilian football team file on to the pitch on the TV above the bar, was the most extraordinary man I had ever met: a man who'd made such sacrifices, had lost the woman he loved and their new-born daughter, had lived with constant threats, imprisonment and beatings and yet simply shrugged and said, "It could be worse."

I looked over at Rosa. Sixteen years old. No longer my little girl, although I knew she never really had been. She'd only ever been on loan, and now I'd brought her back, just as Edson had wanted me to. Was Rosa right? Could he have foreseen events? Could he have guessed what I would find back here? He must've known that I would find out the truth about him, about his past and about Rosa. Had this trip, this whole experience somehow been his parting gift to me and to Rosa? I smiled to myself as I heard the word 'gift' in my head.

'I suppose,' I thought, 'it depends very much on how you look at things.'

I felt such pride, looking at how beautiful, how self-assured Rosa was. She was different. She was no longer the cocky, self-involved teenager that had left London. She'd changed since the stabbing. She was more demure, for a start. She wore hardly any make-up and her fresh face suited her. She looked away when boys caught her eye, she didn't smile at them or flirt, as she would have done before.

"I was just mucking around," she'd told me at the hospital, "I didn't mean anything by it. I thought Tiago," she'd paused – I knew it was still hard to say his name, "I thought he was just a charmer. You know, that we were just flirting, having a good time."

"I know love," I'd said.

"But he wasn't. He came after me, and not because he was jealous, but because he was actually, really, like genuinely worried about me. He was looking out for me. He really cared."

And that's what had changed. Rosa had seen that someone she'd treated as nothing more than a bit of fun had truly cared. So much so that he'd died trying to protect her. And I saw that she'd never really believed herself worthy of that before.

I felt such sorrow too. My little girl had gone, she'd grown up. What had happened had changed her. She was still Rosa, still the same girl to the outside world, but I could see something had changed: the way she held herself, the way she sat. I'd been wrong; she wasn't broken, far from it. She was aware of herself in a way she never had been before, and aware of the effect her looks had on people and that it wasn't something to be played around with.

Things were better between us now. Rosa had apologised to me at the hospital. She'd made conversation and sat with me when I couldn't get out of bed. But a cloud still hung over us; the unanswered question that Rosa couldn't bring herself to ask again, but which I knew I was going to have to answer; the truth about her mother. I still didn't know what to tell her.

I looked out at the ocean. Somewhere, a long way across the water, a nation of Italians were glued to their television sets, praying for victory to the same God as the people around me. Never a strong believer, I wondered how any God could make that kind of decision – who to answer; who to ignore.

'Heaven and Hell are the same place,' I thought, 'it just depends on how you look at it.'

I watched the TV behind the bar as the whistle blew for the start of the World Cup final. Around us people whistled and hooted. Cheering could be heard from the windows and balconies of the apartment blocks across the road, which snaked along the beachfront. From every window, every balcony, hanging from every car door, the green and yellow of the Brazilian flag, although there were hardly any cars on the road now and the street was all but deserted. Everyone was either at home in front of the TV, in a bar like this one, or crowded onto the sand far up along the beach where a giant TV screen had been erected for the occasion. I could make it out from where I was sitting, although the players were no more than dots darting across the screen, especially given that the sun had yet to set properly and the lingering light made the image harder to see.

We were some way up the beach from the crowds but still the bar was packed with men, women and children, all waiting for the expected victory. Behind us, across the street, the foreign customers seemed far less interested in the match being played and more interested in the young girls who were parading themselves provocatively around the tables, intent on distracting the men from the football. From what I could see, the men were quite happy to let themselves be distracted. Disturbed, I looked back at the people around us.

"Why are so many people here wearing black armbands?" I asked, noticing for the first time the black rings around several men's sleeves.

"We're a nation in mourning," he said, "Don't tell me you didn't hear about the death of Ayrton Senna?"

"Who's Ayrton Senna?" asked Rosa.

"Only the motor racing champion of the world!" Ricardo said, genuinely astounded that she hadn't heard of him. "He died in a crash on the track earlier this year. The whole nation's still in shock. He was a national hero."

"And now you all need Brazil to win the World Cup," I said, watching the belief and the hope in the faces of the people around us.

"We all need this, believe me," Ricardo said.

As the half time whistle blew, the score was still nil-nil: still time for countrywide celebration or national despair. Ricardo returned from the bar, cradling four bottles of beer and a soda in his arms.

"You thirsty?" Rosa laughed.

Ricardo handed each of us a beer and put the other drinks on the table in front of him.

"They're not all for me," he smiled and turned to call over one of the young girls who'd been parading herself among the tables at the bar next door. She skipped over, grinning as she evidently recognised him.

"You remember Luciclede," he said to Rosa.

The girl, who I'd at first assumed to be around the same age as Rosa, was, I realised on seeing her closer, not much older than thirteen or fourteen at the most: a child hidden under the make-up, glittery Lycra boob tube and high heels, unsteady in the sand. She cocked her head at us.

"Oi gata," - hello gorgeous - she grinned at Rosa, "you want to come back to see my sewing tomorrow? I've made shorts, you can have them if you like."

I realised that she must have been one of the girls from the shelter.

Rosa laughed, "I'd love to, but we're going home tomorrow."

The girl looked crestfallen. Ricardo bent

down to her level, placed his hand on her shoulder and spoke in her ear. The noise from the people around us was almost deafening. Somewhere behind the bar, drums had started to beat and people were cheering and screaming, gearing up for the victory that no one doubted was theirs for the taking, and which the country so badly needed. Ricardo tapped me on the shoulder.

"Come with me," he said, having to shout now to be heard, "there's someone I want you to meet." He took my hand as naturally as if we were old lovers. Rosa followed us as we left the beach and crossed the road. The girl, Luciclede, skipped ahead, savouring the soda that Ricardo had given her. He still carried the two beers in his hand.

As we reached the pavement opposite, Rosa screamed suddenly and jumped out of the way as a glass shattered on the pavement next to her, dropped from a balcony somewhere in the hotel above us. We edged nearer the buildings to avoid any other falling objects and followed Ricardo, who in turn followed the girl. She led us down a narrow street. I squeezed Ricardo's hand tightly, not wanting to appear afraid but feeling a panic rising in my chest. He squeezed my hand back, understanding my apprehension.

The street led quickly to a parallel road the other side of the block, which I guessed would usually be heaving with traffic and tourists, but which tonight lay hauntingly still, like a frontier town in the Westerns when the bad guy rides in.

It was dark now but between the shadows the street lights lit a handful of women in body-hugging dresses and hot pants, lingering hopefully for the few cars still out on the roads. I leant in closer to Ricardo.

"Where are you taking us?"

"Don't worry, we're nearly there."

"I don't like this, can't we go back?" I held the wound in my side and felt again the pain of the knife as it pierced my skin. I winced and took Rosa's arm, who didn't, for once, resist. Some of the women called out to Ricardo as we passed, and insulted Luciclede, who threw back insults to these women twice her age.

At last she stopped and waved at us to come to her.

"Here," she called.

We followed her pointing finger to two big bins in the mouth of an alley. As my eyes adjusted to the dark I made out a pair of legs sticking out from between them, a silver stiletto falling off one of the heels.

Luciclede called in. "Hey, Mum, get up, we've got visitors!"

The legs folded and scrambled up and a woman emerged, her hands attempting to flatten down her frizzy hair as she wriggled her heel back into her shoe. Her eyes lit up when she saw Ricardo. She straightened her skirt and smoothed down the band of orange Lycra that barely covered her breasts as she walked towards him. As she emerged into the light of the street I could see she must've been in her late twenties, although her skin was marked with deep pink welts and her eyes, although big and dark, were glazed and haunted, hidden under the heavy eye shadow and thick mascara. Ricardo handed the woman a beer and clinked his own against hers.

"Saúde."

"Cheers."

"What have you brought them for?" she asked, jutting her chin at Rosa and me, looking us up and down with distrust.

"They're friends," he said.

The woman was shaking, even in the heat of the night. Her slight frame emaciated, her arms bruised and marked, by drugs, I supposed. Her hair was wild and dark and curly, her face aggressive but looked as if it had once been quite beautiful. A deep pink scar ran the length of her right cheek. I wanted to go back to the beach. My side ached and I was tired.

Ricardo was chatting to the woman and I saw him hand her a small bag. Rosa was still holding on to my arm. He turned to us.

"I'd like you to meet someone," he said.

We sidled forward.

"You've met Luciclede." The girl looked at us without smiling, "Well, this is her mother, Luciana."

I leant forward and shook hands with the woman, aware that I was staring but unable to pull my eyes away. I hadn't a clue what to say, and even if I had thought of something, I wasn't sure I could've articulated it in any coherent manner. What was there to say anyway? 'How are you?' It was perfectly clear how she was – or wasn't. 'How do you know Ricardo?' I knew the answer to that too. The woman's hand felt bony and clammy, like a child's in my own. I felt myself shivering.

Of course, Rosa had no idea of who the woman was. She must've thought it strange that Ricardo had gone out of his way to introduce us, but she didn't show it. The usual indifference and hands-in-pockets sulking had been replaced by a bright, genuinely interested young woman. She followed my example and shook the woman's hand and smiled, actually smiled.

"Que gata," Luciana said, reaching out and stroking Rosa's hair affectionately, "Where did you find such a gorgeous girl Ricardo? She yours?" This last question, I realised, was directed at me.

I nodded, unable to speak. I felt as if I were hovering above the scene, watching speechless as my daughter, Edson's little girl, shook hands and chatted easily to the woman who had given birth to her, asking her where she lived; if she had any other children; why she wasn't watching the match, whilst I stood alongside her, dumbstruck. I heard snatches of their short conversation.

"Where do you live?"

"Here and there."

"Do you live here on the streets?"

"Sometimes, yeah. But it doesn't matter. It's not for long."

"How come? Have you found somewhere to live?"

"Yeah, kind of. We're going to go live in Rio. My brother's sorting it out."

"Just as soon as we've got the money together, right Mum?" added Luciclede.

Eventually it became obvious that Luciana was keen to get back under the streetlight and to send her daughter back to the beach to earn some money. After all, whether Brazil won or lost, it was going to be one of the busiest nights of the year for both mother and child. We said goodbye and left Luciana and Luciclede arguing by the bins.

"She looked ill, Luciana," I said, when they were out of earshot.

"Luciana's HIV positive," Ricardo said.

"Seriously?" Rosa asked.

"She has been for some time."

"But isn't that dangerous?"

"For her and for the men who go with her, yes. And for the wives of those men and the children of those men."

"But don't they at least use protection?" Rosa asked, suddenly aware, I think, of how like me she sounded.

"We give them condoms," Ricardo said.

"Is that what was in the bag?"

"That and her medication. Only she won't take it. I keep trying but at the end of the day they'll do whatever the men want, whatever it takes to get money, and most men seem to practice a 'what I don't know can't hurt me' attitude, especially the tourists. They don't want to come to Brazil without tasting the fruit, it's all part of their exotic holiday experience."

I followed his eyes to a bar where sunburnt men were admiring the young girls flitting around them.

"What about Luciclede?" Rosa asked.

I looked at her concerned face, the face, which wouldn't have shown any concern just a few days ago. How was I going to tell her that Luciclede was her little sister – that she, Rosa, was this woman's daughter?

"Luciclede's clear for now, but then she's been coming to the shelter regularly and we teach them about stuff like that. But she keeps going back onto the street. She says her mum needs her."

"But how can her mum let her do that?" Rosa asked.

I could see she was genuinely upset.

"Rosa, she has no choice," Ricardo said.

"But they're moving to Rio soon, right?"

"I doubt that."

"Why? You don't think her brother's going to sort it out for them?"

"Her brother, Jaru, well, you could say he takes care of them. He cut the throat of the guy who used to 'look after' them; a man called Nelson. This was years ago, and now he's taken over the business, so to speak. But Luciana still trusts him, still believes him. He's her only family now. She's got no one else and he knows it. Rio is the carrot he dangles in front of her – in front of all the girls. But no-one's going anywhere. No-one gets out, not from Jaru."

We walked in silence for a while, each in our own thoughts. As we neared the beach, we had to step into the road to avoid a low, sprawling tree, monopolising the pavement.

"What tree is that?" asked Rosa, reaching up to pick one of the deep red bell-like fruits, "Are these some sort of miniature red peppers?"

"No," Ricardo said, looking back up the road to where Luciana still stood with her daughter, leaning against the metal grille of the closed shop, waiting for the car that would come and take her away for a while, "they're cashew apples."

"Like cashew nuts?" Rosa asked, bewildered.

"Look," Ricardo took the fruit from her, "you see here, at the bottom," he pulled off the small, grey, crescent shaped seed pod that was attached to the bottom of the soft fruit like the clapper of a bell, "recognise it?"

"No, what is it?"

"A cashew nut."

"Seriously? That's how they grow?"

"Yes, only you never get to see the fruit over there, I suppose. It's like so many things here. We take the best part and send it over to you guys in Europe and throw away the rest. You know, the cashew apple has five times more vitamin C than an orange." He held the fruit in his hand and stroked the skin with his thumb, "You wouldn't think it, but it's so sweet under its tough skin. There's so much goodness in this fruit, if people would just bother to look. You can make juice out of it, really good, sweet juice, but more often than not the apple is thrown away, job done, and left to rot at the side of the road."

I looked from the fruit to his face and saw that he was no longer looking at the cashew apple but looking back up the road, watching Luciana as a car pulled up alongside her and she got in.

Back at the beach the second half of the match was already well under way. We didn't go back to where we'd met Luciclede but instead went further down the beach towards the big screen. Tom had arranged to meet us there but we had difficulty finding him. We gave up after a while and sat down on the sand.

As Ricardo watched the match I watched the faces in the crowd: a woman in a faded T-shirt with its sleeves cut off, selling cigarettes on a tray; in front of her crouched a man with headphones, listening to the commentary on a radio in his hand. The rich; the poor; the young; the young at heart; all united in their passion for this game, this symbol of a country's success. Football was their soap opera, a success story, the Brazilian dream.

My eyes came back to rest on Ricardo. I slid my hand into his and leant my head against his shoulder.

"Come back with us," I said, without looking up. He stroked my hand with his thumb, our fingers entwined.

"I can't go to London. You forget - there I am dead."

"I know, and if you think about it, we were married there for nearly fifteen years. That's not a bad run." I joked to hide the fact that I was so miserable at leaving him.

He laughed, and looking up I caught a glimpse of the young lawyer who Edson must have been so in love with.

"Seriously though, I have my work here," he said.

"The work your wife started."

"It doesn't matter who started it – someone has to finish it. I can't leave when there is still someone who needs me."

"Luciana," I said.

"Yes. And all the other Lucianas," he said, looking about him at the girls weaving their way through the crowds.

"Why don't the police do anything?" I asked.

"Apparently they have other things to worry about," he shrugged.

"But what can you do? One person?"

"Oh, I'm not alone. We're just starting to rebuild our country, but it's a long journey and we're not even out of the station yet. I once asked Flavia how she came to be so brave and you know what she told me? She said she started like the rest of us, asking herself why no one was doing anything about this. Then she realised that everyone else was sitting at home wondering the same thing. She realised that she couldn't just sit back and wait in the hope that one of them would get up and act, she had to do something; there wasn't anyone else. Then once she'd got up and started asking questions she found others like her who wanted change. She had a 'better to light a candle that to curse the darkness' attitude, and I guess I've come to understand that. Democracy is still fresh here and the government has enough problems. There are people here who need me. I can't just leave, however much I might want to." He leant his head against mine and I felt it – his desire to be with me. I knew it wasn't just words, he wanted to come back with me.

I inched closer to him, feeling his warmth through his T-shirt, and he put his arm around me. I knew he couldn't come back to London and I didn't want him to, not really. The lyrics of a song flitted into my head; about a fish and a bird who fell in love, but could find nowhere to build their nest. No, I'd already watched one man I loved wither and die far from his beloved Brazil. I understood why he had to stay and I was glad that he had met Rosa. It had been the corroboration he needed that he wasn't fighting a losing battle. I could see that her reappearance had given him new hope, a renewed vigour and determination in his fight.

"But I can't just leave you here."

"This isn't your fight Judith Summers. Go and live. It's your turn now."

"But Luciana?"

"I'll look after her, don't worry."

"But I feel like I'm running away."

Ricardo bent his head and I felt his lips brush my ear.

"Then stay."

Even through the din of the crowds I heard his whisper. I lifted my head and looked at him, "Stay?"

"Here, with me."

I didn't know what to say. "But...no, I couldn't, I mean, I couldn't just leave everything and..." my voice trailed off. Hadn't that been exactly what I'd been asking him to do? "No, I couldn't."

"Why not?"

"Yeah, why not, Mum?" Rosa must have heard the last part of our conversation and her face appeared between us.

"Well, what about visas? We couldn't just move here. It doesn't work like that."

Ricardo smiled. "You forget, you are my wife."

I looked at him, not understanding for a moment.

"I hear we've been married for fifteen years."

I laughed. Surely it couldn't be that easy.

"But you - Edson, I mean you, you died..."

"Not over here, not that I'm aware of."

"And what about me?" asked Rosa.

"I guess to all intents and purposes, at least in the eyes of the law, that makes me your father. If that's okay with you."

Rosa nodded. "That's okay. Dad would be cool with that."

I was still trying to find the flaw in his plan. I wasn't used to things working out. "But what would I do? I'd have to do something."

"We could always use your help at the shelter. Especially now, we're going to need all the help we can get. And someone who speaks English, well, everyone here's going to have to speak English sooner or later. Brazil's going global. It's the perfect time to start teaching English in Brazil."

"You make it sound so easy."

"Maybe it is."

I was scared. Maybe I was scared of being happy.

"But Ricardo," I tried to find the right words, "don't you see? We're two broken pieces of different puzzles. How are we ever going to fit together?"

"I have no idea, but don't you think it'd be fun to try?"

I thought of the kiss. I thought of his bruised body against my own and the feeling of completeness that had enveloped me. Fun. What did I have to lose? What was it I was trying so hard to cling on to? I smiled at him and at the thought of staying with him, of waking up every morning to his smile. It was something I hadn't even dared consider. But this wasn't just about me.

"What about Rosa?" I said, "She ought to go back to school, finish her education. She's only fifteen."

"Sixteen," Rosa said.

"Okay, she's only sixteen." I smiled, pleased that Rosa and I were speaking again.

"Mum, they do have schools in Brazil, you know. And I could come and help out at the shelter in the evenings and at weekends, couldn't I?" This last part was aimed at Ricardo, "I know you could do with the help."

"Why not? And maybe you could work with Luciclede, see if you can convince her to become a mentor for the younger girls. I think you two would get along."

"That'd be good."

I turned to my daughter. "You want to come back?" I said, "After everything that's happened?"

Rosa shrugged. "Like you said, Ricardo, shit happens everywhere. Look at what happened to Dad. What, you think he was safer in London?"

"But you really want to come back?"

"I don't want to just go back to how things were," she said, "This feels, I don't know, scary, but you know…"

It looked as if she was trying not to cry.

"It feels like Dad's near by, doesn't it?" I said, understanding what she wanted to say.

Rosa nodded. I shuffled over and hugged her. I knew what she meant. I felt it too. Rosa had found a family and a country that were a part of her. She still had so much to figure out, and maybe she needed to be here to do that.

"Rosa, there's something I need to tell you."

Rosa looked up, wiping tears from her cheeks. Her eyes looked frightened, like a little child. I looked at Ricardo, who nodded.

"It's about your mother," I began.

Rosa breathed in deeply, her body shivering suddenly with a sob. I felt Ricardo's foot against mine, giving me the courage I needed.

"Your mother was very young when she had you. She hadn't wanted a baby. Her and Dad weren't even together anymore by then, but she didn't know who else to turn to. They went to Ricardo for help and he delivered you, there on the kitchen floor at the shelter, just like he told you. He brought you out to your Dad, who was waiting in the office, and when he got back, your mother was gone."

I looked at Rosa, who was digging her fingers deep in the sand. I was grateful she wasn't looking at me. It was hard enough as it was.

"She left you with Dad," I continued, "She must have known he'd look after you, that you'd be better off with him. He tried everything he could think of to find her but it was no use, she'd gone, and he had a decision to make. He was already in trouble with the law and he knew that if he didn't leave the country, he would most likely end up dead in a police cell. He could have left you there with Ricardo at the shelter, and run, but he didn't. The moment he held you in his arms, he fell in love with you. He gave up everything to make a new life with you. He never heard from your mother again.

Rosa looked up at me, her brow furrowed,

"You don't even know her name?"

I shook my head. "Dad told me her name was Flavia, the name on your birth certificate, but I know now that was Ricardo's wife's name, not your mother's. I guess he wanted to protect you. I asked Ricardo, but he doesn't know either. They didn't exactly have time for introductions the night you were born."

Until the moment I said it, I hadn't known I was going to lie to her. It may not have been the same lie Edson had told me, all those years before, but neither was it the whole truth. The truth was too awful. I finally understood. All this time Edson had been lying to protect us both – protect Rosa from the truth, and me from the burden of concealing that truth from her.

Rosa said nothing but looked at her hands in her lap.

"Dad brought you to England to give you a new life, to help you both move on," I said.

We sat together as the men on the screen fought for their country. I'd been meaning to tell her the truth, about Luciana, about her half-sister, Luciclede, but when it came to it, I couldn't bring myself to break Rosa's heart. Telling her about Luciana would be to tell her Edson was not her father. And I couldn't do that; I couldn't take that away from her, not now. When Rosa eventually looked up she had fresh tears in her eyes.

"Are you okay?" I asked.

Rosa nodded. She looked lost. "I never wanted another mother," she sniffed, "You're my mum. I don't care about the rest, really I don't. And I'm so sorry about what I said, about everything. I've been such a cow."

I reached out and took her hand and held it in mine. "Come here," I said and pulled her towards me.

A shadow over us made me look up.

It was Tom.

"Hey, no one told me there were hugs to be had over here!" he said, grinning, "Can anyone join in?"

"Tom, how did you find us here?" I said, pleased to see him.

He winked at Ricardo, "A little bird told me. You're looking better."

"I'm feeling better," I said and squeezed Rosa's arm.

Tom turned to look at the match, it was almost the final whistle. I looked at his straight back, his strong arms as he took a swig of his beer, his long legs in Bermuda shorts and flip-flops, towering above the people around him. A man called him from further up the beach, towards the big screen.

"Gotta go," he held up his beer bottle, "so, I'll see you at the airport tomorrow," he said.

"Actually, I'm thinking of staying on a while."

Tom swallowed the swig of beer he'd just taken.

"Oh. okay, cool. Nice one."

I thought I saw the briefest flash of disappointment in his face, but before I could be sure he flashed his grin.

"Well, best be going." He winked at us and shouted at his friend to wait for him.

"He likes you," Ricardo said as we watched Tom saunter down the beach towards the big screen.

"I know," I said. I wrapped my arm around Ricardo's waist and leant my head on his shoulder.

The match went to penalties. To me, who knew little about football, it seemed a ludicrous way to decide a World Cup final. The tension in the crowd was frightening. I thought the whole lot of them would combust. And when the first poor Italian struck the ball high over the goalposts, the beach erupted, as if this were it, as if they had already won. And then when the Italian goalkeeper batted the next ball away, saving Brazil's first attempt, it was as if the world were collapsing around us. A woman to my left was crying into her partner's chest, unable to watch. Agony was plastered across the faces around me. Then another Italian was up and this time he scored. Next, Romário, the golden boy of Brazil, as Tom had described him to me during one of his daily visits to my bedside, hit the post, sending the ball, by the grace of God, into the net. The nation clung on to fresh hope.

Another goal went in for the Italians, then another for the Brazilians. I found myself holding my breath as the goalkeeper, Taffarel, punched away Italy's next attempt and the Brazilian captain, Dunga, a funny name I thought, slammed his shot into the back of the net, keeping the hope alive.

I felt Ricardo's hand on mine. He leant over and I felt his lips against my ear once more.

"Thank you," he said.

I turned, shouting above the noise. "For what?"

He leant forward again, his cheek against mine, and kissed me.

"Just, thank you."

And then suddenly it was the decider. As the last Italian player lined up his shot I bit my lip and felt Ricardo squeeze my hand. I didn't know how people could bear to watch. Many couldn't, visibly shaking, holding their heads in their hands, yet still peering through spread fingers, unable to avert their eyes. The beach fell silent. Nothing but the gentle waves lapping the shore, as a nation held its breath.

And then it was over - over the goal posts and into oblivion. Italy had missed. Brazil had won the World Cup. Now four times world champions – another fact that had somehow made its way into my head from Tom's visits. The beach exploded with blaring horns, the thundering of drums, with cheers, with tears, as if everything had been hanging on this moment, as if everything were about to change.

Ricardo jumped to his feet and helped me up. I was still unsteady but he took me in his arms and held me close, our foreheads pressed together, our bodies swaying in unison, giving into the moment, both of us acutely aware of how lucky we were to be there, alive and well, and to have found each other, here, out of all the possible directions our lives could've taken. Music was already blaring out of the speakers on a lorry up on the road, drums were pounding all around us as the crowd moved as one. The beach was scattered with pockets of light and shadows, between which bodies moved like reeds in a river. Barefoot women with bare-chested men swayed together to the music, tripping over each other with the sand and the beer and the contagious euphoria. A drinks vendor skipped where he stood, somehow continuing to balance a polystyrene box on the handlebars of his bicycle. Children danced and attempted to re-enact the penalty shoot out amongst the debris of glass bottles and coconut husks.

I held on to Ricardo, hardly daring to believe that I was there with him and that he wanted me to stay. Despite everything, I had fallen in love with this man and his country. I thought again of Edson, my best friend, my husband, the man I'd known so well, and yet not at all. I watched Rosa laughing at us as we danced and thought about how she had come into this world - her own messed up past - and how, like this country, she undoubtedly had plenty more mistakes up her sleeve, but I had faith in her, just as Ricardo had faith in his beloved country, Brazil.

As the people danced in the sand, the city's lights reflecting on the water under the moon, I reached down and pulled the urn out of my bag. I kicked off my sandals, walked down the sand and waded into the sea.

"Mum, what are you doing?" Rosa shouted after me.

"I'm taking Dad home," I called back, "You coming?"

Rosa kicked off her own flip-flops and waded in behind me. The water was warm and tickled my calves. Sand oozed between my toes as I waded out up to my waist, my skirt floating up like a giant jellyfish. We were not the only ones in the water. Children and adults, drunk on beer and cachaça, high on the victory of their team, were all throwing themselves into the water. I stood and watched them and smiled. Had the young Edson been here, I imagined he would've been doing the same. I waited for Rosa, face towards the dark horizon, the urn hugged to my chest.

As Rosa reached me I gave the urn a final hug, took off the lid and held it out to her. We each took a handful of the man we had both loved and, arms outstretched, let the breeze carry his ashes into the moonlit night. Behind us, the city was alive with music, bodies swarming on to the beach, writhing to the sounds of Forró, their movements a blaze of colour. The smell of meat cooking on barbecues; of roasting corn; the ocean; the crackle of fireworks; a sea of voices, of whispers, cries, singing, shouting, laughing: the voices of a nation come alive, drowning out the sound of the waves that carried Edson out to sea.

Looking back to the shore I saw the beach had become a sea of green and yellow. Beyond, in the high-rises across the street, people on crowded balconies were spraying champagne down on to the heads of the people below.

I looked up into the dark velvet sky, out into the wild openness of the sea and back to the teeming beach and the crazy, vibrant city it merged in to. I felt like a tiny doll in a Lego city – couples kissing; bikini-clad women gyrating their hips; kids drinking guarana; the white, cloud-like tops of the market stalls breaking up the crowds; the line of streetlights curving up the promenade, illuminating the palm trees and parties.

Someone let off fireworks and their light reflected in the water as Edson's ashes settled into the ebb and flow of the gentle waves that would carry them along the coast.

I handed the empty urn to Rosa, who replaced the lid with great care, holding it just for a moment before hurling it out into the water. I watched as the lid flew off and it landed, instantly filling with water, and sank to the sand at the bottom of the sea. I wondered who would find it.

I reached out my hand and Rosa took it. We turned and stood there together, letting the water wash over our legs, as the beach became a flurry of lights and bodies and music, and I knew that for Edson, this was home: this was what he had meant. Edson was finally home, and he had brought us back with him.

-The End-

ACKNOWLEDGEMENTS

I am enormously grateful to so many people for their inspiration, advice and support in the writing of this book. Thank you to my dad for showing me that stories are everywhere, and to my mum for giving me the courage to write them down. To my wonderful friends - Rowena, Anna, Jessica, Imogen, Phyll, Claire, Emma, Becky and Caroline – who took the time to read the manuscript in its various drafts and give me invaluable feedback, thank you for your unfaltering enthusiasm, honesty and encouragement - you are all fabulous. Thank you to my brothers, Gareth and Huw for courageously leading the way and showing me that writers are not mythological creatures after all, but real people with a passion, who knuckle down and write. Thank you to my wonderful agents Maddy and Cara at The Madeleine Milburn Literary Agency for believing in me from the outset and for your impeccable insight, professionalism and warmth. A special thank you to all my wonderful Brazilian friends, both in Brazil and the UK, many of whom are still working selflessly to improve the lives of those around them - you are an inspiration. And last, but certainly not least, thank you to my husband, Matt for his love and support, and to our three wonderful children, who remind me every day of the power of stories.

ABOUT THE AUTHOR

Rebecca Powell was born in Bristol and has a degree in French and Portuguese from the University of Leeds. In her early twenties she worked for a year at a women's shelter in the northeast of Brazil, before moving to London, where she continued to work for a number of national charities. She now lives in the southwest of France with her husband and three children.

www.rebeccapowellbooks.com
@BeccaPowellUK

Printed in Poland
by Amazon Fulfillment
Poland Sp. z o.o., Wrocław